THE LONG AGO

Dan watched a couple of officers load an impressive-looking piece of ordnance onto a horse's back. "Wow," he said. "What's that?" The cartridges gleamed in the sunshine. Each one looked as big as his thumb. The weapon had to come from the Old Time. Nobody nowadays could make anything like that.

"Machine gun—.50 caliber," one of them answered proudly. "We test-fired it, and it shoots great."

"That is so cool!" Dan said. "I didn't know anything like that was left in the armory."

"It didn't come from the armory," the captain said. "Scrounger found it in a house."

"No kidding?" Dan said, and the officer nodded. Dan went on, "Ordinary people could have a piece like that in their houses? Wow! Old Time must've been something else." That gun might beat the Westside all by itself now.

"Old Time *was* something else," the other officer said.

"Oh, yes, sir." Dan knew better than to show he disagreed with any officer, even when he did. But he didn't disagree with this one. "Ordinary people had guns like this, the way folks have belt knives now. Makes you wonder what all the kings—no, they called them presidents—had, though."

"They had the Fire," the first captain said grimly. "They had it, and they used it. And that's how come we don't have so much any more."

Tor Books by Harry Turtledove

Between the Rivers

Conan of Venarium

The Two Georges (by Richard Dreyfuss and Harry Turtledove)

Household Gods (by Judith Tarr and Harry Turtledove)

The First Heroes (edited by Harry Turtledove and Noreen Doyle)

Darkness

Into the Darkness

Darkness Descending

Through the Darkness

Rulers of the Darkness

Jaws of Darkness

Out of the Darkness

Crosstime Traffic

Gunpowder Empire

Curious Notions

In High Places

The Disunited States of America

The Gladiator

The Valley-Westside War

Writing as H. N. Turteltaub

Justinian

Over the Wine-Dark Sea

The Gryphon's Skull

The Sacred Land

Owls to Athens

The Valley-Westside War

Harry Turtledove

A Tom Doherty Associates Book
New York

THE VALLEY-WESTSIDE WAR

A Tor Book
Published by Tom Doherty Associates, LLC
175 Fifth Avenue
New York, NY 10010

www.tor-forge.com

ISBN-13: 978-0-7653-5380-1
ISBN-10: 0-7653-5380-6

First Edition: July 2008
First Mass Market Edition: April 2009

Printed in the United States of America

0 9 8 7 6 5 4 3 2 1

The Valley-Westside War

One

As Dan neared the top of the Sepulveda Pass, he saw the barricade the Westside had built across the 405. His deerskin boots scuffed on the old, cracked, sun-faded asphalt. Weeds, even bushes, sprouted from the cracks, but the freeway was still the best route south from the Valley. Or it had been, till the Westsiders blocked it.

They saw the Valley war party coming. Horns blared an alert. Men ran back and forth behind the barrier. Some of them would have crossbows or longbows. At seventeen, Dan himself was only an archer. Others would carry modern smoothbore muskets. And a few would use Old Time rifles. Those were far better than anything people could make nowadays, 130 years after the Fire came down. But the ammunition was two lifetimes old, too. Sometimes it worked the way it was supposed to. Sometimes it didn't do anything. And sometimes it blew up. You needed to be several different kinds of brave to carry an Old Time gun.

Captain Kevin raised the truce flag. He hadn't brought along enough men to rush the barricade. He couldn't have come without a good escort, though, not unless he wanted to lose face. The game had rules.

Big Louie strode out in front of the flag. He had an even bigger voice. "Parley!" he bellowed. "We want to talk!" He stepped back, looking proud of himself.

A Westside herald shouted back: "Come ahead, with no more than ten!" His voice sounded thin after Big Louie's. The Valley man looked prouder than ever.

Captain Kevin chose two riflemen, four musketeers, and four archers. You had to have some of each. That was what democracy was all about. He pointed to Dan as the last archer. Having a youngster among the veterans helped show he wasn't scared.

The barricade looked stronger than first reports suggested. The Westsiders must have worked hard to make it taller and thicker. Dust kicked up from Dan's boots. It was summer, and hot and dry. Sweat ran down under his broad-brimmed hat. Turkey vultures circled overhead.

Once upon a time, men had flown, too. They could still get gliders into the air, but it wasn't the same. They'd really flown in the Old Time—flown at peace, flown to war. The songs and the old books all said so. And everybody knew the Fire came down from the sky.

"Close enough!" a Westside officer yelled.

"That you, Morris?" Captain Kevin called.

"Colonel Morris, if you please!" Like most of his kind, the Westsider sounded snooty. Dan thought of things that way, anyhow. Westsiders said Valley people were a bunch of hicks. To Dan, that only proved how dumb Westsiders were.

"Well, Colonel Morris, your Wonderfulness, you can tear down this wall," Captain Kevin said. "King Zev and the Council say that's how it's got to be. We have a treaty to keep the pass open, and you people are breaking it. We won't put up with that. We know our rights, we do."

Better believe it, Dan thought. The barricade would cut the Valley off from trade, and from scrounging farther south. If you didn't scrounge, how were you supposed to keep going? So much the Old Time made was better than its modern equivalents: everything from coins to mirrors to guns. People had scrounged a lot and time had ruined a lot, but not everything. There weren't that many people any more, and there'd been even fewer right after the Fire came down.

"Times, they are a-changing," Colonel Morris said. "We've got some things of our own going on. If you want to come south, you'll have to pay to pass."

"That's simple. We won't do it. And if you think you're coming north, you're crazy," Captain Kevin declared.

"Who wants to come north?" the Westsider said scornfully.

"Good luck with your oranges. Good luck with your greens. Good luck with your grain," Captain Kevin told him.

"You need us worse than we need you," Colonel Morris replied. Westsiders always said that. Maybe it was even true back before the Fire fell. Not many Valley people thought it was any more. The way things were going, it looked as if both sides would find out what was really what before too long. They'd find out the hard way, too.

Captain Kevin scowled. "You won't get away with this. I can tell you that right now. We know what our rights are. If we have to, we'll go to war to make sure the pass stays open. And if we go to war, we'll win it."

"That's telling him," Dan muttered. The musketeer next to him nodded.

"You can try." Colonel Morris didn't sound worried. Did that mean he really wasn't, or did it just mean he was a good liar? Most Westsiders were—Valley people thought so, anyhow.

"That's your last word?" Captain Kevin, by contrast, sounded sad and mad at the same time.

"That's my first, last, and only word," the Westside commander said.

"Well, I'm sorry for you, but you'll be sorrier." Captain Kevin nodded to his soldiers. "Come on, boys. If they're going to be dumb, we'll teach 'em a lesson." The soldiers turned around and marched back toward the rest of the Valley company. Behind them, the Westsiders jeered and swore. Dan got an itchy spot right in the middle of his back. If they started shooting, his leather jerkin wouldn't keep out an arrow, much less a bullet.

But they didn't. He breathed a sight of relief when he got out of arrow and musket range. Oh, a rifleman could still hit him, but riflemen would go after important targets first. A kid with a bow was no big deal.

"What's the word, sir?" a waiting Valley sergeant asked.

"War!" Captain Kevin answered.

Liz Mendoza hated this Los Angeles. Being here, working here, was like being best friends with one identical twin and then suddenly having to visit the other one in the intensive-care unit. In the home timeline, where she lived, Los Angeles was one of the great cities of the world. Even a hundred years ago, back in the twentieth century, people said the future happened here first. And they were right.

This Los Angeles had been much like that one up till 1967. Then, in this alternate, somebody got stupid. People in what was left of the USA said the Russians fired the first missile. People in what was left of the USSR said the Americans started the war. It hardly mattered any more. Both sides had fired way too many.

Quite a few alternates went through nuclear wars in the second half of the twentieth century or the first half of the twenty-first. Crosstime Traffic stayed away from most of them. The company that controlled trade between the home timeline and the worlds that happened when history changed didn't see much profit in dealing with them. Why would you want to do business with somebody who'd set his own house and car on fire and then jumped into the flames?

Here, though, UCLA was paying the freight. Indirectly, the government was. The university had got a grant to try to find out just what went wrong in this alternate. Liz's father was one of the historians who'd come here to do research. Her mother was a doctor who specialized in genetic diseases and the effects of radiation. And Liz was . . .

Protective coloration, she thought. Her parents seemed more normal if they had a kid along. And so here she was. She had studied a lot more about the 1960s than she would have otherwise. It was, in the ancient slang of the day, a mind-blowing experience. Except that slang wasn't ancient here. People still used it. They used whatever they could from the days before the war, because they mostly couldn't match that stuff, whether material goods or language, any more. Sad, but that was how things were in this alternate.

She'd start UCLA herself a year later than she would have

otherwise. But she'd start with a year of crosstime experience under her belt. That was good. Or it would have been good if she'd gone to an alternate more different than this one was.

The house where she and her folks stayed was in Westwood Village, a couple of blocks south of the UCLA campus. It was made from the rubble of the stores and apartments that had stood there when the bombs fell. The house was built around a central courtyard. The style came from Rome through Spain to the New World. It gave both light and shade, and worked well in the California climate.

The windows that looked out on the world were small and barred. Liz could see the UCLA campus through the north-facing ones. She could, yes, but she didn't look that way very often. It hurt too much. Most of the big hospital buildings at the south end of campus never got built in this alternate. The war took care of that, as it took care of so many other things. The buildings that did survive were in sad disrepair. Some of the earlier ones, built before there were any earthquake codes, had crumbled in one shaker or another.

Somebody banged on the big brass knocker bolted to the front door. "You want to get that, Liz?" her father called.

Well, no, not really, was the first thing that crossed her mind. But that was the wrong answer, and she knew it. "Okay," she said out loud, and went to the door.

Before she opened it, she looked through the little window set above the knocker. The Westsiders patrolled Westwood Village pretty well, but robber bands still skulked in other ruins and came out to raid every now and then. There were freelance thieves, too.

She relaxed when she recognized the man standing in

the street. Unbarring the door, she said, "Come in, Colonel Morris."

"Thank you, Missy," the Westsider said. In the home timeline, that would have made Liz want to spit in his eye. Here, he was just being polite. His English sounded old-fashioned to her. The language here hadn't changed as much since 1967 as it had in the home timeline.

"Dad!" she yelled. "It's Colonel Morris!"

"Be right there," her father said.

"Hello, Jeff. How are you doing?" Colonel Morris said when Liz's father came to the door.

"Not too bad. Yourself?" Jeff Mendoza held out his hand to the important Westsider. When Colonel Morris took it, his clasp also locked thumbs with Liz's father. Handshakes like that were an ancient joke in the home timeline. They hung on here.

Both men wore baggy wool trousers tucked into boots and equally baggy linen shirts. Colonel Morris used a wide leather belt with a fat, fancy brass buckle. He wore an Old Time windup wristwatch on a broad leather band. Westsiders couldn't make anything that fine, but they could keep some that were already made running.

Dad's belt looked like the colonel's. Some styles here still reflected the ones in fashion when the Fire fell. So did some of the language. Some things had changed, though. Liz's wool skirt reached to the ground. Minis were scandalous. Her shirt was like the men's. It even buttoned the same way, which drove her crazy.

"Liz, why don't you get us some improved water?" her father said.

"Okay," she said once more. Men ordered women around

here a lot more than they did in the home timeline. Women mostly put up with it. The ones who didn't got thumped, and nobody said a thing except that they had it coming. The people who went on and on about how enlightened the Westside was were all men.

Liz poured water from a big earthenware jug into two earthenware mugs. With the aqueducts gone, water was always the biggest worry in this Los Angeles. She added one part strong brandy to about five of water. The brandy was what improved it, not because the booze got you drunk—brandy did that much faster by itself—but because it killed enough germs to keep you from getting the runs.

She politely served the guest first: "Here you are, Colonel."

"Groovy, sweetheart," he said, and she didn't crack a smile. If somebody in 1967 had heard someone else say *Bully, by jingo!*, it would have sounded just as old-fashioned in his ears.

"Thank you," her father said when she gave him his water. You didn't *have* to talk like a hippie here. You didn't have to, no—but you could. Dad turned back to Colonel Morris. "What can I do for you, sir?"

"You'll have heard it's probably war with the Valley?"

"I've heard it. I hoped it wasn't true," Dad answered.

"Well, it is," Colonel Morris said. "We're going to collect a toll at the top of the pass, and they don't like it. I hope we'll be able to buy some more of those fine muskets and revolvers you sell. They're the next best thing to Old Time guns."

"I'll see what I can do," Liz's father said. As far as anyone here knew, the guns he sold came up from a cousin's shop in Sandago. They really came from the home timeline. People there used them as trade goods in several low-tech alternates. Dad went on, "Do you really need the toll enough to fight to keep it?"

"The City Council says we do." The City Council was the band of nine nobles who ran things in the Westside. The title made it sound as if they were elected, but they weren't. A lot of names from the days before the war hung on, even if they pointed to different things now. Colonel Morris added, "I'm loyal to the Council and obey its orders, of course."

"Of course." Dad didn't even sound sarcastic. The Westside officer had to say stuff like that. The City Council's spies were everywhere. Colonel Morris couldn't know Dad wasn't one of them.

"Do you really have to follow orders even when they're dumb?" Liz asked.

Colonel Morris blinked. Dad sent her a look that said she'd got out of line. A mere girl wasn't supposed to challenge authority. For that matter, nobody in the Westside was supposed to.

"That's a heavy question, sweetie," Colonel Morris said, by which he meant it was important. When he said *sweetie*, he meant Liz wasn't. She was only a girl, somebody he could patronize. She wanted to pick up a chair and clout him over the head with it. Maybe that would knock sense into him. Or maybe not.

Instead, she smiled—sweetly—and said, "Well, have you got an answer for it?"

Dad coughed. She wasn't supposed to push like this. She didn't much care, not when the Westsider insulted her without even knowing he was doing it.

"I have the only answer I need," Colonel Morris said. "Whatever the City Council tells me to do, I do it."

I'm just following orders. How many people in how many

alternates said the same thing? How much grief did they cause when they did? Too much—Liz knew that.

"How long will we have to wait for the guns?" the colonel asked Liz's father. He tried to ignore her now. Was that better than patronizing her? Was it worse? Was it as bad in a different way?

"It'll be a while, sir," Jeff Mendoza answered. "Long way down to Sandago." It wasn't even two hundred kilometers. If traffic on the 405 wasn't bad, you could get to San Diego in a couple of hours. You could in the home timeline, anyhow. If you were traveling in a horse-drawn wagon in this alternate, the town with the rubbed-down name was more like a week away.

"Well, do what you can," Colonel Morris said. "We need those guns, especially the six-shooters. See you later." He sketched a salute to Dad, nodded to Liz, and left.

After the door was barred behind the local, Dad turned to Liz and said, "You can't poke him with a pin whenever you feel like it, you know."

"I guess not," she said. "But he ticked me off."

"He didn't even realize he was doing it."

"That's the point," Liz said. "*I* sure knew."

"What am I going to do with you?" Her father sounded half annoyed, half amused.

"Send me home. I don't like it here very much," Liz answered. "Or if you can't do that, let me go up to the campus."

"You know we won't send you home. You know you don't really want to go home, too." Now Dad donned patience like a suit of armor. The most annoying thing was, he was right. She wanted the year of crosstime service on her college applications, even if she didn't like coming here to get it. Dad went on,

"Sending you up to UCLA wasn't so simple, either. What we had to pay to get you a stack pass . . ."

Liz sighed. "What is simple?"

Her father gave her a hug. "Welcome to the world, sweetheart."

"Groovy," she said, as sardonically as she could. He only laughed.

Along with the rest of Captain Kevin's men, Dan marched back to the barracks in the Sepulveda Basin. Piles and piles of sandbags were stacked close to the halls. Most of the time, the Sepulveda Basin was as dry as the rest of the Valley. But it could flood in a hurry when the rains came down. The sandbags had saved the barracks more than once over the years.

No rain now, not in the summertime. The Valley was full of cisterns to hold the rain that had fallen the winter before. Watermasters doled it out to farms and families. In years with dry winters, everyone worried about whether there'd be enough for crops—and for people.

Back in the Old Time, irrigation had brought water from hundreds of miles away. Everybody in Los Angeles had had plenty. All the houses and apartments and factories and shops showed as much. There were far more of them than the people who lived here now could ever hope to fill. All over L.A., in all the little countries that had sprung up since the day the Fire fell, scavengers scrounged through the swarms of abandoned buildings for whatever they could find.

Something occurred to Dan. "Hey, Sergeant!" he said. If

Sergeant Chuck didn't know everything, he didn't know he didn't know it.

"What is it, kid?" The three stripes on his sleeve—genuine Old Time stripes, machine-embroidered—gave him the right to treat everybody below him the way Dan's father treated him before he got drafted.

"Is it true what they say about swimming pools?"

"You mean, did the Old Time people really fill those cement holes in the ground with water and swim in them? They didn't just use 'em for cisterns or put dirt back in 'em?"

"Yes, Sergeant. That's what I mean." Dan nodded.

"Oh, it's true, all right." Sergeant Chuck nodded, too, solemnly. "I've seen pictures in Old Time magazines."

That proved it, all right, unless . . . "Were they for-true magazines?"

"Well, I sure think so," the sergeant answered. "They had other things that sure are real—cars and things, you know."

"Oh, yeah." Dan nodded. You couldn't *not* know about cars. Their rusting corpses filled the streets. To this day, they were the main source of iron for blacksmiths. Their wheels—with tires of wood, not the rubber that had rotted away—still turned on carts and wagons. Glass from their windows gave homes light to this day. "I wonder how they moved so fast all by themselves, though."

"Well, who doesn't?" Chuck said. "Must've been something like a steam engine, I expect."

Big, puffing steam engines pumped water. A few of them moved engines along railroads. But so many rail lines were broken, and so many bandits prowled the routes, that railroads often seemed more trouble than they were worth. "How did Old Time people keep railroads from getting raided?" Dan asked.

"I don't think they did," the sergeant told him. "You know the story of Jesse James and Annie Oakley, don't you?"

"Little Orphan Annie? I hope I do!" Dan said.

"Well, they were train robbers, right?"

"They were," Dan admitted. "But they got caught and paid the price. Jesse did, anyway. Annie married Judge Warbucks and got off. Too many robbers these days never even get caught."

"Too many places for bad guys to slip through the cracks," Sergeant Chuck said. "What you've got to remember is, back in Old Time days this was all one country—the Valley and the Westside and Burbank and Speedro. All the way from Sandago to Frisco. Even Vegas. All one country. Bad guys couldn't just skip over a border and disappear, like."

"Uh-huh." Dan had learned that in school. And there were big stretches of land now that didn't belong to anybody—except bandits and brigands, anyhow. "If people other places would just admit Zev was their rightful king . . ."

Chuck laughed. "Don't hold your breath. The Westside wants the City Council to run everything. Burbank's got a Director and a Producer. All the other countries think they ought to be top dog, too."

"But they don't know what they're talking about. We're the only really civilized one." Dan had learned that in school, too.

"Well, sure." Chuck had probably also learned it in school. Most people in the Valley had four years of education. Quite a few had six or even eight. Dan did. He could read and write and add and subtract and even multiply and do long division. Adding and subtracting always came in handy. He didn't know if he'd ever use the fancier stuff, but he had it if he needed it.

And reading . . . Nothing killed time better than reading.

Back in the Old Time, they'd had TV and the movies and radio and records to make time go by. A few records still played on wind-up phonographs. The other things weren't even memories any more, because nobody still alive recalled using them. But old people remembered their grandparents talking about them, and Old Time books and magazines mentioned them all the time. They had to be for-true.

Sergeant Chuck broke into his thoughts: "If I were you, Dan, I'd start practicing hard. A good archer's worth about as much as a musketeer."

"Do you think there'll be a war, honest?" Dan asked.

"Sure do," the sergeant answered. "King Zev *won't* let the Westside close the pass. That's too big a slap in the face to put up with. If those snooty so-and-so's get away with it, next thing you know Burbank'll start pushing us around, too."

"It's a good thing they put these barracks on Victory Boulevard," Dan said.

"Yeah, that's heavy, all right," Chuck agreed. "Talk about your good omens."

"Can't hardly get a better one," Dan said. Some Old Time books seemed to laugh at the idea that anyone could foretell the future. But the Bible didn't. Whether you were Christian or Jewish, you had to believe in prophets. And plenty of decks of tarot cards floated around, some printed before the Fire came down and others, cruder, afterwards. Dan snapped his fingers. "Talking about omens—can I ask you one more thing?"

"Go ahead." Sergeant Chuck was in a good mood—maybe he looked forward to a war with the Westside.

"Does King Zev *really* have a Magic Eight Ball to help tell him what to do?"

"He doesn't have just one—he's got two," Chuck declared. "My cousin's a preacher's assistant, and he knows stuff like that."

"Two? Wow! Oh, wow!" Dan hadn't dreamt the Valley was so rich.

"You better believe it," Chuck said. "And what he does is, he asks both of them the same question and then he sees how each one answers. If that's not scientific, I don't know what is."

"Scientific." Dan's voice went all dreamy—there was a word to conjure with. And plenty of wizards and fortune-tellers did just that. "Well, if we don't have the vitamins to beat the Westside with *two* Magic Eight Balls, I don't know what else we'd need."

"Soldiers," Sergeant Chuck told him. "Whatever else you've got, you always need soldiers."

Walking up Hilgard to the UCLA campus made Liz want to cry. It was like walking past the skeleton of a good friend. You knew who it was. If you tried, you could picture what the person—or the place—had looked like alive. But all you saw was death.

The asphalt was so old, it was nearer white than black. Here and there, it had washed out altogether. Cobblestones replaced a few stretches. Others were just dirt. Cracks seamed even intact asphalt, like the wrinkles on a great-grandmother's face.

Cracks also marred the concrete of the sidewalk. Back in the home timeline, Liz would have gone past the botanical gardens and some nicely watered lawns across the street. Here, most of the imported plants in the gardens were dead, killed off by L.A.'s summer droughts. No one here had a lawn that was green in the summertime. There was no water to spare for such luxury. From November to March—in a wet year, to May—things were green. Any other time? Brown.

Sorority houses and rich people's homes stood across the street from the campus in the home timeline. Some of the buildings still stood here. A couple of the old sororities even had their Greek letters on the front wall. Nobody in this alternate seemed to know what they meant any more.

They weren't sorority houses and rich people's homes any more, not here. Guards stood outside one of them—it was the Westside jail. Smoke poured from another one—it was a smithy and armory, and made a lot of the weapons the local army used. Several homes were armored with iron—some old sheet metal, some taken from dead automobiles. Members of the City Council lived in those. As far as Liz was concerned, they took *A man's home is his castle* too far. The rulers of the Westside didn't seem to take chances about how well loved they were.

Turning left onto the actual campus was both a relief and a bigger wound. Parts of the north end seemed hauntingly familiar. Everyone in the home timeline called Bunche Hall the Waffle because of the square windows in the south wall that stuck out from the brown stone surface. The building remained intact here, too. Only a few of the windows did, though.

There was also another difference—a subtler one—between the two versions of the same building. Down at the bottom of Bunche Hall in the home timeline, there was a bust of the diplomat, and his name, and the dates of his birth and death: 1904–1971. Everything here was the same . . . except the date of Ralph Bunche's death was missing. He was still alive when the war started, and after that nobody cared. The 1904– that remained seemed asymmetrical. The artisan who put it up had figured it would look fine once Bunche died. In the home timeline, he was right.

Liz wondered whether Ralph Bunche ever saw the building named for him. If he did, what did he think of the way that nameless artisan had laid things out? Wouldn't it have seemed as if the man was just waiting for him to keel over? It felt that way to Liz, anyhow.

Her goal lay beyond Bunche Hall and to the left as she came up from the south. In the home timeline, it was the Young Research Library—the YRL—named after a twentieth-century administrator. Here, it was the University Research Library, or URL. They hadn't got around to naming it for the otherwise forgotten Young before the missiles started flying.

Five stories' worth of books and periodicals . . . What better place to try to figure out why things went wrong in this alternate? The Westsiders had an almost superstitious respect for what they called Old Time knowledge. They took care of what the URL held as best they could. Most of it was still intact.

A guard outside the door nodded to Liz—she'd been here before. He had an Old Time .45 on his hip—that was how important the Westsiders thought the URL was. Liz had sometimes wondered if computer URLs got their name from the University Research Library. That turned out not to be true—only an interesting coincidence.

Once upon a time, the plate-glass door by the guard station had been automatic. No more. No infrared beam to cut. No electricity to power the door even if there were a beam. Nothing but muscle power and fading memories. Liz pulled the door open and went in.

Her eyes needed a few seconds to get used to the gloom in the foyer. Some of the lamp fixtures in the ceiling still had fluorescent tubes in them. Maybe some of the tubes still worked. But no electricity had flowed through them since the Fire fell. The light inside the entrance hall came from the doorway and from the flickering oil lamps and candles. Soot caked thick on the walls above them said they'd burned there for a long, long time.

In the home timeline, students—and other people who needed to find things they couldn't track on the Net—would have bustled through the library and gathered in front of the elevators. Only a couple of people here wandered across the foyer. The elevators, of course, were as dead as the door and the fluorescent tubes.

If you wanted to go upstairs here, you literally had to go up the stairs. A stair dragon waited at the bottom. He called himself a librarian, but he was really a stair dragon. You had to placate him before you could go up, and he'd search you when you came down again to make sure you weren't stealing books.

"Stack pass?" he growled as Liz came up. He breathed smoke, too—he was puffing on a fat cigar. Liz thought he smelled gross. Tobacco was a popular crop and trade good here. And why not? In this alternate, other things were likely to kill you before cancer or heart disease could.

To make sure he didn't start breathing fire, Liz showed him the family stack pass. It had cost her father a pretty penny in bribes, but good whiskey and wind-up alarm clocks and other goodies from the home timeline made getting what you wanted here pretty easy.

"Thank you. Go ahead." The stair dragon actually smiled. The stink of his smoldering cheroot chased Liz up the stairs. She coughed a couple of times, wishing she needed to go all the way up to the fifth floor so she could escape it. But the magazines she wanted lived on the second floor, and the nasty smell was bound to keep coming up after her.

Study desks and chairs and tables all stood near the south-facing windows. Sunlight was the best light by which to work here, and the library shut down after dark. The desks and the tables dated back to the Old Time. A few of the chairs—the plastic ones with metal legs—did, too. Most of those had cracked or worn out since, though. That didn't bother Liz. The wooden ones the Westsiders had made since were more comfortable anyhow.

When Liz did go back into the stacks, the musty smell of old paper filled her nostrils. It was stronger here than it would have been in the home timeline. No climate control here, so the paper aged faster. A lot of books on the top floor were damaged beyond repair because the roof leaked. Down here, that wasn't a worry, anyhow.

She pulled out a bound volume of *Newsweek* magazines that ran from January to March of 1967. The war had started—and ended—in the summer. Nobody at the URL had bound the issues for April to June. Or, if somebody had, the volume had disappeared before Crosstime Traffic discovered this blighted alternate.

Liz wanted those, or the equivalent from *Time* or *Life* or *Look* or *U.S. News & World Report*. She was stuck with what she had, though. She carried the bound volume back to a table. She was the only one there, so she could open the volume—carefully—and start scanning pages with a handheld scanner that sucked up data the way a vacuum cleaner sucked up dust.

If a local did see her doing that, he wouldn't understand it. Neither this alternate nor the home timeline had known how to make handheld scanners in 1967. Transistor radios were still pretty new. She saw an ad for one. It was bigger than an iPod, and couldn't do one percent as much. It didn't even have an FM band, only AM. And the ad said it was a technological breakthrough! The scary thing was, maybe the ad was right.

The Vietnam War dominated the news. It would have done the same thing in the home timeline. Liz didn't know exactly how what had happened here differed from what happened in the home timeline. That was why she was sucking up data. Computers could compare the text here to what the same issues said in the home timeline. Once they figured out how things had changed, they would have a better chance of nailing down where the breakpoint lay.

In the meantime . . . In the meantime, Liz was unskilled labor. All she had to do was slide the scanner over one column after another. It did the real work. If she wanted to stare at the strange clothes and hairdos and the funky lines of the cars, she could. If she wanted to pause and read something interesting-looking, she could do that.

And, as long as the mellow sunshine poured in through the

windows, if she wanted to pretend she was at the other UCLA, the *right* UCLA . . . well, she could almost do that, too.

King Zev wasn't much to look at. Dan had been much younger than he was now when he first realized as much. Zev was short and round, not tall and heroic the way kings in stories usually were. Zev was going bald. His beard was scraggly and streaked with gray. He had a big nose.

But, when he dressed up in an Old Time business suit and necktie, when he put a top hat on his head, he looked dignified even if not quite handsome. And he owned a big, booming voice, the kind of voice a lot of tall, heroic kings would have envied. He hardly needed the gilded Megaphone of State to get what he wanted to say out to the people and the army of the Valley.

Along with the other soldiers who'd gone down to the Westside's barricade across the 405, Dan sat close to the podium from which King Zev spoke. Their tobacco-brown uniforms were a good match for the dirt and the sun-blasted shrubs and bushes all around. Most ordinary people wore homespun, which also went well with the open space. Some richer men, though, had on Old Time shirts of nylon and trousers of polyester. The Old Time fabrics could wear out and fray, but bugs and mildew didn't bother them. And the colors and patterns on some of them drove modern weavers and dyers mad with jealousy.

"The Westside won't get away with it!" King Zev roared through the megaphone. "We won't let the Westside get away with it, will we?"

"No!" Dan yelled, along with the other soldiers. The ordinary citizens shouted, too, but not so loud.

"Down in the Westside, they think they can break treaties whenever they want to," the king said. "They think they can make us pay for what's always been a freeway. They think we're too spineless to care. Are they right?"

"No!" Dan yelled again, louder than ever.

"I can't hear you!" King Zev cupped a hand behind one ear.

"*No!*" This time, Dan yelled so loud, it hurt. All around him, other young men in uniform were shouting themselves hoarse, too.

King Zev smiled. "All right. Good," he said. "Far freaking out. We've told them we won't stand for it, but they don't want to listen. So what are we, like, going to do about it?"

"Fight 'em!" Dan bellowed. The other soldiers were shouting things like "Kill them!" and "Nuke 'em!" and "Smash 'em to bits!"

Zev's smile got wider. "That's just what we'll do. I've given Ambassador Mort his walking papers. He can go down there and tell the Westside City Council our soldiers will take care of their miserable, stupid wall."

Everybody cheered. No one liked the ambassador much. Even for a Westsider, he was pompous. He seemed to think getting sent to the Valley was a punishment, not a diplomatic appointment. He walked around as if everything up here smelled bad.

"Send him back where he belongs!" Dan yelled. The soldiers sitting near him laughed and clapped.

"I'm going to send him back," Zev said, picking up on Dan's shout. That made Dan feel pretty special. All the people in the Valley were special, just because they were lucky enough to live here. He'd learned that in school, too. But he felt *especially* special right now. King Zev went on, "And I'm going to tell him to tell the City Council they can look for our soldiers right behind him!"

"Right on!" Dan thrust his fist in the air in a gesture that came from the Old Time. "Right on, your Majesty!"

"Heavy! That's *soooo* heavy!" Sergeant Chuck agreed. Soldiers and civilians cheered and pounded on things and made as much noise as they could.

King Zev raised his hands. The hot Valley sun gleamed off the golden megaphone. "I thank you, my people, for rolling with me on this one." Now he'd said the closing words. It was official. It was democratic. It was war.

Two

What the Westside called a City Council meeting wasn't like the ones in the home timeline. Liz didn't think so, anyway. The Council decided whatever it decided and then told the people what that was. That was what the meeting was about.

When Liz complained to her dad, he smiled a sour smile. "It's not as different as you think, hon," he said. "They're smoother about hiding what they're really up to in the home timeline—I will say that for them."

The nine members of the City Council knew what they wanted to get across. What had been the UCLA Sculpture Garden was now the Westside assembly area. Some of the sculptures still stood. Others—mostly the abstract ones—had disappeared, probably melted down for the metal in them.

Ambassador Mort was tall and skinny. He wore a double-breasted Old Time sport jacket over baggy modern pants. "The Valley humiliated me!" he shouted to the people who'd come to the meeting. "Humiliated me, I tell you! They put me on a donkey with my face turned towards its tail and rode me to the border that way. It's a shame and a disgrace, that's what it is!"

It was also the standard way to send an ambassador home when you declared war on his country. Mort didn't say anything about that. How many of the men and women listening to him knew what the custom was? Not many—Liz was sure of that. The Council wanted to get people all worked up, and knew how to get what it wanted.

A big man named Cal was the chairman of the City Council. He wore an Old Time jacket, too—an ugly plaid one. He also wore a big white Stetson for no reason Liz could see. "Are we going to let the Valley get away with treating our ambassador that way?" he shouted, his voice high and quick and glib. Liz wouldn't have wanted to buy a used car from him. "I don't think so!"

"No way! No way! No way!" people chanted. They were a claque, a group set up in advance to make the kind of noise their patrons wanted when their patrons wanted it. They were too loud and too smooth to be anything else. When others joined in the chant, they sounded different—less rehearsed, maybe.

"I'm gonna sic my dog on the Valley!" Cal shouted. That was no idle threat. Cal's dog was famed—and feared—all over the Westside. There weren't nearly so many mutations after the atomic war as people had feared. But there were some, and that dog was descended from them. It was a German shepherd about three quarters as big as a horse, with teeth a *Tyrannosaurus* might have envied. It was, mostly, a nice dog. But if it got mad . . .

"Feed King Zev to it!" yelled somebody from the claque. In a moment, that whole group was shouting the phrase. Again, people who didn't belong joined more slowly. But they did join. The stage managing would have been too open, too blatant, to work in the home timeline—Liz hoped so, anyhow. But it did just fine here.

"So shall we show the Valley that they can't tell us what to do?" Cal asked.

"Yes!" "That's right!" "Bet your bippy!" people shouted back. Liz didn't know what a bippy was. She wondered if the men who used the word knew what it meant. Back in 1967, it had probably had a meaning. Now it was just a noise here. People said it without thinking about it. There were words like that in the home timeline, too.

"Is it war, then?" Cal wanted to make it official.

"War!" The word came back as a roar. That seemed official enough to Liz.

It seemed official enough to the head of the Westside City Council, too. "Thanks, folks," he said. "We'll lick 'em. You wait and see. When they got a good look at my dog Pots, they'll be so scared, they'll run away before the fighting really gets going."

Everybody cheered. As the meeting was breaking up, Liz asked her father, "Why does he call that monster of a dog Pots?"

"Because nobody here seems to remember who the Fenris Wolf was," Dad said, which both was and wasn't an answer. He added, "Besides, whatever you call a critter like that, the dog is bigger than the name."

There were old children's books in the home timeline about a dog like that, although he wasn't mean. What was his name? Clarence? That was close, but it wasn't right. "Clifford!" Liz exclaimed.

"Where did you come up with that?" Dad said. "My grandmother had some of those books. She read them to me when I was little. Her mother used to read them to her, she said."

"Oh, wow," Liz said—in the home timeline, a phrase even

more old-fashioned than Clifford books. People still used it here, and it did come in handy now and then. She went on, "Will the Westside win?"

"They sure think so," her father replied. "But the Valley thinks it'll win, too, or it wouldn't have started the war in the first place. I haven't been up there. I don't know what all they've got. I don't know how serious they are about the fighting, either. That's one of the reasons people fight wars—to find out how serious both sides are."

"If the Westside weren't serious, it wouldn't have built that wall across the 405," Liz said.

"Or maybe it just didn't think the Valley would think the wall was worth fighting about." Dad shrugged. "If it didn't, it was wrong. And it looks like a lot of people will get hurt because of that."

If the fighting came all the way down into Westwood, the Mendozas could escape back to the home timeline. A transposition chamber would whisk them away in nothing flat. The locals weren't so lucky. They were stuck here. They had to hope the struggle stayed far away. Liz hoped for the same thing. She didn't want anything bad to happen to the locals, and she really didn't want anything bad to happen to UCLA.

Dan watched a couple of officers load an impressive-looking piece of ordnance onto a horse's back. "Wow," he said. "What's that?" The cartridges gleamed in the sunshine. Each one looked as big as his thumb. The weapon had to come from the Old Time. Nobody nowadays could make anything like that.

"Machine gun—.50-caliber," one of them answered proudly. "We test-fired it, and it shoots great."

"That is so cool!" Dan said. "I didn't know anything like that was left in the armory."

"It didn't come from the armory," the captain said. "Scrounger found it in a house."

"No kidding?" Dan said, and the officer nodded. Dan went on, "Ordinary people could have a piece like that in their houses? Wow! Old Time must've been something else." That gun might beat the Westside all by itself now.

"Old Time *was* something else," the other officer said.

"Oh, yes, sir." Dan knew better than to show he disagreed with any officer, even when he did. But he didn't disagree with this one. "Ordinary people had guns like this, the way folks have belt knives now. Makes you wonder what all the kings—no, they called them presidents—had, though."

"They had the Fire," the first captain said grimly. "They had it, and they used it. And that's how come we don't have so much any more."

He was right about that. The Russians threw the Fire at America, and then the Americans threw it back. That was what the schoolbooks said, and why would they lie? Dan didn't know exactly where Russia was. Somewhere far away—he was sure of that, anyhow. Farther than TJ, farther than Vegas, farther than Frisco. You went a whole lot farther than that, you probably fell off the edge of the world. Schoolbooks also insisted the world was round. Again, why would they lie? But Dan had his doubts. The world sure looked flat to him. Well, bumpy in spots, but basically flat.

The officers with the machine gun looked at him, then at

each other. The second one spoke up: "I bet you've got something you need to do, don't you, soldier? If you have time to rubberneck, we'll *find* you something to do."

"Oh, no, sir. I've got plenty. It was just seeing the fancy gun that made me stop, that's all." Dan saluted and beat a hasty retreat. You didn't always have to be busy in the army. But you always had to look busy. If you didn't look busy, somebody would make sure you were.

He hustled over to the barracks. He had a whetstone in his kit. He started using it to sharpen the points on his arrows. He'd sharpened them just the other day. They couldn't very well have got dull between then and now. Anybody who saw him, though, would think he had plenty of work and didn't need anything more. That was the point, all right.

Had officers and sergeants been so silly back in the Old Time? Dan didn't want to believe it. They'd known so much. They'd been able to do so many things. They wouldn't have wanted soldiers to waste time for the sake of wasting time . . . would they?

Of course, in the end the Old Time folks, the Americans and the Russians, had blown themselves up. They'd thrown away all their marvels, thrown them into the Fire. In school, the books and the teachers said they'd been about to fly to the moon before they went to war instead. The moon! There were still pictures of airplanes, and nobody doubted that the Fire flew before it fell. But the moon! Could people really have gone there?

If they could have . . . If the people of Old Time could have gone to the moon but chose to blow themselves up instead . . . If they chose to do that, were they as smart as everybody always said they were? Or were they amazingly, unbelievably, dumb?

Dan stopped sharpening. He just stood there, file in one hand, arrow in the other. It wasn't against the law to think the people of Old Time were dumb—not quite. It wasn't against any religion to think they were dumb, either—not quite. But if you had a thought like that, you probably didn't want to admit it to anybody, either. People would call you a weirdo or a fruitcake or even a nonconformist. You didn't want to get hung with a label like that. It could stick to you for the rest of your life.

"What's happening, Dan?" Sergeant Chuck appeared behind him at just the wrong moment. Sergeants had a knack for doing that.

"Nothing, Sergeant." Dan started scraping the point against the file again. "I just saw our machine gun. It's too much!" That should be safe.

And it was. "Wait till the Westsiders see it. Wait till they meet it up close and personal. They'll freak out, man—you better believe it." Chuck smiled as if he could hardly wait. That was part of what made him a sergeant.

Dan was ready to go to war, but he wasn't in any big hurry about it. King Zev and his officers were. The next morning, right at sunup, Dan set his helmet on his head. He was just an archer—not a fancy kind of soldier at all. And yet he still wore a genuine U.S. Army steel helmet from the Old Time. If that didn't prove what a rich and powerful kingdom the Valley was, he didn't know what would.

The metal facing on his shield came from an Old Time car door. You could see where, once upon a time, it had said *Falcon*. Falcons were swift, fierce birds, so he thought that was a good omen. His shirt and trousers and boots were modern, but he thought his belt buckle came from the days before the Fire fell, too.

Captain Kevin made a little speech before his company set out. "When we march today, we're going to start marching up Victory Boulevard," he said. "And every step we take till this war is done, we're going to stay on the road to victory. The Westsiders can't stop us, because we're right and they're wrong. We're tougher than they are, too. If they don't know that yet, they'll find out."

Up Victory Boulevard they went, along with the rest of King Zev's soldiers. There had to be two or three thousand men in that army, maybe even more. They sang as they marched, alternating old songs like "Satisfaction" and "Hound Dog" with new ones like "A Mighty Fortress Is Our King." Dan couldn't carry a tune in a bucket, but he enjoyed making noise.

Some of the companies marched south on the 405 when they got to the old freeway. They were going to attack the wall. Dan's unit—and, he was excited to see, the machine gun as well—went south along Sepulveda Boulevard instead. They could support the troops on the 405, because the road and the freeway ran close together.

Still other Valley soldiers kept heading east. From what Dan heard, they would go south by way of Laurel Canyon. The thinking was that the Westsiders wouldn't be looking for a three-pronged attack. The City Council down there didn't know how strong and how determined the Valley was. Captain Kevin had said it best—they'd find out.

It was a hot day, like almost any summer day in the Valley. Wearing a steel hat sure didn't make it any cooler. Sweat ran down Dan's face. "Drink plenty of water!" Captain Kevin called to his men. "Eat some salt, too. But remember to drink. Nobody keels over before we go into action, right?"

"Yes, sir!" Dan shouted along with the rest of the men. He swigged from his canteen and crunched sea salt between his teeth. Sweat was wet and salty. It only stood to reason that salt and water put back what you sweated away.

For a while, stores and apartment buildings lined Sepulveda Boulevard. After the men passed the 101, though, those petered out. There were some houses on either side of the road. Their windows, empty now of glass, looked on the marching men like the eye sockets of so many skulls. Dan wished that hadn't crossed his mind. It gave him the creeps. His free hand twisted in a sign to hold evil away.

His shield and the helmet and his quiver and the long knife he wore on his belt and the pack with his rations in it all started to feel heavy as lead. *Do I really need all this stuff?* he wondered. *Can I throw some of it away?*

He tried to imagine what Sergeant Chuck would say if he did. Then he tried to imagine what the sergeant would do to him if he did. Whatever it was, it wouldn't be pretty. He hung on to his stuff.

Soldiers lined up to fill their canteens at a cistern. Without those, the Valley would have been in trouble. So would the Westside and all the other little countries that made up Greater L.A. You had to save all the winter water you could, or else you'd run low in the summertime.

A medic poured brandy into each canteen—not too much. It kept down the runs. Anybody who improved the water too much caught it from his sergeant. After the men drank, they pressed on.

Along with her father and mother, Liz watched the Westside's soldiers march toward battle. They tramped west along Sunset toward the 405 and Sepulveda. Here as in the home timeline's Southern California, the very richest of the rich lived north of Sunset.

There were differences, though. In the home timeline, hardly any of those super-rich people had children who joined the army. Lots of young officers came from that group here. They were willing to put their lives on the line for what they believed in.

In other words, they were willing to put their lives on the line for the sake of a wall across the top of Sepulveda Pass. The more Liz thought about it, the crazier it seemed. She wondered what would happen if she said so to one of the soldiers in the muddy green, not-too-uniform uniforms. No, actually, she didn't wonder. She had a pretty good idea. She'd get arrested for being unpatriotic, and things would go downhill from there.

So, feeling like a hypocrite, she cheered and clapped her hands. One of the standard-bearers grinned at her. Why not? She was a pretty girl not far from his age. The Westside flag had a bear on it. Part of the bear seemed to come from the one on the old California state flag, part from the UCLA Bruin. That left it looking fierce and friendly at the same time, but the Westsiders didn't care.

"How big is this army?" Liz asked her father.

"I don't know." He shrugged. "A couple of thousand men? Something like that."

"Are they enough?"

Her father shrugged again. "We'll find out," he said, which wasn't what she wanted to hear.

The cheering got louder. Here came Cal and his dog Pots. The beast looked as if it could eat half the Valley's army all by itself. Behind Cal came a horse that carried armor for Pots. The chunks of iron looked like the ones that had protected horses back in the days when knights were bold and life was nasty, brutish, and short. (*Hobbes*, Liz thought, remembering AP Euro.)

Cal waved his big white Stetson. "We'll get 'em!" he shouted to the people. "They won't come past us!"

"*Ils ne passeront pas*," Dad murmured. "That goes back a couple of hundred years. I wonder if he knows."

"Ask not what the Westside can do for you," Cal added. "Ask what you can do for the Westside!"

Liz's father stirred again. That one rang a bell with her, too. She remembered grainy black-and-white video from the middle of the twentieth century. Even across almost a century and a half of changing hair and clothes styles, she remembered thinking how handsome John Kennedy was. Maybe he hadn't been the greatest President. Nobody'd cared much, then or later. An aura of glamour surrounded him to this day.

It did here, too. Kennedy half-dollars weren't just coins in this alternate. They were amulets. Only rich men had them, and mostly wore them on chains around their necks. The coins were credited with everything from magically stopping bullets—more irony, when you thought about it—to curing smallpox.

Smallpox . . . Liz rubbed at her left arm. In the home timeline, the disease was extinct. But she'd had to get vaccinated before she came to this alternate. People here vaccinated, too—they remembered that much. Not everybody got vaccinated, though, and the disease still broke out every now and then. The pocked faces of survivors were . . . appalling.

And people from the home timeline did a brisk business selling perfect copies of Kennedy halves. Yes, it was taking advantage of superstition. But the superstition would have been there whether they took advantage of it or not. In other alternates, Crosstime Traffic sold religious relics of several different kinds. What was the difference, really? Liz had trouble seeing any.

For that matter, what was the difference between superstition and religion generally? Lots of people had spilled lots of ink and killed lots of trees and pushed around lots of electrons trying to define the answer. So far, most of what they said boiled down to *What I believe is religion, and what those foolish people over there believe is superstition.*

There was no evidence that knocking on wood made the world less likely to go wrong. There was no evidence that praying in a church or synagogue or mosque made the world less likely to go wrong, either. That didn't stop people from doing both kinds of things. When it first became plain that science explained how things happened—not necessarily why, but how—better than religion did, lots of "experts," from Karl Marx on down, predicted that religion would wither up and die.

It hadn't happened in the home timeline. It also hadn't happened in any high-tech alternate Crosstime Traffic had found. Most people weren't rational enough, or weren't rational often enough, to be satisfied believing this was all there was. By now, the "experts" doubted they ever would. That might prove as wrong as the earlier experts' certainty that religion would fail.

In low-tech alternates, religion was the only game in town. More and more, that was how things worked in this one. Liz had a hard time blaming the locals for feeling that way. What had science done for them here? Dropped them in the frying pan and turned up the heat, and that was about it.

Oh, the Westsiders still called themselves scientific. But they still called themselves democratic, too. That was another joke, except it wasn't funny.

A priest and a rabbi and a minister marched with the Westside army. No doubt a priest and a rabbi and a minister marched with the Valley's army, too. And no doubt both sides were sure God meant them to win. Some things didn't change no matter what alternate you were in—and no matter how much you wished they would.

Supply wagons made a dull close to a military parade, but no army was much good without them. Mules and horses twitched their ears as they trudged along. It wasn't their war, but people made the work anyway. They didn't like it, not that the teamsters cared. The draft animals got even less vote than the people had at the City Council meeting.

After the soldiers and the wagons passed, the Westsiders started drifting back toward their homes. "Show's over," Liz's mother said. "Now we hope we don't seen the soldiers for a while, 'cause if we do—"

"Something's gone wrong somewhere," Dad finished for her.

"Well, yes." Mom sent Dad a dirty look. Liz didn't blame her. She didn't like getting her lines stepped on, either.

The dirty look sailed over Dad's head the way a badly aimed arrow would have. He said, "Let's get back to the house."

Getting back to the house, of course, meant *walking* back to the house. That was a couple of miles—Liz more readily thought of it as three kilometers—and took more than half an hour. Going from one place to another here was like traveling in the home timeline in one way. Ten minutes of travel was a short trip, half an hour was kind of medium, an hour was long, and two hours was a pain in the neck reserved for something that had better be special.

But how far you went in your time shrank drastically. Here you traveled on foot, or maybe on horseback. If you were very rich, you might have a carriage. Some bicycles survived, but their rubber tires didn't. With wooden tires, riding them was a good way to shake your kidneys loose.

And so you mostly didn't go more than four or five miles—six or eight kilometers—from where you lived. As they had in the days before trains and cars and planes, people lived their whole lives within twenty or thirty miles of where they were born. If this alternate didn't regain its technology, lots of little, very different peoples would sprout from the ruined tree trunk of the USA.

That was already starting to happen. The Westside and the Valley weren't just independent countries. People in both of them spoke English, but it wasn't quite the same English. People from the Valley had a nasal accent that made it pretty easy to pick them out from Westsiders by ear. In another few hundred years, the two dialects might turn into separate languages. Even if they didn't, it was pretty clear that people from Southern California would have trouble understanding people from the upper Midwest. And both those groups would have trouble with the language they spoke in the deep South.

Liz looked around to make sure no locals could overhear. When she saw they couldn't, she asked, "Is what I'm getting out of the library helping you figure out just where this alternate split off from the home timeline?"

"It will help. It's bound to," her mother answered.

"It may take a while, though," her father added. "I envy ancient historians. There's only so much for them to know. It's not like that when you get up into the twentieth century. You're drowning in data. It does seem plain that the breakpoint has to do with the Vietnam War, though."

"We already knew that," Liz said. "Or we were pretty sure, anyhow."

Her father nodded. "It was always a good bet, since the big war started while the Vietnam War was going strong. But it still isn't obvious whether the U.S. escalation here scared the Russians enough to make them start throwing rockets, or whether the United States threw them first when we didn't like what Russia and China were doing."

"Whoever shot first, an awful lot of people on both sides ended up dead." Liz eyed this sorry version of the UCLA campus. "And there's been nothing but trouble ever since."

"Nobody's going to tell you you're wrong, hon," her father said. "At that, they got off lucky here. They got bombed back to the Middle Ages, but they didn't get bombed back to the Stone Age."

"They didn't all get killed, either," Mom said. "That happened in some alternates."

Liz nodded. People really could be stupid. Just in case the home timeline didn't have enough examples of that, the alternates offered even more. People in the home timeline *hadn't* been stupid some ways. They hadn't tried blowing one another off the map with H-bombs, for instance. They were proud of that, and relieved about it, too.

Seeing what other people, people much too much like them, had done in different alternates should have made them prouder of escaping—and also more relieved. To some degree, it did. But only to some degree. Too many people in the home timeline still had axes to grind. Big wars seemed unlikely these days. Terrorist strikes, on the other hand . . .

"I've got a question," Liz said.

"What?" her mother and father asked together.

"What happens if something now makes the home timeline split into two alternates?" Liz said. "They'd both have Crosstime Traffic in them. Which one would be the real home timeline?"

Mom and Dad looked at each other. They walked on for several steps without answering. At last, her father said, "If there are no other questions, class is dismissed."

"Dad!" Liz said reproachfully.

"We're just historians. We can't deal with questions like that," her mother said. "You need to talk to the chronophysicists. If anybody can tell you, they're the ones."

"Talk to them at a convention, after they've got a few drinks under their belts," Dad added. "If you get 'em when they're in the lab, they'll look wise and tell you things like that can't happen. I hope they're right. Everybody does."

"How will we find out?" Liz asked.

"The same way people usually do, I bet," her father answered. "The hard way."

"Come on! Come on! Get moving!" Sergeant Chuck booted Dan in the seat of the pants. He didn't kick him hard enough to hurt, but it was plenty hard enough to wake him.

Chuck went on shouting and booting other soldiers awake. Dan yawned and stretched and looked around. The sun hadn't risen yet, but it would soon. It was already bright enough to see colors. Only a handful of the brightest stars still shone, and they faded out as he watched.

He pulled a square of hardtack and some smoked sausage from his pack. Some soldiers crumbled up their hardtack and fried it in bacon grease. He just crunched on his. You needed good teeth to do that. He had good teeth, and knew how lucky he was to have them. Wounded soldiers got ether before surgeons went to work on them. Ordinary people with toothaches? You needed to be rich to get knocked out before a dentist pulled a tooth that was driving you nuts.

"Everybody ready?" Captain Kevin called. "You better be ready, 'cause we're moving out!"

Dan stuffed a last chunk of sausage into his mouth. As he chewed on it, he probably looked like a hamster with its cheek pouches full. He didn't care. He kind of liked hamsters. They were a lot cuter than rats and mice. They didn't have pointy noses, and they didn't have long, naked tails, either.

Old men and women said their grandparents said there hadn't been any wild hamsters before the Fire fell. There also hadn't been any wild iguanas or parrots. And lakes and ponds hadn't had any piranhas in them. Dan wasn't sure he believed that. Wasn't it like saying there'd been a time without possums and starlings and cabbage butterflies? If there had been a time like that, nobody remembered it now.

"Form up!" the captain shouted. "Chances are we'll be in action later on today."

The soldiers who were about Dan's age hurried into place. They were as eager as he was. Older men, men who'd gone to war before, didn't move so fast. Dan thought that was because they were old. That it might be because they'd already seen battle and didn't much care for it never crossed his mind.

As carefully as if handling gold and precious jewels, the machine-gun crew loaded their lovely weapon onto the pack horse's back. Extra ammunition went onto another horse. When the men waved to Kevin, he got the company moving.

"Be alert—the enemy may have pushed scouts forward," he warned.

That made Dan try to look every which way at once. Old Sepulveda gave scouts plenty of places to hide. One could lurk in any of those dead houses, watching the Valley soldiers with field glasses. But if one was, how would he get word back to his commanders? This wasn't the Old Time. He wouldn't have a television or a radio or a telephone handy.

Here and there, people did still use telegraphs. Could a scout have strung wire out behind him so he could click away and pass on information like that? Dan supposed it wouldn't be impossible, but he didn't think it would be easy.

And how much did it matter? As they started to march, they moved uphill, toward the top of the pass. The Westsiders were already looking down into the Valley. If they didn't know King Zev's army was moving toward them, they were even dumber than Dan thought. Could you be that dumb and live? He doubted it.

That set him looking toward the top of the pass. He already knew there was a wall across the 405. Was there one across Sepulveda, too? Squint as he would, he couldn't tell. Sepulveda was lower than the freeway, and didn't show up so well against the sky.

Something howled, up ahead in the distance. The noise seemed to echo from the brush-covered walls of the pass. The hair at the back of his neck stood up. "Is that a coyote?" he asked, trying not to sound scared.

"If it is, it's a coyote the size of the Coliseum," Sergeant Chuck answered. The saying reached back to Old Times. The Coliseum didn't exist any more. One of the bombs that got L.A. and ended the good days came down not far from it.

"Does Cal really have a dog the size of a house?" Yes, Dan was nervous.

"*I* don't know. We'll see what comes out of the tunnel, that's all," Chuck said. Old Sepulveda went through a cliff near the highest part of the pass. The Westside held both ends of the tunnel. Dan would have liked it better if the border went through the middle. Then either side could have blocked the other from using that way through. As things were, the Westside had the edge.

We've got to beat them, that's all, he thought. *Then we'll hold both ends of the tunnel, and let's see how they like that.*

A cannon boomed. He thought the sound came from near the barricade the Westsiders had built. It was a black-powder boom, not the sharper crack of Old Time explosives. If you were on the wrong end of a cannonball, though, you wouldn't care one way or the other.

"Come on! Step it up!" Captain Kevin shouted. "Our friends, our neighbors, are in action. We'll help them out! Hurrah for King Zev!"

"Hurrah for King Zev!" Dan yelled. Along with the rest of Kevin's company, he trotted forward.

Another boom, this one from near the mouth of the tunnel. Dan could see this cannonball flying through the air. He ducked. He couldn't help himself. He felt ashamed till he realized the other Valley soldiers were ducking, too. The cannonball hissed over his head and smashed into an empty house with a noise like a thunderclap. Startled crows flew up, screeching.

"Spread out!" Kevin and Chuck yelled the same thing at the same time. "That way, they won't be able to get so many of you with one round," Chuck added.

Oh, boy, Dan thought. It didn't mean they wouldn't be able to get him. It just meant they'd have to work a little harder, or he'd have to be a little less lucky. He wished he hadn't thought of that.

There wasn't a whole lot of room to spread out in, either. The cracked asphalt of Old Sepulveda and the wider expanse of the 405 were the only good routes through the pass. Wreckage and undergrowth clogged the rest.

That horrible howl came again. "Holy moley!" somebody shouted, pointing south. "There he is!"

The dog had to be enormous to be noticed from that far away. Was it really as big as a house? Dan wasn't sure. It was plenty big enough—he was sure of that. Some Westside soldiers ran forward with it, to guide it toward the Valley men. Then, as it saw them or smelled them or did whatever it did to know they were there, it ran on by itself. They just wore uniforms, while it had on armor like a cavalry charger's. It easily outdistanced them even so.

Dan reached back over his shoulder for an arrow. A heartbeat later, he started to laugh at himself. As if an arrow would do anything to a creature like that even if by some accident it hit! He wanted to run. The fearsome Westside dog could bite him in half with one chomp.

A couple of Valley soldiers *did* run. Their sergeants swore at them, which didn't make them stop. They'd get in trouble later on. They had to think that was better than getting eaten right now.

Then Dan heard a sharp, repeated hammering noise: *bang! bang! bang! bang! bang!* The reports were bigger and louder than any he'd ever heard from an Old Time rifle. He looked around. The machine-gun crew had got their weapon down from the pack horse. They were banging away at the Westside monster dog as if their lives depended on it—and they did.

The dog-monster's growls changed to yelps of agony. The beast's armor would have turned arrows, maybe even musket balls. Dan didn't know about ordinary Old Time rifle bullets. He did know the armor had zero chance against the enormous slugs the .50-caliber machine gun spat.

In spite of its wounds, the dog was brave. It kept coming up Sepulveda till it couldn't move any more. It didn't finally go down till it got within a couple of hundred yards of the Valley soldiers. By then, Dan could clearly see the holes the bullets had chewed in its armor, and the blood that poured from the holes in the animal's hide. His stomach wanted to turn over—it wasn't pretty.

That cannon up near the mouth of the tunnel boomed once more. The big iron ball it fired clanged off a boulder not far from the machine gun and crazily ricocheted away. One of the men in the gun crew had some Old Time field glasses. He peered through them, then pointed. The machine gun started banging again.

Dan had no field glasses. Some of the machine-gun rounds were tracers, though. He could see where they went. The red flashes of fire led his eye straight to the cannon. The Old Time machine gun had at least as much range as the modern artillery piece. One after another, the men serving the cannon fell.

When the machine gun stopped shooting, some of the Westside artillerymen stood up. Replacements ran forward to help them fire the gun. The Valley machine gunner with the binoculars was waiting for that. As soon as the enemy gun crew was complete again, the machine gun roared back to life. More Westsiders went down. Dan didn't think they would rise till Judgment Day.

"Let's go!" Captain Kevin yelled. "They won't give us any trouble now!"

Cheering, the Valley men ran forward. Dan charged past the enormous dog's corpse. Blood puddled underneath it. Flies buzzed up in annoyance as the soldiers went past. They'd already started feeding on the body.

A few shots rang out from the Westsiders. They must have counted on the dog and the cannon to hold back the Valley troops. Now that that wasn't working, they didn't seem to have another plan. The pitiless machine gun picked off their men at a range from which they couldn't answer.

Some of the Valley soldiers started climbing up to the 405. Dan was one of them. What he saw when he got up there made him whoop and stomp his feet. The Valley men had outflanked the wall, which didn't stretch all the way across the pass. And the Westsiders were running as fast as they could.

Three

Sound really carried here. That was one of the first things Liz had noticed about this alternate. It had much less background noise than the home timeline did. No streets and freeways full of cars here. No TVs. No radios. Only a handful of windup record players. No factories, not really.

And so, when the fighting in the Sepulveda Pass got going, Liz and her family could try to figure out what was going on from what they heard. So could everybody else in Westwood.

One particular set of bangs made her father frown. "Somebody's got a heavy machine gun," he said. "For a place like this, that's a very nasty weapon."

"It's a very nasty weapon anywhere," her mother said.

"Well, yeah." Dad nodded. "But we've got even worse ones in the home timeline. Here, it's liable to be king of the hill. King of the pass, I mean."

"Do you think it belongs to the Westside or the Valley?" Liz asked.

"Yes," Dad said, deadpan.

"Thanks a lot." She gave him a dirty look. "Which one, please?"

"Well, I didn't see it in Cal's parade," her father answered. "If he had one, he would have been proud to show it off, I think."

"If the Valley has it . . ." Liz's voice trailed away.

"If the Valley has it, the people here were really dumb to go to war," Dad said. "Unless their hat has a rabbit in it, too."

"Do you think it does?" she asked, adding, "I don't want anything to happen to UCLA."

After some thought, Dad shrugged. "Hon, I just don't know. If they've got more stuff than they were showing, I haven't heard about it. But I don't know if I would. I'm just a tradesman, after all. If the big bosses have any brains, they'll keep secrets from people like me."

"If the big bosses had any brains, they would've known the Valley's got a heavy machine gun, right?" Liz said.

Her father spread his hands. "Can't argue with you. I wish I could. I've never thought King Zev was real smart, but it's amazing how brilliant you look when you can shoot your enemies and they can't shoot you back."

"Right," Liz said.

When she went out into what had been Westwood Village to shop for produce, everything seemed normal enough. People weren't paying much attention to the bangs and booms coming out of the north—or, if they were, they weren't letting on.

Apricots. Peaches. Oranges. Lemons. Avocados. Eggs. Chickens. Live baby pigs. Fish—some smoked, some salted, some you'd buy if it smelled okay. The sellers—mostly women—sat under awnings or Old Time beach umbrellas to protect themselves from the sun. Seeing what amounted to a farmers' market just south of the UCLA campus made Liz sad.

In 1967, Westwood Village had probably been the coolest

part of L.A., the way Melrose was a generation later. In the home timeline, it got commercial. Then it got grimy. Then it got redeveloped and turned cool again, even if not quite so cool as the first time around. Then the cycle started over.

In this alternate, time might as well have stopped when the bombs came down. And after it stopped, it might have started running backwards. Without running water to fight them, fires flattened a lot of the shops and restaurants and apartment buildings that had stood in the Village. The buildings here now—the house where she was staying included—were built from rubble and wreckage. The market had sprung up in one of the fire-born open spaces.

"How much for those avocados?" Liz asked an old lady in a broad-brimmed straw hat—not quite a sombrero, but close.

"Dime apiece," she answered. "Three for a quarter."

Liz had all she could do not to giggle. Old Time money still circulated here. So did newer coins on the same standard. Prices were ridiculously cheap, at least by the home timeline's standards. Liz had had to learn about pennies and nickels and dimes and quarters before she came here. In the home timeline, a dollar—the smallest coin around—wouldn't come close to buying what a penny bought here. And a benjamin—a hundred dollars—was worth somewhere between a dime and a quarter.

No matter how cheap things seemed, you couldn't take the first offer. That was an insult. "I'll give you a quarter for five," Liz said. "They aren't very big." She'd had to practice sounding that snotty.

The old lady let out a squawk. She told Liz what a snippy, rude thing she was. All this was as formal as a dance. They settled on four avocados for twenty-five cents, the way they'd both known they would. But social rules had to be followed even when they made no sense—maybe especially when they made no sense.

More bangs and booms came from the north. "Are those getting closer?" Liz asked. That wasn't in the rules about haggling, but it was liable to be more important.

After cocking her head to one side to listen, the avocado seller said, "I sure hope not. That would be a stone bummer."

"Yeah, wouldn't it?" Liz said. She wasn't sure, but she did think the noises from the north were louder than they had been. Maybe that was just her jumpy imagination talking. She could hope it was, anyhow.

Carrying the avocados in a cloth sack, she wandered through the market looking for a chicken to buy. Meat here didn't come neatly packaged in a refrigerated case at the store. If you wanted chicken stew, you bought a live chicken and whacked off its head with a hatchet. Then, after it stopped spewing blood and thrashing—which could take *much* longer than Liz would have imagined before she watched the first time—you had to pluck it and clean it. Cleaning it was a polite way to say cutting it open and taking out the guts and the lungs and whatever else you didn't want to eat.

The first time Liz helped do that, she got sick. She could handle it now, but it didn't thrill her—not even close. So she dawdled instead of buying a bird right away. Carrying one back to the house by its feet while it clucked and squawked wasn't much fun, either.

Hoofbeats drummed up the road from the west. That was more interesting than looking at one more beady-eyed chicken, so Liz turned to see what was going on. A mounted soldier galloped his horse toward the market. Liz had seen the look on his face before, back in the home timeline. People who'd just been in a traffic accident had that same air of stunned disbelief.

"What's happening, man?" somebody called.

"They beat us." The soldier's voice was eerily calm, the way those of accident survivors often were. "They beat us," he repeated, as if he'd forgotten he'd said the same thing a moment earlier. "They rolled us up. That stinking machine gun of theirs . . ." He shuddered. "They're coming. We'll try to stop them, but they're coming."

Before anyone could ask him more questions, he rode on. He left chaos in his wake. Men groaned. Women screamed and wailed. Some of the buyers and sellers decided they didn't want to hang around any more. Several of them looked to the north as if they expected a million Valley soldiers to follow hard on the horseman's heels.

That didn't happen, of course. Little by little, the ones who stayed realized it wouldn't. But by the time Liz bought a mean-looking chicken (so she wouldn't mind so much when the bird got it in the neck), several more Westside soldiers made it back from the fighting in the pass. Some rode horses. Others were on bicycles with the wooden tires they used here instead of rubber.

They all told the same story, near enough. They would have easily beaten the men from the Valley if not for that machine gun. With it, King Zev's soldiers could do no wrong. "They could kill us from ranges where we couldn't even touch them," said a man on a bike. "How are you supposed to fight a war like that?"

"Why didn't Cal know they had it?" somebody asked.

"Beats me," the soldier answered. "He didn't, though—never

in a million years." He paused, then added one more telling detail: "Pots is dead. That gun chewed up his armor like it wasn't there. Chewed him up, too."

People moaned and wept when they heard that. The monster mutant dog had been a symbol of Westside strength for years. What did he symbolize now? The collapse of Westside strength? It sure looked that way to Liz.

Sack of avocados in one hand, chicken legs in the other, her head full of news, she headed back toward the house. She was glad to give her mother the chicken. She wasn't so glad to pass the news along.

Mom's mouth tightened. "I was afraid of that. Remember how your father said a heavy machine gun would be big trouble?"

"Well, he was right." Liz didn't say that every day. She got on well with her father, but she didn't always agree with him—not even close. She paused, gulped, and asked, "What do we do if . . . if the Valley soldiers come here?"

"Try to stay out of their way," her mother answered. "Try not to make them notice us. Try not to get in trouble. Try to protect UCLA, if we can."

"How do we do that if we're doing all those other things, too?" Liz asked. This time, Mom didn't answer. Liz wondered why. She thought it was a mighty good question.

Dan was over the top of Sepulveda Pass. The wall the Westsiders had run up—the wall that had started the war—lay behind him. Prisoners the Valley troops had taken were already starting to knock it down.

"All downhill from here!" Captain Kevin shouted. The men in his company cheered.

The captain meant it both literally and figuratively. Dan figured the fight would get easier from here on out, too. And it *was* downhill from here, all the way into Westwood and Brentwood, the Westsiders' most important northern centers.

Not all the enemy soldiers had given up and run away. Somebody fired a musket from behind a boulder. A cloud of black-powder smoke told where he hid. The bullet hit the asphalt maybe twenty feet from Dan and ricocheted away.

"Shall we hunt him down, sir?" Sergeant Chuck asked.

Captain Kevin shook his head. "No. It would only waste our time, and that's what he wants. Spread the men out so they're harder to hit, that's all. Once we finish taking the Westside apart, this guy will have to surrender, too."

"Yes, sir," the sergeant said. Dan didn't think he liked the order, but he obeyed it. Before long, the musketeer fired again. He missed again, too. A musket would shoot farther than a bow, but it was less accurate. If he'd had an Old Time rifle, now . . . But he didn't, and Dan was glad he didn't.

Before long, the Valley men came to another barricade across the 405. This one was made of rubble, and plainly brand new. Some Westside soldiers crouched behind it, aiming to stop the troops from the Valley—or, more likely, to delay them, anyhow. A couple of the Westsiders did have Old Time weapons. They opened up too soon, though, and warned the Valley men. Dan and his comrades scrambled off the freeway into the brush to either side. If they had to work their way past the men with the dangerous weapons, then they did, that was all.

And then the machine gun started hammering at the Westsiders again. With that gun reaching for you, you had to be crazy, or at least crazy-brave, to expose yourself to the death it spat.

Some of them were. They held their ground and tried to shoot back. But the machine gun was too much for most of them to face. Some of its bullets even punched through the junk they'd piled up to protect themselves. So was it any wonder that a lot of them ran away to fight somewhere else another time—or maybe just to save their own lives?

Wonder or not, one of the Westsiders dashed past Dan without knowing or caring that he was close by. The enemy soldier couldn't have been more than a year or two older than he was himself. Dan set an arrow on his bowstring, drew, and let fly all in one smooth motion. The string scraped across his leather wristguard.

The arrow caught the Westsider in his right calf. He went down with a wail. Dan had aimed at his chest. Still, a hit was a hit. Drawing his shortsword, Dan ran forward. "Surrender!" he yelled. "You're my prisoner!"

"It hurts!" the Westsider said. "It hurts!" He hardly even knew Dan was there. Pain twisted his face. Blood ran from the wound—Dan could smell it as well as seeing it. All at once, gulping, he was less proud of what he'd done.

"You give up?" Dan said roughly, and then, "You better give up. You reach for that musket, it's the last dumb thing you'll ever do."

"It hurts!" the Westsider wailed again. After that, he blinked and seemed to realize he had company. He looked from Dan to the musket he'd dropped. "Stupid thing isn't loaded anyway."

He could say that, which didn't make it true. "Do you surrender?" Dan demanded. "This is your last chance." That sounded tough, but what would he do if the Westsider said no? Kill him in cold blood? He wasn't sure he could.

He didn't have to find out, because the Westsider answered, "Yeah, I surrender. What else can I do? Will you put a bandage on my leg?"

"Sure," Dan said. "Want me to push the arrow through first? Otherwise, the surgeon will have to cut for it, and I don't think we've got ether for prisoners."

"Oh, wow." The captured enemy sounded bleak. Dan would have, too, were it his leg. Only luck that it wasn't, luck and a heavy machine gun. If one of those slugs had hit this guy, he wouldn't be freaking out about a nice clean wound. He'd likely be dead. Dan had gone past some Westsiders who'd stopped .50-caliber rounds. Even if the bullet didn't hit a vital spot, the shock of getting smacked by something moving that fast could kill.

"Well, do you?" Dan asked when the Westsider didn't give him a straight answer.

"Yeah, go ahead." The other youngster set himself.

But before Dan could, Sergeant Chuck said, "Come on, kid—get moving. Throw his musket some place where he can't grab it, and get yourself in gear. He won't be your personal slave, even if you did shoot him. You're here to fight. We've got other people to clean up the mess afterwards."

"Okay, Sarge." Dan wasn't sorry to have an excuse to get to his feet. He knew what you were supposed to do about an arrow wound, but he'd never tried it before. He didn't much want to, either. Hurting somebody on purpose, even if you were helping at the same time, seemed harder than shooting at the same person had been. That was crazy, but it was true. He nodded to the Westsider. "Uh, good luck."

"Thanks a bunch," the wounded soldier said. Dan grabbed the musket and flung it into the brush. The Westsider wasn't likely to go after it.

"Let's move." Chuck gave Dan a shove. Dan got moving. The sergeant asked, "First one you shot?"

"First one I know I did, anyway," Dan answered.

"Yeah, sometimes you can't tell," Chuck agreed. "How do you feel about it?"

Dan wanted to brag about how heroic he was. He found that the words wouldn't come out of his mouth. What did come out was, "I almost barfed." He waited for the tough sergeant to laugh at him.

But Chuck only nodded. "Well, that's honest," he said. "I felt the same way the first time I did it. People who aren't soldiers think war's a game. The ones who have to fight know better."

"Some soldiers brag about what they do," Dan said.

"Most of the ones who brag haven't really done it," Chuck replied. "Some of the others . . ." His mouth tightened. "Well, some people get off on hurting others. They're good killers. They usually aren't good soldiers. There's a difference."

"I guess." Dan hadn't really thought about that before.

A few hundred yards ahead, some Westsiders were making another stand. They couldn't hope to stop the Valley army now—or they were flipping out if they thought they could. But they could slow down the advance through the pass. That would let more of their own men get away.

"Come on! Come on!" Captain Kevin shouted. "We have to

outflank them. They'll be sorry they tried to mess with us then. They—" He broke off with a howl of pain, clutching at his right upper arm.

"The captain's hit!" Chuck shouted. He and Dan weren't especially near the wounded Valley officer.

One of Kevin's lieutenants spoke up: "We have to go on! Our medics will see to the captain!" That deep voice had to belong to Hank. He made a pretty good number two man. Dan had never thought of him as a commander, but now he had the chance to show what he could do.

For the moment, he did what Captain Kevin had been on the point of doing. He led the Valley men around the makeshift scrape of earth and rubble the enemy had thrown up. He didn't wait for the heavy machine gun to make the Westsiders keep their heads down. Instead, he used riflemen and musketeers for the same job. They did what needed doing, too. There weren't that many defenders, which helped.

When the Westside soldiers saw the Valley men were starting to slip around behind them, they fled. Dan shot at one of them. He wasn't too disappointed when his arrow missed. He did think he aimed honestly—he didn't want to let his kingdom down or anything. But he still wasn't sorry not to be responsible for hurting somebody else.

Some of the other Valley men were hurting the Westsiders. Dan watched a man go down, clutching at his side. A Valley soldier ran over to him, picked up a loose chunk of asphalt, and bashed in his head. "For the captain!" the Valley man yelled. He kicked the Westsider—who had to be dead after that—and ran on.

If they'd won, they would have done the same thing to us,

Dan thought. He knew that was true. The Westsiders wouldn't have turned Cal's huge, horrible dog loose on anybody they loved. Even so, seeing what war was all about and what it did to people didn't make him happy.

Then a bullet cracked past his head. It came so close that he felt, or thought he felt, the wind of its passage. While he was being sorry war was so savage, somebody on the other side was doing his level best to kill him. And the enemy soldier's level best was almost good enough.

If the Westsiders were going to fight, how could he do anything else? He saw no way. They were probably asking themselves the same question about King Zev's troops, but Dan couldn't do anything about that.

He'd been fighting and scrambling forward all day long. Even so, he realized, he wasn't nearly so hot and sweaty as he would have been back home. People said the weather on the Westside was cooler than it was in the Valley. They talked about the sea breeze. Dan had never seen the sea. He knew it was there, but he'd never gone down Topanga to see it. That was an all-day journey. A lot of the time, what people said was a bunch of bull. Here, though, it looked as if those people—whoever they were—knew what they were talking about. It really *was* cooler once you started coming down the south side of Sepulveda Pass.

"*Jeep! Jeep! Jeep!*" A scrub jay yelled at him from a bush. He almost jumped out of his skin. Scrub jays lived in the Valley, too—he saw them all the time. But he hadn't noticed this one till it started screeching. The way ice ran through him told him how jumpy he was.

Firing picked up again. The pass widened out as it got

lower. There wouldn't be many more places for the Westsiders to make a stand before the Valley men came to Brentwood.

A cannon boomed. The smoke that poured from the muzzle looked like thick fog. Dan saw fog every so often in the Valley. There was supposed to be more of it down below the pass. The cannonball slammed down onto the 405, scattering chips of asphalt that probably bit like bullets. It bounced up the freeway, not much bigger than a softball.

A Valley soldier stuck out a foot to try to stop it. "Don't do that!" Sergeant Chuck screamed. The startled man jerked back his foot just in time. The cannonball bounced on.

"Why shouldn't he stop it, Sarge?" Dan asked.

"Because he wouldn't, that's why," Chuck answered. "It's still going fast, and it's solid iron. If it hit him in the foot, they'd likely have to amputate, 'cause it'd smash him to the devil and back again."

"Really?" Dan had trouble believing it. Had he stood where the other soldier was, chances were he would have done the same thing. He eyed Chuck. Was the sergeant pulling his leg?

But Chuck solemnly raised his right hand. "By King Zev's name, I swear it's true," he said. "I haven't seen it, but I know somebody who did. He wouldn't lie, either—he's not that kind."

"Okay, Sarge." Dan believed that Chuck believed it. Whether it was true . . . Who would want to find out by trying it?

The Westside cannon roared again. A horse shrieked and toppled, spouting blood. The man on the horse yelled, too, when its weight came down on his leg. Dan had been amazed to find out how much blood a man's body held. A horse's held much more, and it was just as red, just as scary.

From behind the advancing Valley soldiers, the heavy

machine gun started up again. Those big, nasty slugs probed for the cannon crew. The machine gun had at least as much range as the miserable modern gun. The muzzle-loading cannon fired one ball at a time. After that, the crew had to go through a fancy dance to reload it. It got off maybe a round a minute. Maybe. The machine gun, on the other hand . . .

One after another, Westside artillerymen went down. The cannon stopped shooting. The Westsiders brought up horses to haul it away so it could fight somewhere else later on. The machine gunners waited till the Westsiders hitched the horses to the gun carriage. Then, cruelly efficient, they shot them down.

"You hate to do that," Chuck said. "The poor horses don't know what's going on. This isn't their fault. But if they can help the bad guys hurt you . . ."

Down there in the Westsiders' shattered lines, were they calling the machine gunners *the bad guys*? They probably were. The gun had done more to smash their hopes than the rest of the Valley army put together.

Bang! . . . Bang! Bang! That wasn't a machine gun. But it was an Old Time rifle, fired from the Westside position. Dan needed a few heartbeats to figure out what was going on. Then he did. The Westsider was trying to pick off the machine gunners the way the Valley men had nailed the artillery crew.

He tried, yeah, but he didn't have much luck. The machine gun was just at or just past the extreme range of his piece. His bullets could reach about that far, but not with any accuracy. And he could also fire only one round at a time, though he managed several shots a minute.

When the machine gun answered, it put out a lot of lead. If one bullet didn't get the rifleman, the next would, or the one after that. A Westsider threw up his hands and then flopped down limply over the rough barricade behind which he was shooting. Was that the troublesome fellow with the rifle?

The machine gunners must have thought so. They kept shooting to make sure he'd been killed. Dan watched the body jerk several times. By the time the Valley machine-gun crew turned the weapon in a new direction, the Westsider had to be dead.

Another Westside soldier scrambled over the barrier to rescue the valuable Old Time rifle. The machine gunners shot him before he could get his hands on it.

"Serves him right," Sergeant Chuck said. "There's a time to show how brave you are, and there's a time to use your brains. You don't go sticking your head in the cougar's mouth, not more than once you don't."

Dan nodded. The machine gun was much more deadly than any cougar ever born. Cougars would have climbed trees to get away from the Westsiders' mutant dog. The gun had killed it easy as you please.

"Oh, wow!" Somebody pointed ahead. "Look at all the houses and stuff."

Some of those buildings were too big and fancy to be houses. UCLA was down there somewhere. Its bear had gone into the Westside flag—Dan knew that much. It was supposed to be a store of wisdom, too.

How much good had its wisdom done the Westside, though? If the people who lived there were wise, would they have picked a fight with the Valley? Dan didn't think so. The Westsiders were probably sorry now. Being sorry was easy, but it usually came too late to do any good.

The other soldier pointed again, this time to the southwest. "Oh, wow!" he repeated. "Is that the ocean? Can it be?"

Dan's eyes followed the man's outstretched index finger. Off in the distance, where things got blue and hazy, the land did seem to end. Something even bluer lay beyond it. The Pacific? "The sea," Dan murmured, awe prickling through him. "The sea!"

In a moment, all the Valley soldiers were chanting it: "The sea! The sea!" How many of them had ever seen it before? Maybe a few of the officers had, and some who came from widely traveled merchant families. But for most of the Valley men, the sea was only a vast mystery—or it had been, till now.

One reason they could see it was that a bomb had flattened Santa Monica. Whatever tall buildings had stood there were nothing but melted stumps now. Dan wondered why no bomb had come down on the rest of the Westside. That would have taken care of those people once and for all.

Did the Westsiders feel the same way about the Valley? Wondering whether they did never occurred to Dan.

More and more panicky Westside soldiers ran through Westwood Village. All of them went from north to south. None seemed interesting in fortifying the area against an attack from the Valley. Was that good news or bad? Liz wasn't sure.

"I think we're going to get occupied," her father said.

Liz thought so, too. "What will the Valley soldiers do?" she asked nervously.

"Well, they won't shoot up the village and smash things with cannonballs," her mother answered. "If the Westsiders tried to make a stand here, they would."

As the sun set, somebody knocked on the Mendozas' door. Dad opened it. There stood Cal in his trademark white Stetson and plaid jacket. A couple of bodyguards with rifles followed him. "You boys can wait outside," he told them as he stepped over the threshold.

"But—" one of the guards began.

"It's okay," Cal said flatly. "If I have to worry about these people, no place is safe for me." As Liz's father closed the door, Cal muttered, "And maybe no place is. The way things are going . . ."

"What can we do for you, sir?" Dad asked.

"I hear you have a way to keep things safe for people," Cal said. "Is that so?"

A stout safe, one that looked as if it came from the Old Time, was hidden in a storeroom. In fact, it came from the home timeline. The locals wouldn't be able to break into it . . . though they might torture the combination out of someone. Dad *could* also take stuff back to the home timeline if he had to or wanted to.

He picked his words with care: "There's safe, and then there's safe. If someone puts a gun to my head, I won't get killed to hang on to something for somebody else."

"No, no. I understand that," Cal said. "But within reason, you can, right? And you can make things hard to find, right?"

"Sometimes. If things work out the way they should." Dad was playing it as cagey as he could. Liz didn't blame him a bit.

Cal didn't seem to be fussy. "Here." He thrust a large leather pouch at Liz's father. "Hang on to this till I can come back and get it. I hope that won't be long. I hope I can rally our forces and lead us to the victory we deserve. I aim to try." He suddenly ran out of bluster. "But you never can tell. Hang on to it, like I said. If I don't come back for it, I'll see if I can find some kind of way for you to get it back to me. Is that a deal?"

"That's a deal," Dad said. It wasn't one that committed him to much.

"Good!" Cal stuck out his hand. Dad shook it. Cal made as if to tip his hat, then went out the door and hurried away. He and his bodyguards trotted around a corner. After that, Liz couldn't see them any more.

"What did he give you?" she asked her father.

Dad hefted the pouch. "A lot of what's in here has to be gold. Nothing else that takes up so little room is so heavy." He grinned wryly. "Oh, it could be lead, but I don't think so."

"Why don't you look?" Liz said. "He didn't tell say you couldn't or anything. He didn't even ask you not to."

She watched Dad fight temptation and lose. The expressions chasing one another across his face were pretty funny. "You're right," he said after maybe ten seconds. "Let's go in the kitchen, where we can spread stuff out."

Mom was chopping up tomatoes when Liz and Dad came in. Everything here got done by hand. Liz had found out about chickens the hard way. But there were no food processors here. No fancy bread machines, either. Making food was work, a lot of work. Keeping it fresh was even more work—no refrigeration, either. If you didn't want to eat it the day you made it, or the day after that, you had to salt it or smoke it or dry it.

"What have you got there?" Mom asked. She seemed glad of any excuse to knock off for a while.

"Cal gave it to Dad," Liz answered.

"He's heading into, ah, political exile," Dad added. "He

hopes he'll be back, but he's not making like Douglas MacArthur."

"He'd better not, not with that hat and that coat," Mom said. "So what did he leave behind?"

"We're going to find out." Dad opened the pouch and spilled its contents onto a table with a Formica top and iron legs with peeling chrome trim: an Old Time relic. Some of the gold that spilled out was old coins. Some was rings and bracelets and necklaces. Some was just lumps, where a goldsmith had melted stuff down.

"So you're deeper into the banking business," Mom said to Dad.

"Looks that way," he agreed.

"Anything else in the pouch? Hope, maybe?" Liz had been studying Greek mythology, and it rubbed off.

"I'll find out." Her father reached inside. He pulled out a folded sheet of paper. It was modern, not from the Old Time. Ironically, that meant it would last better. It wasn't cheap wood pulp that started turning brown the day it got made. Instead, it came from old rags, the way paper had when it was just invented.

As Dad turned it over, Liz saw a wax seal and some upside-down writing on the other side. "What does it say?" she asked.

" 'Open only if you know I'm dead,' " Dad answered.

"Are you going to pay attention to that?" Mom asked.

He thought about it, then nodded. He didn't look very happy, though. "I guess I am," he said. "Cal *might* come back and get his stuff."

"Yeah, and then you wake up." Mom wasn't sarcastic very often, but she could be dangerous when she let fly.

As if to underscore what she said, bursts of gunfire came from the north—from not nearly far enough away. Screams said somebody'd been wounded. Running feet and galloping hooves added to the racket outside. As far as Liz could tell, they were all going from north to south. If those weren't more Westsiders getting out while the getting was good, Liz would have been amazed.

"See?" Mom said.

Dad spread his hands, palms up. "This is now. Who knows what things will look like next year, or even next week? Maybe the Valley's machine gun will break down. Maybe it'll run out of ammo. Or maybe the Westsiders will scrounge one of their own. Cal won't be happy if he comes back and finds out we've been snooping."

"You're no fun," Liz's mother said. "Besides, can't we match the seal and put it back so he never finds out we peeked?"

"It's not as simple as you make it sound," Dad answered. Liz happened to know he was right. Sealing wax was low-tech, which didn't make it a bad security device. Oh, you could beat it. If you took a mold of the existing seal before you broke it, you could replace it with one that looked the same. If you didn't put the replacement in *just* the same spot, though, somebody with sharp eyes or a suspicious nature could tell what you'd been up to.

"Hold it!" Somebody out there yelled. Was that the nasal whine of a Valley accent? The man went on, "Don't you move, or you'll be sorry!"

Somebody must have moved, because a musket boomed a second later. And an anguished cry from right in front of the house said whoever had moved *was* sorry now.

"Search that man!" ordered the fellow who'd warned against moving.

"For sure, Sergeant!" That had to be a Valley soldier talking. They were here in Westwood Village, then. Cal had got out just in time. A moment later, the soldier said, "He's got silver!"

"Well, save me my share," the sergeant said.

"I wouldn't hold out on you—honest." The soldier sounded offended.

"Okay, Dan. Keep your shirt on." The sergeant, by contrast, seemed to be doing his best not to laugh. He went on, "That guy need a doctor?"

"Nope," Dan answered. "You got him in the neck, and he's dead. Nice shot."

"Thanks."

They both seemed casual about death. How much of it had they seen before? How much had they dealt out? Liz's stomach did a slow lurch as she thought about that.

And then her heart leaped into her mouth, because the soldier—Dan—was banging on the front door and yelling, "Open up! Open up in the name of King Zev!"

Four

"Open up!" Dan shouted. "Open up in the name of King Zev!"

He didn't know what he would do if the people inside didn't. He couldn't shoot through the door, not with a bow and arrows. The windows were narrow, shuttered slits. Like most modern houses, this one rejected the street. It would have a courtyard inside from which to draw light and air.

He might start a fire if the people inside proved stubborn. That would fix them. Trouble was, it might fix them too well—them and all their neighbors, and maybe the Valley soldiers, too. Starting fires was easy. Putting them out once they got going . . . That was a different story.

Back in the Old Time, there'd been underground pipes full of water. The pipes were still there. The water wasn't. You couldn't fight fires with buckets and cisterns, not if you expected to win. Everybody dreaded them.

And so Dan dropped any thought of arson, even if he was in the enemy's country. He banged on the door again, louder this time. "Open up!"

Sergeant Chuck had a gun. He could fire through the door if he felt like it. Would he? Dan doubted it. Why should this house be more important than any of the others around here?

Then, to Dan's surprise, the door opened. A middle-aged man with glasses—not common these days, but not unknown—looked out at him. "Yes?" the fellow said in a mild voice. "What do you want?"

"Uh—" Dan felt foolish, which was putting it mildly. He'd been making noise and acting tough—that was all.

Chuck knew what was what. He pointed his musket at the local and growled, "Who are you? What have you got in there?"

"My name is Mendoza," the man with the glasses answered. "I'm a trader. I'm a peaceable man. I don't want any trouble. All kinds of things are here. If you want them, take them. Things are just—things. They aren't worth getting killed over. I won't try to fight you."

"Like you could," Dan said scornfully.

But Sergeant Chuck was thoughtful. "He might cause trouble if he felt like it, Dan," he said. Then he spoke straight to the trader: "You've seen the elephant once or twice, I expect."

"Could be," Mendoza said. "I've fought bandits. Not a lot of traders who haven't. But only a fool or a desperate man takes on soldiers."

"Especially after they've won," Chuck said.

"Yes, especially then," the trader agreed. "So come in—you would anyhow." He stepped aside. "Take what you want—you'd do that anyhow, too."

His voice still easy and calm, the sergeant went on, "Suppose we don't just feel like plundering? Suppose we still feel like killing?" Dan didn't, and looked at Chuck in surprise. He'd had his fill of killing for a long time, maybe forever. But if the sergeant hadn't . . .

"I hope you won't, not in cold blood," Mendoza replied, a

certain bleak calm in his voice. "But if you do, well, if that wouldn't make me a desperate man, I don't know what would."

How dangerous would he be in a fight? Maybe more dangerous than he seemed at first glance. He was worried, plainly. He might well be afraid. But he wasn't panicked—that seemed obvious. And anybody who could keep his head in a tight spot could cause a lot of trouble.

Was Sergeant Chuck making the same calculation? If he brought up his musket now, what would Mendoza do? What *could* the trader do?

Two or three more soldiers from the Valley pushed up behind Dan and Chuck. That made everybody relax. The trader might have had some chance against two men. Against so many more? Not a prayer, and he had to know it.

He did. With a sigh, he said, "Well, come on. Here's what I've got. I hope you'll leave me something when you're through."

"You stay here, Jerry," Chuck told one of the new arrivals. "Guard the door. Don't let anybody else in." Jerry didn't look happy. Chuck slapped him on the back. "Don't get all bent out of shape, man. We'll share with you, and you won't get any less than these guys." He didn't say anything about what he would get himself. He was a sergeant, so he was entitled to more. If you didn't believe it, you just had to ask him.

But his promise did make Jerry happy—or happier, anyhow. "Okay, Sarge. I guess that's fair," he said.

The trader led the Valley soldiers from the entry hall out into the courtyard. Standing there were a woman about Mendoza's age and another one who couldn't have been any older than Dan. "My wife and my daughter, Liz," Mendoza said carefully. Even more carefully, he added, "They aren't loot. That's part of the deal."

What could he do about it if Sergeant Chuck decided they *were* loot? He could get himself killed, that was what. But how much of a ruckus could he (and the women?—they looked uncommonly alert) stir up beforehand? Maybe Chuck decided he didn't want to find out, because he nodded and said, "Sure. Plunder's one thing, but that'd be something else."

Dan nodded, too, toward Liz. "Hi," he said. She might not be gorgeous, but she was a long way from ugly.

"Hello," she said soberly.

"You're not, like, real friendly," he said.

She shrugged. "I bet I'd like you better if you weren't robbing my house."

She sounded polite and matter-of-fact, so he couldn't even get mad at her. She was telling the truth, too. One of the other soldiers had gone into a storeroom. He came out with a big grin on his face, a box in his hand, and a cigar in his mouth. "They've got *smokes*, Sarge!" he exclaimed.

"Far out!" Chuck said. Tobacco was an expensive luxury. The Valley didn't grow much, because it needed land and water for crops that didn't just go up in smoke. But it traded for cigars and pipe tobacco when it could. Old people said the stuff wasn't good for you, but that didn't keep a lot of them from smoking. Dan figured other things were more likely to do him in than a cigar every once in a while.

When the other soldier gave him a handful of them, he stuck one in his mouth and the rest in a front pocket. Chuck had a flint-and-steel lighter. Dan leaned close to get his cigar started. It was a good one, the flavor fine and mild. He blew out a happy cloud of smoke. Then he offered Liz one of the other cigars.

"No, thank you," she said, her voice still polite but now with an edge in it. "For one thing, I don't smoke. For another thing, don't you feel funny about trying to give me something that's really mine to begin with?"

His ears got hot. "I didn't think of it that way."

"I guess not," she answered. Three words, and she made him feel about three inches tall. Not even his mother could do that.

When the soldiers found bourbon and brandy, Chuck limited the plunder there to one bottle apiece. "We are not going to get too drunk to do our jobs," he growled. "We are *not*—you hear me?"

"Yes, Sergeant," Dan chorused along with the rest of the men. Like most people, he drank beer or wine instead of water when he could get them. He would mix wine with water if he didn't have enough wine to drink by itself. Drinking water without something in it was asking for the runs.

But brandy and whiskey were a lot stronger than beer and wine. You had to make a pig of yourself to get drunk from beer or wine. Not with the distilled liquors. No wonder Chuck warned his men to go easy.

"What other goodies have you got?" the sergeant asked Mendoza.

With a sigh, the trader said, "I'll show you my cash box. You'd find it anyway."

Chuck shared out the money. He took more than he gave any of the soldiers he led, but not a lot more. He eyed Mendoza. "This is all the bread you've got, right?"

"Of course it is," the trader answered, deadpan.

He was lying. Even Dan could see it. But Chuck only

laughed. He slapped Mendoza on the back. "You've played pretty fair with us. I'm not going to try and squeeze you for whatever you're holding out."

"Gee, thanks." Mendoza somehow managed to sound sincere and sarcastic at the same time.

"I'll even post a guard outside to keep you from getting it twice," the sergeant went on. "Dan, you take that slot. Anybody else tries to do a number here, send 'em to me."

"All right, Sergeant," Dan said. "But what if it's an officer?"

"Send officers to Lieutenant Hank," Chuck said. "I'll let him know where it's at with this place."

"Okay." Dan nodded. He had his orders. He would follow them. And maybe—who could say?—Liz would come out while he was standing watch. That could be interesting, too.

The shooting was over. They'd got robbed by some of the politest thieves Liz had ever not enjoyed meeting. The Valley soldiers didn't even try to pretend they weren't looting. They took what they wanted and acted as if the Mendozas ought to be grateful they didn't do worse. The devil of it was, Liz knew how many different ways they *could* have done worse if they'd wanted to.

"They didn't hurt us," Dad said for about the dozenth time. "Thing are just things. We're all right. That's the only thing that matters."

Would he have said that if he truly depended on making his living from what the Valley soldiers stole? Liz wouldn't have bet a dollar on it, let alone a benjamin. Playing the role of merchant lent him a certain detachment a real trader wouldn't have had.

Mom winked at Liz. "I think the kid outside on guard duty likes you."

"Oh, boy. That's all I need," Liz said. They trained you not to get involved with people from the alternates where you worked. Being people themselves, men and women from Crosstime Traffic sometimes ignored their training. From everything Liz had heard, those affairs almost always ended badly.

She wouldn't have wanted anything to do with even a Westsider. The best of them were dirty and ignorant, racist and sexist and homophobic—by home-timeline standards, anyhow. Those were the standards she had, and she stuck to them.

And the invaders were bound to be worse. The Westsiders saw them as country cousins, people who weren't very bright. Besides, they *were* invaders. Wouldn't a proper Westsider feel like a traitor for having anything to do with them?

Liz got her answer to that the first time she went to the market. She saw several Westside girls walking and talking with the occupiers. They hadn't wasted any time figuring out which side their bread was buttered on. Older Westside women sniffed at them, but not too loud. Liz was reminded of old black-and-white pictures of German soldiers with Parisian girls during World War II.

She wondered what would happen if Cal and the Westsiders farther south drove the Valley men out of Westwood Village again. How much trouble would these girls be in? Plenty, unless she missed her guess.

Sergeant Chuck had been right—that cash box wasn't the only money the Mendozas had. The Valley soldiers hadn't found the safe, for instance. Even if they had cleaned things out, Dad could get more with the transposition chamber under the house. No wonder he hadn't worried too much about getting robbed. But if somebody took your life, it was gone forever.

With some old coins and some new ones, Liz bought coffee—imported up from Mexico—and some green onions. The onions were local. She carried the purchases back to her house.

The soldier named Dan was doing sentry duty outside. He nodded as she came up. "Hello," he said.

"Hello," she answered. When somebody with a bow and arrows talked to you, you couldn't very well pretend he wasn't there.

"How are you?" Dan asked.

"I'm all right." Liz wanted to push past him and go on in, but didn't have the nerve. Bad things could happen if he decided she was rude. So she asked, "How are you?" too.

The kid soldier's face lit up. "I'm fine," he said. "Is it always cool like this here?"

"A lot of the time," Liz said. Westwood could be ten degrees Celsius cooler than the valley in the summertime. Nobody in America used Celsius in this alternate, though. Some thermometers from Old Time survived, but they were all in Fahrenheit degrees. Liz thought they were dumb. Why 180 degrees between boiling and freezing? Why was freezing thirty-two degrees and not zero? Because Fahrenheit was a weird man—that was the only answer that occurred to her.

"Is it colder in the winter, too?" Dan asked.

"I don't think so. It doesn't snow or anything," Liz said.

"I saw it snow once," Dan said. "I was just a little kid. It was like the snowflakes were dancing in the air. It was so pretty. But boy, it was cold!"

Liz couldn't remember the last time it had got cold enough

to snow on the Westside. She wondered if her parents could. That wasn't obvious, either. If you lived up in the Valley, you faced weather extremes both ways.

Nodding as politely as she could, Liz went into the house. She felt Dan's eyes on her as she closed the door. How much of a nuisance would he be? Or, on the other hand, how hot and bothered about nothing was she getting? If you shot every guy who looked at a girl and tried to talk to her, the world would get empty mighty fast. She understood that.

But Dan wasn't just a guy back at high school. He was a soldier in a conquering army. If he got angry at her, he could do things a guy at high school never dreamt of. After a moment, Liz shook her head. High-school guys probably did dream of things like that. But they could only dream. Dan didn't have to. He had King Zev's army behind him, after all.

King Zev! Liz didn't know whether to laugh or cry. He ruled a kingdom that wouldn't even be a county supervisor's district back in the home timeline. (Not that the Westside was, or had been, any bigger.) He was the most petty of petty tyrants—except maybe for whatever was left of the Westside City Council. But his men were here, which was what counted now.

She brought the coffee and the onions into the kitchen. "Thanks," her mother said when she set them down. "Any trouble?"

"Trouble? No, not really," Liz answered.

Mom shot her a sharp look. "Something, though. What's up, Liz? Is that Dan outside the door again?"

"Uh-huh. He's not really trouble. Not *trouble* trouble, anyhow."

"I sure hope not," Mom said. "Do you want to stay inside

the rest of the time we're here? If bad things happen while you're away from the house, your father and I can't do much about them till it's too late."

Liz shook her head. "I don't want to do that. I'm here to learn how to take care of myself in the alternates, right? Hiding like a turtle in its shell is no way to go."

"We try not to get stuck in the middle of wars. It doesn't always work, but we do try," her mother said. "If the choice is between staying in and getting raped or murdered, you stay in."

"Dan's not like that—or I don't think so, anyway," Liz said. "He's just . . . interested, you know what I mean? And I'm so not interested in him. He's a local, and he's not even a cute local." She made a face.

"Cute isn't always the only thing that matters," her mother pointed out. "Is he smart? Is he nice?"

"He's nice enough, I guess," Liz said. "Smart? I don't know. We haven't talked about anything much more complicated than the weather." That was literally true. She glanced over at Mom. "Do you think I ought to act friendlier to him? Protective coloration, like some of the girls in the market square?"

"Not if you really can't stand him. And I didn't mean throw yourself at him or anything. There are lots and lots of good reasons why Crosstime Traffic doesn't want us to get involved with the locals."

"I know. I was thinking about that a few minutes ago. These people couldn't do anything with the crosstime secret even if we handed it to them on a silver tray, though."

"Sure, but that's not the only reason why the rules are there. They keep people from getting hurt, too," Mom said. "No matter how you slice it, we're way different from people in the alternates, especially in low-tech ones like this. But if you can be friendly without . . ." Her mother paused, looking for the right words.

"Without acting like a floozy?" Liz suggested, acid in her voice.

Her mother made a face much like the one she'd pulled a moment before, but then nodded. "That's close enough. If you can, it might make things easier all the way around."

"As long as you're not asking *me* to be easy," Liz said.

"No, no, no. No, even." Mom made pushing-away motions. "I want you to be able to live with yourself and to live in a world with Dan in it. Both at the same time, if you can."

"That'd be good," Liz said.

Her mother fed some of the roasted coffee beans into an old-fashioned—and very old—coffee grinder, all brass and wood and glass. In the home timeline, it would have been a fancy antique on a shelf. It still worked for a living here. Mom turned the crank. Freshly ground coffee started to fill the hopper. A wonderful aroma wafted through the air. Liz couldn't help smiling as she sniffed. What a shame coffee smelled so much better than it tasted! She thought so, anyhow. Her folks guzzled the stuff.

"Get me a canister, would you?" Mom said, still cranking.

"Sure." Liz pulled a small one off the shelf. It was yellow plastic. Most of the decal of a green and red hen still survived to show which side was the front. Liz thought it was ugly. Most people from the home timeline would have. She would have bet that most people from the 1960s would have, too.

But nobody in this alternate could make plastic any more. Here, the ugly little canister was a symbol of better days. All the locals who saw it exclaimed over it. And it had an airtight lid. It would keep the ground coffee fresh.

"There we go." Mom put the coffee in, then made sure the lid was on the way it should be. "Now your father and I can pry our eyes open in the morning."

"I wish I could," Liz said. In the home timeline, she got her caffeine from Cokes and chocolate. Cokes and other sodas survived here only as legends. Once in a blue moon, chocolate came up from the south, but it was much rarer and more expensive than coffee. And, once in a blue moon, a CARE package from the home timeline included real Cokes. Those had to stay—and be drunk—in a concealed basement storeroom. It lay behind reinforced concrete and had a passworded voice lock the locals weren't likely to figure out. So she mostly stayed decaffeinated in this alternate. When she had to have a jolt, she put up with coffee's bitterness.

"I don't know why you don't like coffee better," her mother said. Liz stopped listening. Mom had been telling her that since she was twelve years old and first started trying to drink the nasty brew. What was the point of *I don't know why you*? The only answer was, *Because I don't, that's why*. Liz had said it again and again. It didn't seem to help, because Mom didn't want to hear it.

A lot of the time, Dad would be sensible when Mom wasn't. Not here. He liked coffee, too, and couldn't see why other people didn't. Where coffee was concerned, Liz couldn't win.

(And sometimes Mom could be sensible where Dad wasn't. Anything that had to do with boys . . . Dad wasn't as bad as some of her friends' parents, but he wasn't good, either—not even close. Liz hadn't said much about Dan to him. She worried what he would do if she did.)

"It'll be okay, Liz." Her mother might have picked her fretting right out of her head. She wondered if somebody'd hooked up a news crawl above her eyes and connected it to her brain while she wasn't looking.

"Well, I hope so." She let it go at that.

Guard duty in front of the Mendozas' didn't last as long as Dan wished it would have. Pretty soon, things in Westwood Village settled down. The Westsiders started getting used to the idea that King Zev's men were there to stay. And the Valley soldiers stopped carrying off everything that wasn't nailed down.

A lot of men went farther south, to hold the Santa Monica Freeway line against any Westside counterattacks. Maybe they'd push past the old freeway themselves. That would be something! Captain Kevin's company stayed behind in Westwood, though. Somebody had to remind the locals that they'd changed hands.

One Valley soldier got knocked over the head, and nobody owned up to it. Not long after that, five Westsiders were hanged from lampposts. (A lot of the posts still stood, as they did in the Valley, but their lamps hadn't shone since the Old Time.) "Next time, it will be ten," Lieutenant Hank warned. "You can't play those games with us, not after your soldiers lost."

Nobody bushwhacked any more Valley soldiers.

Dan was glad of that. He didn't want to walk his patrols always looking over his shoulder, wondering if some Westsider with a brick or a knife was sneaking up behind him. He was starting to realize he didn't make a great soldier. Oh, he could do the job. But he liked people too well—he didn't want to hurt anybody. Some of the men in his company seemed to think the Westsiders had it coming just because they were Westsiders. Dan didn't feel that way.

Liz, for instance . . .

He got assigned to patrol the UCLA campus because he could read a map and wouldn't get lost. UCLA had a reputation even up in the Valley. It was supposed to be a place where Old Time knowledge still lived. Not everybody liked that—too many people remembered what Old Time knowledge had done to the world.

But when you thought about cars and planes and light that made nighttime bright as day and medicines that made people healthy all the time and all the other lost marvels, hadn't there been at least as much good as bad in those days? Dan thought so.

And then he stopped thinking about stuff that would never be anything but pictures in books with yellowing pages. (Even the pictures were marvelous. He knew what photographs were, but hardly anyone could take them any more.) There was Liz, walking south from the direction of the tall building that looked like a waffle on its side.

He waved. "Hi! What are you doing here?"

"I was in the library." She pointed toward the lower, plainer building to the left and in back of the big waffle.

"What were you doing there?"

"Reading things. What do you think I'd be doing in a library, fishing?"

Dan's ears heated. He'd got zinged, and he knew it. "What were you reading about?" he asked, figuring that was safe enough.

When Liz paused before she answered, he wondered if he was right. What *was* she doing there? Looking for ways to make Valley soldiers' uniforms catch fire or something of that sort? Dan didn't think anyone could do anything like that, but he wasn't sure. He also wasn't sure where science stopped and magic started, or which worked better. Few people he knew were.

After that hesitation, Liz said, "I was trying to find out why the Fire fell from the sky."

"The Russians did it," Dan said automatically. That was one of the first lessons you learned in school. He'd never seen a live Russian. He didn't think anybody from the Valley—or the Westside—had. They lived far, far away, if any of them were still alive. The Fire fell on them, too—lots of it. Schoolbooks went on and on about the revenge America took.

"I've heard that the Russians say we did it," Liz said. Before Dan could even get mad—the nerve of some people!—she went on, "But that's not what I meant, anyhow. Even if the Russians did do it, I was trying to find out why they wanted to blow up the whole world."

"Because they were evil, godless Communists." Dan parroted another lesson. He didn't know just what Communists were, only that they were evil and godless.

Liz's sigh made him feel as if he'd got zinged again, but he didn't understand why. She sounded very patient, though, when she asked, "What would they say about us?"

"Who cares?" Dan blurted. The idea that anybody might care what the Russians said had never crossed his mind till this moment. Neither had the idea that the Russians might say anything at all.

"Well, if that's how you feel . . ." Liz started to turn away.

That wasn't just a zing. Again, she made Dan feel about three inches tall.

"Wait!" he said. If she didn't like him, he could deal with that. If she scorned him, if she thought he was a jerk, that was a different story. He desperately cast about for a way to go on which wouldn't leave her with the notion that he drooled whenever he wasn't careful. He surprised himself by finding one: "How do you know what the Russians say?"

Liz pointed back toward the library again. "A lot of it's in there. The records are still pretty good."

"Those would be records for the Old Time, though," Dan said, and Liz nodded. *See? I'm not so dumb after all!* He wanted to shout it. Instead, he went on, "How do you know what the Russians say now about what happened way back then?"

This time, the look she gave him was cautious and measuring. *No, you aren't so dumb. Does that make you less of a pest or more?* Dan didn't *know* that was what she was thinking, but he would have bet on it. "Traders talk to other traders," she said, picking her words with care. "News comes in from farther away than you'd think sometimes. It doesn't move fast, but it moves."

"News ordinary people don't hear?" Dan asked, an edge in his voice. Most of the time, he liked being ordinary fine. Ordinary people were what democracy, even King Zev's democracy, was all about, weren't they? But sometimes being ordinary meant not finding out what the secret stuff, the good stuff, was all about. He didn't like thinking he was on the outside trying to look in.

"No, it's not news ordinary people don't hear," Liz told him. "You're hearing it from me, aren't you? But sometimes traders do hear it first."

Dan thought about that. His nod was grudging, but it was a

nod. "I guess that's fair," he said, and then, "Do you have any trader news on where Cal's hiding? Big reward for whoever catches him."

"No, I don't know about that." Did Liz speak too quickly now? *Or am I imagining things?* Dan wondered. After a moment, he decided he probably was. He didn't know Liz well enough to be sure how she usually talked.

"Well, go on," he said, and pointed south toward her house. "Nobody told me people couldn't look in the library. I'm not sure how much point there is to it after all these years, but it doesn't hurt anything."

"Wow! Thanks a bunch!" When Liz was sarcastic, she was really sarcastic. She walked—stalked—past Dan with her nose in the air. If she'd wounded him with weapons, not words, she would have left him dead on the half-overgrown paving stones. As things were, he watched her get smaller and smaller till she finally walked around a building and disappeared. Even then, he had to remind himself to get back on patrol.

"I messed up," Liz said when she got back to the house. "I think I talked my way out of it, but I messed up."

"What did you do?" Dad asked. He was arranging a tray of fancy brass belt buckles. The Valley soldiers liked them well enough to pay through the nose for them.

Liz explained how she'd told Dan what the Russians in this alternate thought about who started the nuclear war. "We learn that when we go through training," she said. "It didn't occur to me till too late that he wouldn't know anything about it."

"I should have these on belts." Dad pointed to the buckles. "Then I could take a belt and give you a whipping with it."

Hardly anybody in the home timeline spanked even little children. It was thought of as the next thing to child abuse, or maybe not the next thing but the abuse itself. But things were different in this alternate, as they were in so many. Kids here got walloped all the time, walloped and worse. And so, for a split second, Liz thought Dad meant it. Then, when she noticed the twinkle in his eye—too late, as usual—she could only glare.

"You're impossible!" she said.

"Thank you. I do my best," he answered, not without pride. "But you did talk yourself out of it?"

"I'm pretty sure," Liz said. "He didn't seem suspicious when we got done. Jealous, maybe, but not suspicious. I wasn't even lying, or not very much—traders *do* get news before other people a lot of the time."

"I know that, thank you." When Dad was sarcastic, he didn't lay it on with a trowel the way Liz did. He underplayed instead. A lot of the time, that made him more dangerous, not less. After a moment, he went on, "I don't mind if he's jealous. Envy's a nice, ordinary feeling."

"It can be dangerous, too," Liz said. "When the Valley soldiers were stealing things here—"

"I know. That was bad, and it might have been worse. Sometimes you get stuck, that's all."

"It's not supposed to work this way," Liz said. "We've got the subbasement where the transposition chamber comes. If we can get down there—"

"Everything's golden. But that's if we can," Dad reminded

her. "Remember all the stuff they tell you in training, 'cause it's true. Life doesn't come with a guarantee. Anything that can happen can happen to you."

Remembering that stuff and liking it were two different things. "I don't know how many releases I had to sign before I could get in a transposition chamber at all. Enough to get sick of them—I know that," Liz said. "But I figured it was all—"

"Lawyer talk?" Dad interrupted her again.

She nodded. "Uh-huh."

"Well, it is and it isn't." Her father sighed. "They make you sign those releases because doing this is dangerous. Sometimes people don't come back. If anyone going out to an alternate didn't promise ahead of time not to sue if something went wrong, Crosstime Traffic couldn't stay in business. Some alternates look safer than others, but you never can tell. Your mother and I wouldn't've brought you here if we'd known this stupid war would start."

"Would you have come yourselves?" Liz asked.

Dad sighed again. "Yeah, probably. But that's different. We're grownups. We can figure the odds for ourselves."

That made Liz mad. "You think I can't."

"You're not as good at it," he said, which only made her madder. He held up a hand. "Don't start throwing things at me. You're as smart as you'll ever be—I'm not saying you aren't."

"What *are* you saying, then?" Liz hoped she sounded dangerous. She sure felt dangerous.

"If we were computers, you'd have as much RAM as I do. But I've got more programs and files on my hard disk than you do. That means I can judge some things better than you can, because I've got more data than you do." Dad grinned one of his patented crooked grins. "And one of the things you have trouble judging is the idea that you have trouble judging things."

"So how am I supposed to get better at it?" Liz demanded.

"Do things. Sometimes you'll be right. Sometimes you won't. With a little luck, you'll start figuring out why, and how you can do better next time. It's called growing up. There's no way to hurry it much. Sometimes your folks need to give you a hand where you may not know enough to make a good choice by yourself."

"If you were so smart, you would have seen the war coming yourselves," Liz said. "You can make mistakes, too, and calling them bad choices doesn't make them anything but mistakes."

"I didn't say it did. I'm not perfect—even if I can play perfect on TV." Dad winked. Liz made a face at him. He went on, "Somebody who's a little older has more experience and a better chance to get things right, that's all. But it doesn't matter how old you are—sometimes you'll still mess up. That's part of being human."

Liz wanted to stay angry, but he didn't make it easy. If he'd said he had all the answers and she didn't have any . . . But he hadn't said anything like that. He'd just said he probably had more than she did. And he was probably right, no matter how little she cared to admit it.

"Okay," she said. Sometimes life was too short for a quarrel. "I scanned some more *Newsweek*s at the library today."

"That's good." Her father seemed relieved to talk about more ordinary things, too. "What kind of shape are they in?"

"Not real good," Liz answered. "The paper's getting crumbly. They're not as bad as something like *TV Guide*—those fall apart if you look at them sideways. But I've got to be careful handling them just the same."

Back in the home timeline, magazines like that were preserved in a nitrogen atmosphere. They were also scanned, so electronic images would survive even if paper didn't. Here . . . Considering what had happened here, it was a miracle that anything from before the big war was still around.

The librarians at this UCLA didn't fully understand what a treasure they had. They did their jobs as much because their parents and grandparents had done them as because they loved books themselves. But, in the end, why they did them didn't really matter. As long as they could preserve things till civilization revived and appreciated them again, they were doing something worthwhile.

"What's the name of that book? You know—the one with the funny title," Liz said, not quite out of the blue.

Dad knew which book she meant, too. "*A Canticle for Leibowitz*," he said. "Yeah, that one fits this alternate pretty well. And you know what else? It was written before the war started, so there's probably a copy in the URL."

"I wonder if the librarians ever found it," Liz said.

Five

Dan gave the little old lady in the market square a dirty look. "Fifteen cents for a sandwich?" he said. "What do you think I am, rich or something?"

"No, sir," she said. "But I have to live, too, you know."

"I'll give you a dime," he said. Now she gave him a dirty look, but she nodded. He handed her the little silver coin. She tucked it away and gave him the sandwich, thick with ham and cheese and avocado. He took a big bite. Almost in spite of himself, he smiled. It was a mighty good sandwich.

And thinking about sandwiches made him think about money. Most dimes and quarters and almost all half-dollars *were* silver. But some were sandwiches themselves, copper at the core with gray metal like the stuff from which they made nickels on the outside. People argued and argued about what those sandwich coins were worth. Nobody nowadays could turn out anything like them, which made some people think they had to be very valuable. But they didn't have any truly precious metal in them, so others preferred real silver. Even wealthy traders quarreled over that one.

The question mattered less to Dan than it did to those wealthy traders. His big problem with coins—silver or sandwich—was that he didn't see enough of them. Common soldiers in King Zev's army made three dollars a month. Yes, he would haggle over every nickel, even if it made little old ladies dislike him.

She's only a Westsider, anyway, he thought as he walked along, munching. *Who cares whether she likes me or not?*

Sergeant Chuck waved to him. Pointing to what was left of the sandwich, the underofficer said, "That looks tasty. Where'd you get it?"

"That old gal there, the one in the blue-and-yellow bell bottoms." Dan pointed back toward her. "She'll try and get fifteen cents out of you, but she'll settle for a dime."

"Cool," Chuck said. He made more money than Dan—here as anywhere, rank had its privileges, all right—but he wouldn't end up with a fancy house and a four-horse carriage and a bunch of retainers, either. Nickels mattered to him, too. He hurried off to collect his sandwich.

Everything in the market square was peaceable enough. On the surface, Westwood seemed resigned to coming under King Zev's rule. Some people had told Dan that King Zev's taxes were lower than the ones they'd paid the City Council before. He thought they were dumb to admit it. That would only make Zev more likely to bump things up.

But you never could tell, not for sure. Captain Kevin was back on duty, with his arm in a sling. He went on and on about watching out for spies. Some of the Westsiders didn't want—*really* didn't want—to be ruled by the Valley. They would pass on whatever they could find out to their friends south of the Santa Monica Freeway line. That would mean trouble for the Valley soldiers in Westwood.

So Captain Kevin said, anyhow. He also said you had to remember that spies looked like ordinary people. You couldn't tell who they were by the way they acted, either. They were supposed to act like everyone else—that let them do their spying. So you had to be careful about what you said around any Westsider.

Dan supposed that made sense. It wasn't easy, though, no matter how Captain Kevin made it sound. Dan looked around. Yes, there were Westsiders within earshot. There almost always were. Unless he talked only when he was in the Valley soldiers' encampment, Westsiders would probably hear him. And he couldn't *just* talk about things that didn't matter.

He looked north, toward the UCLA campus. That was probably worth more than the knowledge any number of spies could steal from the Valley soldiers. Whatever they'd known in the Old Times, the secrets were hidden somewhere in the library . . . weren't they? And now those secrets belonged to King Zev. If he could figure them out. . . .

Then what? Dan wondered. Would cars start running again? Would airplanes fly? Would refrigerators keep food from spoiling? Would filter tips make cigarettes taste great?

Maybe. But if they would, why hadn't the Westside City Council made all those wonderful things happen? Dan was a good Valley patriot. He was sure King Zev knew more about such things than Cal and the other councilmen. But Zev didn't know enough now to make any of those things happen in the Valley.

A slow smile crossed Dan's face. King Zev's men knew enough to get that heavy machine gun working. Without it, chances were they wouldn't have beaten the Westsiders. If the UCLA library held a book about old machine guns, the locals either hadn't found it or hadn't paid any attention to it.

That Liz . . . Dan smiled again. She hadn't even thought about machine guns. She'd worried about *history*, of all the useless things! That would have been funny if it weren't so sad.

The smile faded faster than it had formed. Liz *said* she was interested in history. *How do I know that's true?* Dan wondered. He realized he *didn't* know it, not for sure. Maybe she'd been looking up stuff about machine guns or bazookas or cannons or tanks. (He wasn't quite sure what tanks were, but he knew they were supposed to be very bad news.)

He didn't want to believe that about her. But how much did what he wanted to believe have to do with anything? She could talk about history all she wanted. If she was really studying flamethrowers or even A-bombs, what she talked about didn't matter.

Dan shook his head. She could study A-bombs as much as she wanted. Nobody nowadays was able to make them work. Maybe that meant God loved mankind too much to let it blow itself up twice. (But why didn't He love mankind too much to let it blow itself up once, then?) Or maybe the people of Old Times had used up all the atoms there were. Whatever the reason, the Fire hadn't fallen from the sky since 1967. All kinds of other bad things had happened since then, but not that one.

He pulled his thoughts back to Liz. He needed to ask her some questions about what she was really doing at the UCLA library. Then he started to laugh. If he truly believed she was trouble, wouldn't he turn her over to his superiors? Sure he would. A good, dutiful soldier would, anyhow.

Maybe I'm not a good, dutiful soldier, then, he thought. But if he were a bad soldier, he wouldn't pay any attention to her at all, would he? He didn't want to think of himself as a bad soldier. All he wanted to do was get through the time when he had to wear King Zev's uniform. If he could do that without getting hurt, he could go on with the rest of his life once he took off the uniform.

And if the rest of his life happened to involve Liz . . . He laughed again. Down deep, he knew why he was paying attention to her. And it had nothing to do with whether he was a soldier—good, bad, or in the middle.

Liz was about as happy to see Dan come to the house as she would have been to come down with a toothache. For people in this alternate, toothaches were no joke. No biological repair here—not even any high-speed drills. No novocaine to let dentists work without hurting their patients. A few dentists did have ether or chloroform to let them pull teeth without causing pain. What that meant, though, was basically that, whenever anything went wrong with a tooth, out it came. Lots of smiles here had gaps in them.

"Sure must be a bunch of books in that big old library." Dan stretched before he sat down on a bench in the courtyard.

"There are," Liz agreed. She could tell he was sweet on her—she recognized the signs. Maybe, if she didn't encourage him, he would take a hint and go away. Maybe.

"Must be books about all kinds of heavy things," Dan went on.

"I guess." Liz wasn't sure just what he meant by *heavy*. She wasn't sure he was sure, either. *Important* probably came closest, but that wasn't right, either.

"All that stuff in there from the Old Time," Dan said. "I bet you could find out a lot about what they knew back then if you could just figure out where to look."

"That's what I've been trying to do," Liz answered, interested in spite of herself. "I want to know what really kicked off the war."

"Yeah, that's what you said." Dan nodded. "Surprises me, like, that you worry about history and not something you could really use."

"Huh?" Liz didn't get it. And then she did. He thought she was looking for high tech in the University Research Library. That would have been funny if it weren't so sad. By the home timeline's standards, the ones she was used to, nothing in the URL *was* high-tech. Technology from 1967 here was as old-fashioned and out-of-date to her as it would have been there. But people here had been able to do much more in 1967 than they could nowadays.

Her understanding must have shown on her face. Nodding again, Dan said, "Now you can dig it, right? I mean, who cares about history when you can look up machine guns?"

"But I don't care about machine guns," Liz said—which was nothing but the truth.

"Sure you don't," Dan said—which was anything but agreement. "If you made them, don't you think you or your father could sell them?"

He didn't understand about factories. How could he, in this poor, sorry alternate? "I couldn't make a machine gun. Neither could Dad," Liz said.

"I bet the Westside could, if it found out how in a book."

Dan might have been right about that. Liz wasn't sure one way or the other. "If they were looking in the library for things like that, they wouldn't send somebody like me to find them," Liz said. "Use your head, man. They'd send a gunsmith who already knew most of what he needed. He'd be after the last few clues—he wouldn't be starting from scratch, the way I'd have to."

By the look on Dan's face, he might have taken a big bite out of a lemon. He hadn't thought of that ahead of time, and it plainly made more sense than he wished it did. "Well, maybe," he said.

"Not maybe—for sure," Liz said. "Because I don't know diddly squat about machine guns, and I don't care, either."

"You should care," Dan said seriously. "If the Westside had a couple of machine guns, you wouldn't have lost the war."

"Well, sure." Liz knew she was supposed to be a Westside patriot. Taking the idea seriously wasn't easy. Why would anybody want to fight and die for a silly little excuse for a country like this? But the question, once asked, answered itself. People had fought and died for little tiny countries all through history. Athens. Sparta. Venice. Singapore. Lots of others. She went on with the truth: "Like I told you, I still don't know anything about machine guns."

"You're a trader." Dan made money-counting motions. "Where's the profit in finding out about Old Time history?"

Liz started to answer that, then stopped before she stuck her foot in her mouth. She sent Dan a sharp look. He sat there in the courtyard, soaking up sun like a lizard. He had a patchy, scratchy-looking beard. He didn't bathe or wash his uniform often enough. (Liz didn't bathe often enough, either. Nobody in this alternate did. That made it a little easier to take. People said that, where everybody stank, nobody stank. It wasn't quite true, but it came close enough.) He didn't have much education—nobody here did. But he wasn't stupid after all. He might be dangerously smart.

She hoped her pause wasn't too obvious. Then she said, "There isn't much profit in Old Time history, or there hasn't been yet."

"So why do you do it, in that case?" Dan pounced like a cat jumping on a hamster.

"It's my hobby, I guess," Liz answered. "Some people collect teacups or stamps or Old Time baseball cards. Some people have windup trains. Some of them even still work, or I've heard they do, anyhow."

"Yeah, I've heard that, too," Dan said. But he didn't sound convinced. He looked at her in a way she didn't like at all. She would rather have had him following her with his eyes because he thought she was pretty. She knew how to deal with that, and also knew it wasn't dangerous in any serious way. This intent, thoughtful stare, on the other hand . . . He went on, "I'll tell you what bothers me about your—hobby, like. It gives you the excuse to go to the library and look for things that could hurt my kingdom. I don't want anybody to get away with anything like that. Can you blame me?"

You bet I can, Liz thought. What irked her was, she was telling the truth—mostly, anyhow. She didn't care about machine guns or hand grenades or tanks. The home timeline had far better weapons than the ones anybody had imagined in 1967. The history of this alternate, finding out exactly where its breakpoint was . . . that really mattered—to her, anyhow. But she could see she wouldn't be able to explain why in any way that made sense to Dan.

So she didn't try. She just said, "If you're going to think like that, you'd better put guards around the library and keep everybody from going in and out. It's not just me, you know. Lots of people use the books there. That's what they're for. And you'd better take away all the Old Time encyclopedias you can find. I'm sure they talk about weapons and things, too. Or do you think I'm wrong?"

He looked too unhappy to think she was wrong. "You're saying everyone who can read may be a spy," he said slowly. He also sounded plenty unhappy.

Liz shook her head. "Most people aren't spies. *I'm* not a spy, for heaven's sake. I'm just saying you're on my case for no good reason, and I wish you weren't. It really bugs me, man." Talking that way really bugged her, too, but she couldn't let on. To herself, she sounded like somebody from an ancient sitcom.

"Sorry," he said, but she knew he wasn't. He went on, "You got me interested in you, and now I can't help noticing the things you do."

That's what I was afraid of—one more thing Liz couldn't say. She did say, "Like, try. Try as hard as you can."

He gave her a nasty look. "What would happen if we did search this place as hard as we could?"

She glared back at him. She couldn't let him see the threat worried her. "You'd rob us again, same as you did when you came in here the first time. Just 'cause we can't do anything about it doesn't mean we have to like it."

"That's what you get for ending up on the losing side of a war," Dan said.

He wasn't even wrong. Five thousand years of history and countless alternates proved he wasn't. To the victors went the spoils. That was as old as the hills and as new as next week. It could have been worse, too. The Valley soldiers could have decided that Liz and her mother were part of the spoils. Lots of soldiers would have decided exactly that, and then things really would have turned ugly.

"I'm not a soldier, and I'm not a spy," Liz said. "I didn't do anything to you. I didn't do anything to the Valley or to King Zev, either."

"I guess not." Yes, Dan agreed, but he didn't seem convinced. "But there's something funny about you. I don't know what it is, but it's there. You can't tell me it's not. You're . . . more foreign than most Westsiders. How come?"

"*I* don't know," Liz lied. She knew much too well. No matter how much she'd trained and practiced, she wasn't a real Westsider, and nothing could make her one. Somebody who really did belong to this alternate was liable to notice if he looked closely enough. Dan had. His reasons for looking closely weren't the ones that usually tripped up Crosstime Traffic people—he *liked* her. But that made him wonder about her in the same way as if he hated her.

He scratched the side of his jaw. Those wispy whiskers rasped under his fingernails. She thought the noise was gross, but she couldn't tell him so. "Well, something funny's going on," he said. "Something fishy. You know stuff you aren't telling. You're just lucky it's me asking the questions—that's all I've got to say."

Liz shook her head. "That's not true." He glared at her. For a split second, she saw what he would look like if he did hate her. It wasn't pretty. But she made herself go on: "If I were lucky, nobody would be asking me questions, because I haven't done anything to deserve it." Her voice broke on the last couple of words. She hadn't planned that, which probably made it even more effective.

"Don't cry!" Dan exclaimed, which almost made Liz laugh instead. Yes, he liked her, and yes, her cracking voice had done her some good. He really sounded alarmed. "I have to ask you these questions, you know," he said. "It's my Patriotic Duty." She could hear the capital letters thud into place.

"I think you're using your patriotic duty as an excuse to push people around," Liz said. And how often had men and women done *that* in all the different histories of the world? Millions of times, more more likely billions. Most of them would have had the purest motives imaginable—in their own minds, anyhow. The people they pushed around might have had a different opinion.

"I am not," he said angrily. "You tell me all this weird stuff about the Old Time—it's not what I learned in school, that's for sure. And you know too much about the Russians, and everybody knows how bad they are. So what am I supposed to think, anyway?"

"I know what I know," Liz said with a shrug. *And how I know it is none of your business, pal.* "I don't know what schools are like in the Valley, or what they teach you there. I don't know what Westside schools are like, either. I'm a traders' brat. Maybe that's what makes me seem different to you. We travel around a lot, so if my folks didn't teach me nobody would. If you want to blame anybody for the way I think, blame them."

If Dan did decide to blame them . . . well, so what? They could disappear back to the home timeline, and so could Liz.

"Where all do you travel?" Dan asked. "Have your folks ever seen real, live Russians with their own eyes? Have you?" He might have been talking about demons with horns and fangs and tails. By the way he asked the question, he probably thought he was.

"*I've* never seen any Russians," Liz said. "How could I? They're across the ocean." She gestured toward the west. You could see the Pacific from the tops of tall buildings in Westwood. You could, if you felt like climbing all those flights of stairs to get that high off the ground. You took elevators for granted . . . till you had to do without them. When you were climbing stairs, who wanted to go more than four or five flights' worth?

"What about your folks?" Dan didn't want to let it alone. *Do they worship devils?* He didn't say that, but it was what he meant.

"I don't think they ever have. Like I said, how could they?" Liz answered. "But if you really want to know, you'd do better asking them yourself."

She wondered if he would. Talking with somebody your own age—even grilling somebody your own age—wasn't so hard. Taking on somebody as old as your parents had to be a lot tougher. Sure, Dan wore the uniform of a conquering army. But Dad and Mom wore a different kind of uniform: the beginnings of gray hair and wrinkles and the invisible armor of experience.

She could tell he felt the burden. "Maybe I will," he said, but not in a way that suggested he was looking forward to it. He got to his feet. "I guess you aren't trying to hurt the Valley. I guess." He didn't sound sure about that, either—nowhere close. "I don't know just what you *are* up to, but it's something funny. History!" He shook his head and walked off toward the door. He didn't quite slam it behind him, but he also didn't shut it gently.

Liz didn't know whether to laugh or to cry. The only thing that interested her about this alternate *was* its history. Dan wouldn't believe her if she told him so. And she couldn't tell him *why* it interested her, or that she was from the home timeline. She had to go on pretending to be something she wasn't, even if it got her into trouble. The trouble she'd get into if he ever found out what she really was would be even worse.

A rock and a hard place. The devil and the deep blue sea. Damned if you do and damned if you don't. They were all clichés, of course. But now Liz understood how they'd got to be clichés. They put truth into a handful of words.

She said a handful of words herself. None of them helped much. Saying them made her feel better—for a little while, anyway. Sometimes you took what you could get, even if it wasn't much.

Dan stood in line, waiting for a cook to give him bread and fried chicken and sauerkraut. He hated sauerkraut. It was supposed to be good for you, so the cooks dished it out a couple of times a week. Sergeants kept an eye on you to make sure you really ate it, too.

The stuff even smelled foul. One of the Valley soldiers in front of Dan pointed at the kettle where the sauerkraut bubbled and asked, "Who died?"

"Oh, you're funny," the cook said. "Funny like a broken leg, you are." He also got his revenge. He gave the mouthy soldier a burnt piece of bread and a chicken back with more bone than meat. And he gave him a big helping of sauerkraut.

If the other soldier hadn't, Dan might have joked about the sauerkraut. Sure, he knew annoying the cooks wasn't the smartest thing you could do. But there was a difference between knowing and *knowing*. When the other soldier popped off and paid for it, that drove the lesson home. Dan didn't say anything at all. He just held out his mess kit. He got a plump thigh, some unscorched bread, and . . . less sauerkraut than the joker had, anyway.

He sat down on what had been a concrete bus bench. They had those in the Valley, too. The benches survived, while buses were nothing but pictures in Old Time books and magazines and stories that granddads said they'd heard from their granddads once upon a time when they were little kids.

No, no buses on the streets now. No cars. No trucks. Some rich people's carriages had wheels and axles taken from motor vehicles. Some—the super-fancy ones, pulled by big teams of horses—were made from car bodies, with the front part, the part that had held the now-useless motor, cut off to save weight. King Zev had a carriage like that. Its windows still went up and down, even. A few Valley nobles were also lucky enough to travel in style. So were some traders.

Dan hadn't seen any carriages like that here in Westwood. He was sure there were some. The big shots here were just as rich as the ones in the Valley, probably richer. But most of them didn't get rich by being dumb. They weren't showing off what they owned, not when King Zev ruled this place now instead of their pet City Council.

Sergeant Chuck came up. He had two juicy-looking drumsticks in his mess kit. A sergeant didn't need to butter up the cooks the way ordinary soldiers did. A cook who got in trouble with a sergeant would pay for it.

"What's happening, Dan?" Chuck asked.

"Not much, Sergeant." Dan stood up so Chuck could sit down on the bench. The sergeant did. Dan didn't have to give up his place—nothing in the rules said he did, anyhow. But Chuck would have remembered if he didn't. Sergeants had long memories, too.

"How's that chick at the traders' house?" Chuck grinned as he asked the question. That meant he knew Dan liked Liz. A sergeant who was worth his pay kept track of what was going on with his men.

"She's okay. She's kind of weird, though," Dan said.

"Well, Westside chicks are supposed to be that way," Chuck said. That was an article of faith among Valley men. The Westsiders thought people from the Valley were a bunch of hicks, but what did *they* know?

"Not weird like that. Not *weird* weird." Dan wondered if he was making any sense at all. Chuck nodded, so maybe he was. He went on, "I mean, she's into *history*, if you can dig that."

"History?" Chuck gnawed the meat off one of those drumsticks. Then he shook his head. After he swallowed the fried chicken, he said, "Yeah, that's pretty freaky, all right. How'd you find out?"

"She was coming back from the UCLA fancy library. I asked her what she was doing, and that's what she told me," Dan said.

Chuck's eyes narrowed. So did his mouth. "Could be a cover for something else, something nastier."

"I thought so, too," Dan answered. "But she really does

know stuff about Russians and things, and she doesn't know much about guns. If they were trying to get stuff out of the library, wouldn't they have picked somebody who does?"

"We would—that's for sure," Chuck said. "The Westsiders, though . . . they're kinda far-out, so who knows for sure?" He paused. "Russians, eh? How does she know about Russians?"

"I'm not quite sure," Dan admitted. "The way she made it sound, traders hear stuff ordinary people don't. Do you think that's true?"

Chuck scratched his head. "Don't know for sure. I guess it *could* be. They travel more than most people do, that's for sure." He cocked his head to one side, studying Dan. "I bet you've been trying like anything to find out what she does know."

"Well . . . yeah." Dan was embarrassed. He didn't think he'd done anything wrong, but he didn't want his private likes and dislikes to get in the way of his duty, either.

"Don't sweat it, man," Chuck said, understanding his tone. "If you want to like her, you can like her. Plenty of our guys have got Westside girlfriends for themselves. Long as you remember you're a Valley soldier, everything's cool."

"You know I wouldn't do anything else!" Dan exclaimed.

"Sure, sure." Chuck nodded. "I'd really hassle you if I had anything to worry about there." He paused for a bite of bread. "She say anything about what's going on south of the Santa Monica Freeway line?"

"No, Sergeant," Dan answered truthfully. "What *is* going on south of the freeway, anyhow?"

"Beats me," Chuck said. "But we can't push any farther—the Westsiders are still hanging tough down there. If they make a deal with Speedro . . . Well, that could cause everybody a lot of trouble."

"Could cause the Westside a lot of trouble," Dan said. "If they let Speedro's soldiers in to fight us, how do they chase 'em out again afterwards?"

"Sounds like the $64,000 question to me," Chuck said. "But I've heard some talk about it, so I wondered if your girlfriend said anything."

"She's not my girlfriend," Dan said, so sorrowfully that the sergeant laughed. Ears hot, Dan changed the subject: "The $64,000 question . . . People say it, but can you imagine anybody who's really got that much money?"

"I bet the king does," Chuck said. After a moment's thought, Dan nodded. That might be true. Of course, the king collected taxes from all over the Valley. Chuck added, "I wonder *why* we say it. And why $64,000? Why not $65,000—or $75,000?"

"Beats me," Dan said. "Do you want me to see if I can find out what Liz knows about whatever's happening down south?"

"Sure. Maybe the Russians will tell her all about it." Chuck laughed loudly at his own wit. Dan laughed, too. When a sergeant made a joke, any common soldier who knew what was good for him thought it was funny.

Chuck dug into his sauerkraut. He ate every bit that the cook had given him, and he didn't complain or make faces, no matter how bad the pickled cabbage tasted. In his own way, he was setting an example for the men under him. If Dan had noticed he was setting an example. . . .

But Dan's mind was on other things. He did his best not to grin from ear to ear. Now he had another excuse to hang around

Liz, to see what she knew, and to see if he could get her to like him. He couldn't have been happier. He didn't even stop to ask himself how happy she'd be.

"How do I get rid of this guy, Mom?" Liz asked. "This side of shooting him, I mean. He hasn't been any bad trouble, but he sticks like glue."

Her mother was plucking a chicken. No, no neatly wrapped plastic-covered packages in the butcher's shop at the supermarket, not in this alternate. If you wanted meat, you had to deal with it yourself. Mom paused for a moment. "As long as he's not bad trouble, why worry about it?"

"*Because* he sticks like glue." Liz wondered why Mom couldn't see how obvious that was. "He likes me, and I don't like him—for sure not *that* way. He doesn't know much, and most of what he thinks he knows is wrong, and he doesn't take enough baths, either. *And* he thinks I'm some kind of spy or something."

"Nobody's perfect," Mom observed. The look Liz sent her said she wasn't perfect herself—not even close. For a wonder, Mom noticed. She stopped plucking pinfeathers and added, "Now you see why we've got all these rules against getting involved with people from the alternates."

"Sure." Liz had long since figured that out. She threw her hands in the air. "But what we really need are rules to keep people from the alternates from wanting to get involved with us."

Her mother smiled, which made Liz want to throw the mostly plucked chicken out the window. She needed sympathy, and what was Mom doing? Laughing at her! "If you could put on a mask that made you ugly and if you talked like an idiot, that might do the trick," her mother said. "Hand me the cumin there, would you?"

Liz did, but doing it only made her angrier. For one thing, Mom seemed to think getting the chicken ready for dinner was more important than the way Dan kept bothering her. For another, she was tired of cumin and cilantro. The locals used them in everything this side of apple pie, and her mother naturally cooked the way people here did. (Apples were rare, imported luxuries in this Southern California. The trees grew fine, but they needed frost to make fruit. Even in the Valley, where it got colder than it did on the Westside, freezes didn't come every year—or every other year, either.)

Her mother started braying cumin seeds in a brass mortar and pestle. You didn't buy them already ground, the way you would in the home timeline. You didn't punch a button on a food processor, either. Here, you were your own food processor. If you didn't do the work, it didn't get done.

"Since I'm sorta stuck being me," Liz said, as sarcastically as she could, "what do you think I should do about Dan?"

"I told you—put up with him as long as you can," her mother answered. "If he really gets to be a pain, we can always send you back to the home timeline and say you went away."

"I suppose." But Liz didn't want to go back. "That'd put a black mark on my record, wouldn't it?"

"Well, it wouldn't look good." Mom brushed the plucked chicken with olive oil. That was also a local product, and surprisingly good. Unlike apples, olives did great here. She started spreading the ground cumin and some chopped cilantro leaves over the bird. "Part of the reason you come to the alternates is to learn how to deal with the people who live in them."

"Yeah." Liz couldn't have sounded gloomier if she'd tried. "That's what I figured. Maybe I just ought to hit him over the head with a rock."

"If you think you can get away with it, and if people here don't talk about you afterwards, why not?" Mom thrust a long iron spit with a crank handle at one end through the chicken's carcass and set the bird above the fire. "You want to turn that for a while?"

"Okay." You were your own rotisserie here, too. Before long, the chicken started to smell good. Cooking over wood gave more flavor than gas or electricity did in the home timeline, though it polluted more, too. The work didn't keep Liz distracted more than a minute or two. "He's a pain, Mom, nothing else but. I *ought* to wear an ugly mask. If I pulled out two of my front teeth, he'd forget I was alive."

"Mm, maybe not," her mother said, which wasn't what she wanted to hear at all. "By now, you know, he doesn't just think you're pretty. You've fascinated him with your mind, too. Look at the questions he asks you."

"He's trying to trap me, you mean," Liz said. "He can tell I'm not from here. My cover isn't good enough. I don't think the way these people do. He knows."

"Well, turn the chicken anyhow, dear," Mom said. Liz did, feeling foolish—her attention *had* lapsed. Her mother went on, "I just think he thinks you're weird and he thinks you're pretty and he thinks the combination is interesting."

She'd put enough *think*s in there to make Liz need a few

seconds to realize what she meant. When Liz did, she shook her head. "I wish you were right, but it's more than that. I can tell."

"In that case, maybe you *should* go back to the home timeline," Mom said. "Nobody here can do anything with the crosstime secret—we both know that. But the company sure wouldn't be happy if the locals worked it out."

That took no time at all to understand. If Crosstime Traffic wasn't happy with you, you'd be stuck in the home timeline forever. If Crosstime Traffic *really* wasn't happy with you, they'd throw you out on your ear. And who'd ever want to hire you if you couldn't hack it with the biggest, most important company in the history of the world?

Washed up at eighteen, Liz thought. She knew she was being silly, to say nothing of melodramatic. Part of her did, anyhow. The rest . . . She'd broken up with a boyfriend the summer before. It wasn't the end of the world, even if they'd dated for most of a year. She'd known that, or most of her had. It wasn't, no, but it sure felt as if it were. And this felt the same way. If you lost one boyfriend or one job, how could you be sure you'd ever land another one? You couldn't.

"Turn the bird, sweetheart," Mom said gently. "The secret *won't* come out, and Crosstime Traffic *won't* blackball you forever. Right?"

"Right." Liz knew she sounded shaky. She thought she was entitled to. For one thing, she couldn't be sure the secret wouldn't slip out by accident. She couldn't be sure she wouldn't get in trouble. And, for another, what business did Mom have reading her mind like that?

"We all may have to go back to the home timeline, and it

won't have thing one to do with you," her mother said. "If the war heats up again, if the Westsiders try to come back, staying won't be safe."

"We're lucky. We *can* get away," Liz said. "Everybody who lives here is stuck in the middle."

"Turn the chicken," Mom said one more time.

Six

"Attention!" Captain Kevin shouted. Dan straightened and froze in place. Morning inspection. It came every day, and he hated it every time.

Captain Kevin didn't inspect the company in person. Sergeant Chuck prowled through the ranks. Whenever he found somebody with a dirty weapon or ungreased boots or a missing button, he let the unlucky soldier hear about it. Chuck cursed as well as anybody Dan had ever met. No—he cursed as well as anybody Dan had ever imagined, which covered a lot more ground.

Chuck stared at Dan with red-tracked eyes. Dan looked straight ahead and pretended the sergeant wasn't there. After what seemed like forever, Chuck went on to share his good cheer with the next soldier. Dan didn't let out a sigh of relief. That might have brought the sergeant back, which was the last thing he wanted.

After the inspection was over and punishment handed out to soldiers who'd fouled up, Captain Kevin said, "And now we have some good news."

Dan blinked. He didn't hear that every day. A buzz ran through the company. "Silence in the ranks!" Chuck yelled.

Somehow, though, he seemed less ferocious than usual. "You better listen up now!" he went on. "Captain Kevin's got something important to say."

Anything the company commander said was important, just because he said it. So it seemed to Dan, anyhow. He couldn't imagine any common soldier wouldn't think the same.

Kevin strode out front and center. The sling he still wore somehow lent him extra authority—it showed he'd been through the worst war could do. "We aim to be a modern army," he said. "We aim to have the best weapons we can get. Now we've captured a big Westside arsenal, and so our army gets to take their weapons. Only fair, since we won—right?"

"Yes, sir!" the soldiers chorused, Dan loud among them. Who would say no?

"Cool," the company commander said. "Because of that, we get to retire fifteen bows and arrows in this company and replace 'em with matchlocks." He gestured. Two ordnance sergeants wheeled up a cart that probably went back to the Old Time. On it gleamed the modern muskets and their gear. Kevin fished a scrap of paper from his tunic pocket. "The following soldiers will turn in their bows and arrows and become musketeers." He began reading names.

Dan wanted to hear his. He didn't really expect to—he was very junior—but he wanted to. A matchlock of his own! That would be something. It might even impress Liz. A musketeer had to be a much more important person than a mere archer.

Soldiers came up to claim their muskets and powder horns and leather bullet boxes and ramrods and lengths of slowmatch—string soaked in water and gunpowder that burned at a set, reliable rate. One by one, they returned to the ranks, their faces glowing with pride. Each of them thought he was a much more important person than a mere archer.

Then Captain Kevin said, "Dan!"

Dan jumped. He *hadn't* expected to hear his name. But here he was, getting a matchlock of his very own! He hadn't been so happy since . . . since forever, as far as he could tell.

Sergeant Chuck poked him in the ribs. "Go on, kid, get moving," the sergeant stage-whispered. "You don't put your fanny in gear, he's liable to decide to give somebody else the gun."

Kevin wouldn't do that . . . would he? Dan didn't want to find out. He hurried forward. One of the ordnance sergeants took his bow and bowstrings and his quiver full of arrows. Just for a second, he wondered what would happen to them. Maybe some gray-bearded home guard would get them. Or maybe they'd sit in the arsenal for years and years.

But then Dan forgot all about them, because the other ordnance sergeant handed him his matchlock and everything that went with it. "Take good care of your new stuff," the sergeant growled.

"I will!" Dan shouldered the musket and returned to the ranks.

The first thing he noticed was that the gun and the bullet box were heavy. The musket weighed a lot more than his bowstave had. Maybe the bullet box wasn't heavier than the quiver full of arrows, but it packed its weight into much less space. Matchlock bullets were balls of lead, each one as thick as his thumb. They weren't so deadly as the long, pointed rounds Old Time rifles fired, but you still didn't want to stop one with your face or your chest.

Chuck snorted like his father when Dad was exasperated.

"Here—you wear them like this." The sergeant put the bullet box on Dan's belt. The ramrod went there, too. He looped the powder horn over Dan's left shoulder. He wrapped the slow-match around Dan's right upper arm. Dan knew where everything was supposed to go, but he'd never had to worry about it himself before. Now he did. Now he was a musketeer.

"Thank you, Sergeant," he said. Chuck only snorted again. Dan asked, "Now when do I really get to shoot?"

"New musketeers will start practicing this afternoon," Chuck answered. "These aren't like Old Time rifles. We make the guns and the bullets and the powder ourselves. They aren't gone forever once we use them up—we can get more whenever we need them. So you'll have plenty of practice." His smile turned nasty, even for a sergeant's. "And you won't have any excuses for missing what you aim at, you hear?"

"Yes, Sergeant!" Dan said loudly. Saying *Yes, Sergeant!* as loud as you could was almost always the right answer.

Sure enough, the Valley army had set up a firing range not far from the archery targets. Chuck scowled at the men who stood in front of him, and at the uncertain way they held their matchlocks. "I'm supposed to turn you into proper musketeers?" he growled, rolling his eyes. "It's like asking me to turn a bunch of jackasses into racehorses, and that's the truth. But it's what they told me to do, so I've got to do it."

Sergeants always said common soldiers were the dumbest things on two legs, so Dan didn't get uptight about one more insult. He'd heard too many. He knew they didn't mean much. If Chuck didn't say crude things about the men under him, he probably wouldn't know what to say.

"Ground your muskets!" he ordered, and held his vertically with the stock on the ground so they would know what he meant. "Now pour a charge of powder!"

Dan had already discovered that the tip of the powder horn came off. It made a miniature horn, one that held a single charge of powder. He poured in the gunpowder, and then carefully poured it down the muzzle of his musket. One luckless fellow spilled his powder instead. Chuck reamed him up one side and down the other. Dan thanked heaven *he* hadn't goofed.

"Stuff in your wads!" Chuck said.

In the bullet box, along with the musket balls and a flask of priming powder, were little squares of cloth. Dan took one, folded it up, and stuffed it down the muzzle. He used the ramrod to force it down toward the bottom of the musket barrel.

"Now the bullet!" Chuck said. A couple of men laughed. Chuck glared at them. "Think it's funny, do you? When you're really fighting, you can forget. You can—unless you're trained so you do it right without thinking about it. Most of you lugs don't think real good anyway, so you better get it down pat."

The bullet in Dan's hand felt heavy, as if it meant business. It was a tight fit when it went into the muzzle. It had to be, or the gas from the burning gunpowder would get around it and not push it forward.

Chuck used the ramrod again. "Ram that baby home," he said. "Really ram it down there. Don't be shy—you've got to seat it firmly."

Dan imitated him in that step as he had in the others. He felt the sweat spring out on his forehead as he thrust with the ramrod again and again. You could shoot arrows faster than musket balls. Musket balls carried farther, though. And you were supposed to need less practice once you got the hang of using a matchlock, too.

Once you did, yeah. Till you did . . .

"Fix your match in the serpentine," Chuck commanded. The swiveling piece that brought the match down onto the touch-hole had a groove into which the thick string would fit. "Leave a couple of inches sticking out. Now pour your priming powder into the touch-hole. Just a little, mind."

The priming powder from the small flask in the bullet box was much more finely ground than the ordinary black powder in the powder horn. That made it burn faster and more reliably.

"Now if you were in battle, you'd already have your match burning, right?" Chuck said.

"Yes, Sergeant," Dan chorused along with the rest of the new musketeers. When it rained, matchlocks weren't good for much. Luckily, that wasn't a worry very often in the Valley or on the Westside.

Chuck had a lighter—a real Old Time Zippo. "I have a devil of a time finding flints for this now, but I manage," he said. He flicked the Zippo—and it lit. There was no more Old Time lighter fluid. He used strong spirits instead. The flame was blue and almost invisible. "Now nobody pull the trigger till I give the order, you hear?" he warned. "You'll be sorry if you do. Got it? Dig me?"

"Yes, Sergeant," Dan said again. Chuck walked along the line of musketeers, lighting one length of slowmatch after another. The smell of burning gunpowder didn't make Dan think of battle. It smelled like fireworks, and reminded him of the Fourth of July and of October 23, the day the Valley's first king broke away from Los Angeles after the Fire fell.

"All right!" Chuck shouted. "Aim at the target!"

Along with the rest of the new musketeers, Dan did just that. It wasn't much more than a hundred yards away, but suddenly it seemed very small. He tried not to let his hands shake. He wanted a bull's-eye more than anything.

Chuck got behind the soldiers with the matchlocks before he gave his next order: "Fire!"

Dan pulled the trigger. Down came the serpentine. The burning match set off the priming powder around the touch-hole. The priming powder hissed and fizzed. Half a heartbeat later, the main charge went off—*Boom!* The heavy matchlock bucked against Dan's shoulder. Flame and a big puff of gray smoke burst from the muzzle.

"Wow!" Dan said, coughing from all the sulfurous smoke. When matchlocks fired a volley, they almost hid what they fired at. Was that where the phrase *fog of war* came from? Dan wouldn't have been surprised. But now he'd shot off a gun. He really and truly had. He felt proud enough to burst.

"Now it's safe to stand in front of you people again," Chuck said. "I'm going to go over to the target and see how you did."

"We slaughtered 'em!" a musketeer said.

"Yeah!" Dan nodded. He thought so, too. If he hadn't put his musket ball right through the center of the target. . . .

Chuck walked over, took the paper down from the mound of earth that caught bullets, and carried it back. "Three hits," he said, displaying the target. It was a lot bigger close up. "Fifteen of you shooting at it, and three hits. Maybe the rest of you would've scared the bad guys a little. Maybe. But three out of fifteen! I know a matchlock's not a real accurate gun. Even so, you can do better than that. You can, and you will, or I'll know the reason why. Reload!"

As Dan started the complicated job of getting another bullet into the matchlock, he realized being a musketeer wasn't just an honor. Like anything else, it was a lot of work.

The first thing Liz noticed when she opened the door and saw Dan standing in the street was the matchlock on his shoulder. The second thing she noticed was how proud of himself he looked. She didn't laugh, though she wanted to. He would have got mad—she could see that.

"You had a bow before," she said gravely.

"I got promoted," he said. "I'm a musketeer now."

Athos, Porthos, or Aramis? she wondered. He might get that. *The Three Musketeers* was a book here, too. The breakpoint between this alternate and the home timeline lay more than a century after it was written.

But Liz didn't want to talk about Alexandre Dumas with Dan. She just wanted him to go away. "Congratulations," she said, and then spoiled it on purpose by adding, "I guess."

"I think I was the youngest soldier in my company to get a musket." Yes, he wanted to brag about it, no matter how much that made him sound like an idiot. He thought he was hot stuff. All he needed was a plume in his hat, and he could make like d'Artagnan. Never mind that his weapon would've been obsolete in 1750. He didn't care. It was more up-to-date than a bow and arrows, which was all that counted for him.

"Well, good for you," she said. If he knew how pathetic he was . . . But she was judging him by the home timeline's standards. He wasn't pathetic here. By the standards of this alternate, he was way cool, and he knew it. A girl who took those standards for granted would think he was way cool, too.

Tough beans, Liz thought. *I ain't that girl, even if Mr. Musketeer thinks I am.*

And, all too plainly, Dan did. "Can I come in?" he asked. He didn't even dream she would say no. What he really meant was, *Can I show off some more?*

Liz wanted to tell him to get lost, at least as much to see the look on his face as for any other reason. She wanted to, yes, but she didn't dare. You were supposed to try to get along with the locals when they weren't impossibly obnoxious. If you didn't, you got a black mark in your database, one that would stay there forever. And Dan wasn't . . . quite . . . impossible. He ran his mouth, yeah, and he wondered whether Liz was some kind of spy, but he'd always kept his hands to himself.

She almost wished he wouldn't. If he tried feeling her up, that would give her a real excuse for having nothing to do with him afterwards. His silly talk and strutting weren't nearly enough, not by themselves. And since they weren't . . .

"I guess you can," Liz said with a sigh she didn't even try to hide. Dan never noticed it. She hadn't thought he would. She would have bet a hundred benjamins against a dollar that he wouldn't, in fact. But winning the almost worthless dollar wouldn't have mattered to her.

Once he walked into the house, she had to be more polite. This alternate had rules about hospitality. A guest was a guest. She brought Dan orange juice and bread and olive oil, and had some herself. They sat on a bench in the courtyard. She wasn't going to take him to her room—no way. That would have given him ideas he didn't need. Oh, he probably had them already, but he wouldn't do anything about them, not out here. She couldn't be so sure of that in a more private place. There was such a thing as asking for trouble.

But right this minute Dan was too full of himself—and of his super-duper matchlock musket—to turn into that kind of nuisance. He unslung the musket and asked, "Do you want to know how it works?"

"Oh, I'm dying to," Liz said in a tone that couldn't mean anything but, *You must be out of your mind, Charlie.*

Dan didn't get it. She might have known—she *had* known—he wouldn't. He walked her through the whole complicated process of loading and firing the gun. The only reason she would have wanted to know that was so she could shoot him with it. If he couldn't buy a clue, could he at least rent one?

Not a chance. After he'd gone through his rigmarole, he said, "And then, after you've been shooting, you have to clean the inside of the barrel. Gunpowder builds up in there—we call it fouling." By the way he said it, he might have coined the word himself.

Liz knew she had to give him some kind of answer. *Big deal* was the first thing that came to mind. Somehow, she didn't think he'd appreciate it. She tried something safer: "How about that?" You couldn't get into too much trouble with three little words that didn't mean anything.

"Did you know any of this stuff before?" Dan didn't ask it quite smoothly enough. He wasn't just interested in her. He still halfway thought she was some kind of spy. Maybe more than halfway.

She shook her head. "No, not really. I told you—I'm not into guns."

"No. You're into history. And that's just freaky," Dan said.

Who was it who'd said, "History is bunk"? Henry Ford, that was who—Liz remembered it from a question on an AP test, and from reading *Brave New World*. Lots of people—most people, even—in the home timeline had thought so, right up into the middle of the twenty-first century.

But when you could go from one alternate to another, when you could see how one change in history altered everything that sprang from it, and when you needed to figure out how the changes worked, history wasn't bunk any more. Along with chronophysics, history was one of the underpinnings of Crosstime Traffic. In the home timeline, that made it a very big deal indeed.

But not here. Here, it was still bunk. People were still trying to get out from under the disaster history had dropped on them 130 years before. Understanding exactly why the disaster happened was a luxury they had no time for.

She couldn't explain that to Dan. So she pointed to his precious matchlock and said, "Do you think you'd be carrying that if somebody wasn't interested in history?"

He looked at her as if she'd started speaking Russian. "Huh?" he said.

"It's true," she told him. "We can't make guns like the ones they had just before the Fire fell, right?"

"Well, sure. Everybody knows that," Dan admitted. "But what's it got to do with history? Or matchlocks?"

"Matchlocks come from a time hundreds of years before

the Fire fell. They aren't a new invention. They're a, a re-invention, I guess you'd call it," Liz said. "After the Fire fell, somebody who knew the history of guns must have figured, *Well, let's use these—they're the best we can make with what we've got left.*"

She waited. Would he think she was crazy? Would he understand any of what she was talking about? Or would he think she was making things up to freak him out?

He looked at the matchlock, and at the powder horn on his belt. "I guess the same thing's true about machine guns, huh?" he said after a few seconds.

Liz nodded. "Only more so, because they're more complicated."

"Okay. I guess you make sense. I hadn't thought about it like that before," Dan said. But before Liz could get too happy about enlightening him, he went on, "You sure know a lot about guns for somebody who says she doesn't know anything about guns."

Oops, she thought. She threw her hands in the air, playacting only a little. "I don't know squat about guns. I don't care about guns—"

"But—" Dan interrupted.

"I don't!" Liz interrupted right back. "I know something about history. It's not the same thing. Can't you see that?" It wasn't quite the same thing, anyway. She hoped he wouldn't think it was.

She watched him wrestling with it. "Well, maybe," he said. "But you know about Russians, too."

He'd never let her live that down, would he? "I don't know a whole lot about them—I really don't," she said.

"You know more than any right-thinking American's got any business knowing," Dan said.

Most of the time, he thought of himself as belonging to the Valley. It was his kingdom, and Zev was his king. The Westside was a different country to him and to his fellow soldiers—and to the Westsiders, too. But he remembered the murdered United States on the Fourth of July . . . and whenever he talked about the Russians.

"It's a democracy, isn't it?" Liz said. Democracy was still a potent word here, even if it didn't mean what it had before the Fire fell. Duties got split up so lots of people did them—that was democracy. The rulers on the Westside called themselves city councilmen and not dukes—that was democracy, too. Liz went on, "So I have the right to find out about whatever I want to, don't I?"

"Maybe you do." Dan sounded troubled. "But just because you have it doesn't mean you should use it. We gave the Russians what they deserved. After all, they hit us first."

Not if you listen to them. But he wouldn't want to hear that. And nobody knew who'd launched the first missiles. After 130 years, it mattered only to historians. This alternate was too busy trying to take care of itself to have the time to train historians and give them a chance to work. If not for people like her family, people from the home timeline, nobody would try to find out till all the best evidence had crumbled to dust.

A lot of evidence had already crumbled. Liz wasn't sure she and her folks would ever be sure what had happened here. At least they were trying to find out, though. The survivors of the nuclear exchange—here and in Russia—were too busy blaming each other to care about the truth, whatever it turned out to be.

She frowned at Dan. "You're saying I shouldn't try to know what's so if that doesn't go along with what people believe."

"Right on!" He didn't try to deny it. "If all the people believe it, it's so. That's democracy, too, isn't it?"

No! She wanted to scream it. But that *was* democracy, at least the way they used the word here. "I'm sorry, but I want to know what's what no matter what," she said. She knew she could have put it better, but too bad. "Everybody here on the Westside thought we'd beat your army, but we didn't turn out to be right enough, did we?"

"I should say not. We creamed you." Dan frowned again, this time at himself. "Okay, though. I guess I see what you're trying to say."

Liz breathed a silent sigh of relief. She'd wondered if he would. A lot of the time, if somebody knocked a hole in your argument, you just pretended it wasn't there. She was glad Dan would admit there was a difference between what everybody thought and what was true.

"A long time ago, people thought the earth was flat. They thought it was the middle of things, too, and the sun went around it," she said.

"It sure *looks* flat," Dan said. "They teach us in school that the earth goes around the sun, but I'm dogged if I understand why. I don't know if I believe it, either. It looks like it ought to be the other way around, doesn't it? I mean, you can see the sun move and everything. Just, like, watch our shadows."

Tears stung Liz's eyes. In another 130 years, people in this alternate probably *would* think the earth was flat again. They *would* think the sun went around it. If your own eyes told you so . . . If everybody's eyes said the same thing . . . That was democracy, wasn't it?

Sure it was. And it was wrong, wrong, wrong.

"If you try to figure out the phases of the moon, or how the planets move, you get better answers if you put the sun in the middle than you do if you put the earth there," Liz said.

"But I don't much care about the phases of the moon. I don't care about the planets at all," Dan said. "How do you figure that stuff out, anyway?"

"It takes more math than I know how to do," Liz admitted.

"There you go," Dan said. "Even if it's true, it's complicated. But I can see the sun. There it is, right up there." He pointed at it, squinting and blinking. "If you watch for a while, you'll see it move, too."

"No, you'll see the earth turning." Liz wasn't about to quit.

"You sound like my teacher." Dan laughed. "She taught what was in the book, but who says the book was right? Maybe it was one of those waddayacallits—fiction books, that's what I want to say. I mean, it just stands to reason. You can see how little the sun is, and how big the earth is. How could we go around that and not the other way around?"

Instead of walking over to a column and banging her head on it, Liz said, "A mountain looks little 'cause it's a long ways off. The sun's a lot farther away than any mountain. Of course it looks small."

"Ninety-three million miles," Dan said. "That's what the book said in school, anyhow. But how could there be that many miles? And even if there were, how would anybody know how many there were? You couldn't go all that way yourself. You'd be traveling forever."

And you would run out of air. And you would roast as you got closer to the sun. And a lot of other things. Liz didn't mention any of them. She didn't remember how you went about learning how far it was from the earth to the sun. Since she didn't, she couldn't very well explain it to Dan.

What she did say was, "Well, if they knew that stuff back in the Old Time, chances are they were right about it."

Dan grunted. "Yeah, I guess that's true," he said.

Liz had won the argument. Then she wondered if she'd cheated. He was trying to be logical about things, to argue from what he could see. She'd hit him over the head with authority. Wasn't that like the Church coming down on Galileo because he said the earth moved?

The difference, she told herself, was that the Church was wrong and she was right. But the churchmen had thought they were right. And they'd had authority on their side, too.

So she felt pretty rotten when Dan left. But he didn't give her any more trouble about Russians, anyhow. Whether the sun went around the earth or vice versa wouldn't get him so excited.

She hoped.

After practicing like a maniac, Dan could load his matchlock almost fast enough to keep Sergeant Chuck happy. He was no slower than the rest of the new musketeers. Chuck screamed at all of them impartially.

"You have to keep up with the men who've been doing this for years!" the sergeant shouted. "A volley's not a volley if everybody doesn't shoot together. So move, you stupid, clumsy lugs! Move!"

Dan rammed his bullet home and brought the musket up to

his shoulder. So did the rest of the new men, all at about the same time—except for one luckless fellow who dropped his ramrod. What Chuck called him would have curdled milk.

"I'm sorry, Sergeant," the soldier said miserably.

"You do that in the middle of a real battle and you'll be sorry you're dead, you—" Chuck found a few more compliments to pay the luckless musketeer. Then he growled, "Are we ready at last? We'd better be, don't you think? Let's find out. Ready . . . Aim . . . Fire!"

Dan pulled the trigger. The match came down on the priming powder in and around the touch-hole. Hiss—*Boom!*—Kick. He coughed as the smoke went up his nose.

The musketeer just to his left puffed on a cigar. A lot of the men who carried matchlocks smoked either cigars or a pipe. That meant you usually had a hot coal handy if you needed to get your match going again. Dan didn't usually smoke all that often, but he knew a good idea when he saw one.

Chuck walked out to the target and brought it back. He showed the soldiers the punctures their musket balls had made. "Well, you're starting to scare the enemy, even if you don't always hit him." But he wasn't about to let them think that was good enough. He went out to the far end of the range and set up a new target. "Now let's see how fast you can give me another volley. I want everybody ready when I give the command. *Go!*"

It would have been easier if Chuck hadn't gone on yelling at them while they reloaded. Dan wanted to hate him for that, but found he couldn't. He'd been in battle by now. He knew how much noise and chaos there was. You had to block it all out if you were going to do your job. If you let it rattle you, you endangered yourself and your buddies.

Nobody dropped his ramrod this time. If anyone had, Chuck would have eaten him raw—probably without salt. And the volley went off in a close-packed set of thunderclaps that left Dan's ears ringing. People who'd used guns a lot also tended to use hearing trumpets. But what could you do?

"Well, you weren't *too* slow," Sergeant Chuck said. That was about as much praise as the underofficer ever doled out. He retrieved the target. When he came back, he looked like somebody trying hard not to smile. "Seems like some of those . . . people would have stopped lead, that's for sure. Now let's see you do it again, so I know it's no fluke."

Some of the musketeers groaned—but none of the men at whom Chuck was looking directly. He would have blistered them if they'd tried getting away with that. Dan didn't want to fire another volley, either. But he wanted to do the shooting and not get shot if he had to fight some more, so he kept practicing without making any noise.

Several volleys later, the smoke was making tears run down his face from eyes that felt as if they had ground glass in them. "Well, that'll probably do for today," the underofficer said. He grinned a crooked grin. "If I told you to load for another one, chances are you'd aim it at me. And you *might* even hit what you were aiming at. I don't think it's real likely, but I don't want to take the chance, either. So we'll knock off for the day."

He stood only a few feet from his weary students, not a hundred yards down the range. If they turned their matchlocks on him, he would have more holes than a colander, and he had to know it. But he didn't want to admit, to himself or to the musketeers, that they were getting the hang of it.

They were plenty glad to knock off for the day. The sun was sliding down the western sky toward the nuclear glass and rubble of Santa Monica and toward the Pacific beyond it. Supper soon, and then sleep, except for the ones unlucky enough to draw evening sentry duty.

Dan always looked forward to sleep. He did enough on any day of soldiering to leave him tired. Garrisoning Westwood wasn't so bad as the strike through the Sepulveda Pass, though. Then he'd always wanted to curl up and grab what rest he could. He'd always wanted to, and never been able to. He didn't know how much sleep he'd got in that mad dash south. He did know it wasn't enough.

Fowls were roasting on spits above cookfires. Cooks basted them with chilies and cilantro and other spices in olive oil. The delicious smell made Dan's stomach growl. He could hardly wait till the savory birds got done.

Sergeant Chuck reacted differently. Pointing to the birds, he said, "I wonder whose goose they're cooking."

"Oh, wow!" Dan groaned. "After a joke like that, Sergeant, it ought to be yours." You could be rude to a superior as long as you used proper military courtesy when you did it . . . and as long as you picked your spot with care.

Chuck grinned at Dan. "I've got no shame. How's your girl, and what's she really pulling out of the UCLA library?"

"She's not my girl," Dan said regretfully. Liz was polite, but he could tell she liked him less than he liked her. He didn't know what he could do about that. So far, he hadn't been able to do anything. Sighing, he went on, "You know what we talked about the last time I was over there?"

"Tell me," Chuck said.

"You're gonna laugh," Dan said. The sergeant shook his head and held up his right hand, as if to swear he wouldn't. Thus encouraged, Dan went on, "Whether the earth really does go around the sun like you learn in school."

Chuck stared at him, then threw back his head and let loose. He didn't just laugh—he howled. "I'm sorry," he said at last, not sounding sorry at all. "You go visit a pretty girl, and you talk about *that*? The moon and the stars and how pretty they are, sure. But the sun and the earth? C'mon, man! You can do better than that."

"See? I told you you would." Dull embarrassment made Dan's ears burn. It also heated his defiance. "And you know what else? It was interesting, too." *So there*, he thought.

"Okay, okay. Don't get all uptight about it. I said I was sorry," Chuck replied. Dan realized you didn't get an apology out of a sergeant every day, not if you were a common soldier. "So what does she think about that? Me, I don't know if the teachers are as smart as they think they are."

"I'm with you," Dan said. "If the people in the Old Time were all *that* smart, would they have let the Fire fall? So they didn't know everything there was to know—you can bet your sweet bippy on that."

"There you go," Chuck said. "That sure makes sense to me. How'd Liz like it?"

"Not even a little bit," Dan answered. "You hear her talk, the earth spins around to make days, and it goes around the sun to make years."

"You know what?" Sergeant Chuck said as they lined up to get their pieces of chicken or duck or whatever the cook dished out. "The real deal is, so what? I mean, who cares? It doesn't make a penny's worth of difference in your life or mine. It wouldn't matter if the earth was shaped like a .50-caliber bullet. We're just going to see this little bit of it, and that's all."

"Yeah," Dan said. Back in the Old Time, you could fly all over the world. Those people might not have been all *that* smart—must have been human, in other words—but they knew more than their modern descendants. That seemed unfair to Dan. He wondered what Liz thought about it. She knew a lot. Did she miss not knowing even more?

Seven

Luke was a ginger-bearded trader up from Speedro. Liz didn't know whether the Valley soldiers knew he'd come up to deal with her folks. She would have bet against it. Luke had the air of a man who dodged authority whenever he could. And Speedro and the Valley weren't the best of friends anyhow.

"Got me some of the things you said you were looking for," he said now, puffing on a nasty pipe and sipping from a glass of raw corn whiskey Dad had given him.

Dad had a drink of his own, though he didn't smoke. There was such a thing as taking authenticity too far. Wrecking your lungs crossed the line. "Well, let's have a look," he said.

"Sure enough." Luke had a knapsack on his back and two stout flintlock pistols and a Bowie knife on his belt. Ignoring the guns, he slid off the knapsack. "Don't quite know why you want these, but I found 'em."

"Oh, come on," Liz's father said. "You never ask that question. Maybe I'll make a profit selling them to somebody with more money than sense. Maybe I want 'em for myself, just because of how far out they are. Long as you make money selling them to me, what's your worry?"

The other trader gave him a crooked grin. "Well, I know

how that works, all right. One fellow's trash is another guy's treasure." The grin grew more crooked yet. "And we're all living in the middle of the trash from the Old Time, and I expect we will be from now till doomsday, or maybe twenty minutes longer."

"Wouldn't be surprised," Dad said, and then, "Well, well. How about that?"

Luke displayed a dozen popular-science and science-fiction magazines from 1965, 1966, and 1967. The UCLA library's files on those were less complete than they might have been. Sometimes the library's holdings were less complete than the card catalogue said they should be. Some time between the fall of the Fire and now, people had made things disappear.

To Liz, stealing from a library wasn't just a crime. It was a sin. And this library's card catalogue fascinated her. All the equivalents in the home timeline were electronic, of course. The idea of a room full of actual, physical files you could shuffle through struck her as extremely slick. And, surprisingly, once you got the hang of it, it was almost as fast as accessing a database.

That wasn't fair. Using the card catalogue *was* accessing a database. You couldn't do it with just a computer and a keyboard or a mike, but you could do it. Some of the things you could do without electricity startled her. They still had working windup phonographs here. In the home timeline, vinyl was a teeny-tiny niche market. Liz didn't think she'd ever heard a real record there. It was nearly all downloads. Here, records were all they'd known about when things went boom. Hearing a classic like the Doors' first album coming out of a tinny speaker that looked like a giant ear trumpet, and hearing it all full of scratches and hisses because it was so ancient, was almost enough to make her cry.

Dad sorted through the magazines. He handled them with great care because the pulp paper was ancient, too. Comparing these issues to the almost-matching ones from the home timeline would—or at least might—give researchers a few more clues about what had gone wrong here.

"Well, I can use 'em," he said at last. "How hard are you going to rip me off?"

"Two dollars apiece." Even Luke sounded amazed at how much he was asking. Two dollars, here, could buy as much as a couple of hundred benjamins—$20,000—back in the home timeline.

Liz's father had the money. It meant no more to him than Microsoft Monopoly money did. But you couldn't make a deal—especially not a big one—without haggling. And haggling was a full-contact sport here. Luke called Dad some things . . . Well, if he'd said anything like that to Liz, she would have done her best to murder him. But her father only grinned and gave back as good—or as bad—as he got.

They finally settled on a dollar and a quarter per magazine. Luke was one of the people who preferred silver quarters to the copper-and-nickel sandwich ones that had replaced them. "Yeah, I know we can't make anything like those nowadays," he said when Dad asked him which he wanted. "But silver's *silver*, confound it. I'd like it even better if you gave me cart-wheels."

A cartwheel was a silver dollar, and it weighed more than four quarters or two half-dollars. To Liz, it was a just a symbol. It was worth what it said it was worth, and that was that. To

Luke, and to a lot of people here, it was worth what it said it was worth because it had so much precious metal in it. They came from different worlds not only literally but also in their minds.

"You know what?" Dad said. "I can do that, and I will, because you've gone to some trouble for me." The difference in weight wasn't enormous. It was as if he were giving Luke an extra-nice tip at a restaurant.

But the trader's eyes lit up when he got his hands on those fat, sweet-ringing silver coins. "Much obliged to you, sir," he said, and tipped his broad-brimmed hat. "You didn't have to do that, and I know it. You're jake with me, and that's the truth. I take back all the stuff I called you—till I need it again next time we dicker, anyways."

Dad laughed. Even Liz thought that was pretty funny. Dad said, "Don't get yourself in an uproar, man. If you don't help your friends, you don't have friends for long, right?"

"Right on!" Luke said. "And I'm mighty glad you put it that way, on account of those funky magazines weren't the only reason I came all the way up here."

Speedro was a couple of days away from Westwood in this alternate: no small journey. In the home timeline, you could hop in your car and get there in a little more than an hour . . . if the freeways weren't jammed. If they were—and they often were—it took two or three times that long, and felt like a couple of days.

"Well, what's on your mind?" Did Dad sound cautious? Liz thought so. She would have, too—she was sure of that.

Luke, by contrast, was cagey, almost coy: "You've got a friend with a big old dog, isn't that right?"

"Not any more," Liz blurted. Not even the enormous and

ferocious Pots could stand up to machine-gun bullets. The Westsiders—and Pots himself—had learned that the hard way. Losing the terrible dog went a long way toward breaking the Westside's morale. It must have gone just as far toward pumping up the Valley's soldiers.

The trader nodded to her. "You're right, Miss. That's the straight skinny, all right. But you sure know somebody who did have a big old dog, don't you?"

"What's Cal got in mind?" Here, unlike in a haggle over money, Dad didn't have to waste time beating around the bush.

"Well, he aims to throw these Valley squares back where they belong, and then another mile further," Luke replied.

"People can aim at all kinds of things. 'A man's reach should exceed his grasp,/ Or what's a heaven for'?" Dad quoted old poetry—Liz remembered the lines from Brit Lit. He went on, "But just 'cause he aims to do it doesn't mean he can. And where do I fit into all this?"

"Well, he was hoping you could let him know where the Valley soldiers are at and how many they're keeping down here," Luke said.

"Through you?" Dad asked.

"No, man. Through the Easter Bunny." Luke snorted like a horse. "Of course, through me. You gonna write him a letter, like, and stick a stamp on it?" People remembered stamps, the way they remembered cars and TVs. Unlike cars and TVs, stamps still did get made by some of the larger, more stable kingdoms in this shattered alternate. None of the ones in Southern California qualified, though.

And the idea of putting stuff that dangerous in writing wasn't anything to jump up and down about, either. Nor was the idea of taking sides in the petty struggles here. That was the last thing people from Crosstime Traffic were supposed to do.

On the other hand, people from Crosstime Traffic *were* supposed to act as much like locals as they could. And a local trader might well want to help Cal against the Valley soldiers. If your instructions started quarreling with themselves . . . Liz waited to see what her father would do.

"I don't usually go looking around for soldiers, you know," Dad said.

"Cal says he'd make it worth your while if you did," Luke answered.

Cal didn't have anything that could make it worthwhile for someone from the home timeline . . . and Dad was holding a lot of his assets. Without a doubt, Cal could make a trader here—or a couple of traders here—rich. From what Liz had seen of him, though, there was a big difference between *could* and *would*. Maybe he'd just say Dad could keep what he was already holding.

Dad also took a jaundiced view of the Westside City Councilman. "I'm sure Cal's word is worth its weight in gold," he said dryly.

Luke needed to think about that for a couple of seconds before he got it. When he did, he gave a snaggle-toothed grin—no orthodontists here—and snorted again, this time on a higher note. "You're a funny fella—you sure are. Worth its weight in gold! I got to remember me that one."

"You see what I mean, then." Dad spread his hands.

"Well, Cal's slipperier'n smoked eels packed in olive oil, no two ways about that," Luke allowed, and Dad smiled in return. The trader from Speedro went on, "Chances are he'd pay off for this, though. He purely hates those Valley dudes, and he wants to get rid of 'em."

"Now that you're up here, you could look around as well as we can," Liz said.

"I could." By the way Luke stretched the word, he didn't want to. He explained why: "I'm a stranger in these parts, and they'd get hinky about me in a hurry. I bet they don't even look at you people twice." He paused. "Well, they'd look at *you* twice, honey, but not on account of they figured you were spying."

Liz's cheeks got hot. She'd thought Dan's attention was the last thing she wanted. Now she found it was next to last. Having this hairy, smelly, old trader notice her, that was way worse. And she could tell him, "Some of them already do think I'm spying."

Luke grunted. "That's not so hot."

"If I find anything out, I'll let you know, Luke," Dad said. "I'm sorry, but I just haven't paid that much attention till now."

"Too bad. Cal was hoping you would have." Luke heaved himself to his feet. "Well, I'll be on my way. Much obliged for the silver dollars, my friend. Like I say, you didn't have to do that, and I know it." He touched a callused forefinger to the brim of his hat.

Liz sat in the courtyard, wishing she were ugly. Life would be so much simpler if she were.

Dan was coming up Glendon when a trader left the house where Liz and her folks lived. The fellow looked tough, and wore not one but two pistols. That meant, in case of a miss, he could fire again while Dan was still reloading. Muskets were nice, but they were slow.

The trader didn't want any trouble, which was a relief. He nodded politely to Dan and said, "Hello, kid. How ya doin'?"

Don't call me kid! Anger automatically flared in Dan. Then it faded, and not just because the man was heavily armed. Gray streaked the trader's hair and whiskers. To him, Dan, with his own thin, scraggly, scratchy beard, *was* a kid, no two ways about it. So Dan nodded back and said, "Not bad. You?"

"Tolerable." The trader considered, then nodded. "Yeah, I'm just about tolerable."

"Cool," Dan said. "Ask you something?"

"Well, you can always ask." The older man's eyes narrowed. "I don't promise to answer, mind you. Your business is yours, and my business is mine."

That wasn't necessarily so. The trader represented nobody but himself. Dan served the Valley and King Zev. Somehow, he didn't think the trader would be much impressed if he told him so. Instead, he said, "Did you do any of your business with the people there?" and pointed to Liz's house.

"What if I did?" No, the trader wouldn't give anything away.

"Look, I'm not trying to get money out of you. I don't care about money," Dan said. That wasn't exactly true. He cared plenty about his own money, but he was willing not to worry about the trader's. "There aren't any new taxes for trading here"—if there were, chances were they would have sparked an uprising—"and I'm not trying to shake you down."

"Says you," the trader answered. "If you knew how many lines I've heard . . . But I haven't heard one just like this, anyways. So if you aren't trying to shake me down, what the devil *are* you doing?" His leathery face was watchful, wary. He kept his hands well away from the pistols, but Dan would have bet he could have one in his grip in a hurry. And the matchlock wasn't even loaded.

"What I want to know is, what did you bring up here to trade with those people?" Dan said.

"You won't believe me if I tell you."

"Try me."

"Okay. Remember, you asked for it. I unloaded some magazines from Old Time, from the days just before the Fire came down."

Dan *did* believe him. He sounded too pleased with himself to be lying. Dan was sorry he'd said he wouldn't ask about money—he wondered how much this guy had got. But what the man said fit in pretty well with what Liz had told him before, which also made him think the trader was telling the truth. So all he asked was, "What kind of magazines? Did they have to do with Old Time guns and stuff?"

"Nah. I could see people wanting those." The trader shook his head. His greasy hair flipped back and forth under his hat. "These were just weird, man. I think they were mostly pretend stories. Why would you care about those?" He sounded honestly puzzled.

Dan was puzzled, too. "That's all?" he asked.

"That's it. Cross my heart and hope to die." The trader made the required gesture. For the first time, though, his eyes slipped away from Dan's. Was he hiding something? If he was, Dan saw no way to make him turn loose of it. And the older man was impatient to be gone. "You gonna hassle me any more?"

"I wasn't hassling you," Dan said. "You want to get hassled? I'll take you to my sergeant. He'll show you more about hassling than you ever saw."

"That's okay, kid, if it's all the same to you." The trader's tone warned it had better be okay with Dan. Even so, he sounded amused as he went on, "I have met up with a sergeant or three in my time, and it's a fact that they can hassle better'n just about anybody."

"You can say that again!" As soon as the words were out of Dan's mouth, he wished he had them back. Now he'd given the trader something to use against him. That wasn't smart. But he didn't think Chuck would do much more than laugh. He hoped Chuck wouldn't, anyhow. Sounding as gruff as he could, he said, "You can go."

The trader touched the brim of his hat in what wasn't quite a salute. "Much obliged, buddy. You know, that trader's got a daughter about your age." He jerked a thumb toward the house from which he'd come.

"I've met her." Dan bit off the words.

"She's smart, too." The older man didn't know how much trouble he was causing—or maybe he did know and didn't care. "If I were as young as you are, I'd try and spend some time with her, I would."

"Right," Dan said. If looks could have killed, the trader's fancy pistols wouldn't have done him a nickel's worth of good. Didn't he know that Dan wanted nothing more than to spend as much time with Liz as he could? And didn't he know that Liz didn't seem the least bit interested in doing the same thing?

Of course he doesn't know any of that, Dan realized. The trader had just set eyes on Liz for the first time. (Unless he'd come up here before the Valley took Westwood. But Dan thought that unlikely. The man would have talked about her differently if he had.) How could he know that Dan went over there whenever he found the chance? How could he know Dan was on his way over there now? Simple—he couldn't.

Or could he? His leathery, weathered face was much too cunning as he said, "Well, have a nice day, pal," and ambled off.

He didn't look back over his shoulder to see whether Dan knocked on Liz's door. Maybe that meant he didn't care. Then again, maybe it meant he already had a pretty good notion of what Dan would do.

Steaming, Dan tramped right past that door. He was, after all, supposed to be on patrol. But he looked back over his shoulder after he'd gone half an extra block. No sign of the trader. If the miserable fellow had hung around to see what Dan would do, he was gone now. And if he was gone now . . .

Dan hurried back to Liz's house and knocked on the door. The barred little telltale at eye level opened up. Dan didn't think those were Liz's eyes on the other side of it. He turned out to be right, because a man's voice said, "Oh, it's you. Wait a second."

A thud meant the man was taking down the bar that held the door closed. When it swung wide, Dan found himself looking at Liz's father. "Hello," he said politely—he couldn't bring himself to call anybody in occupied Westwood *sir*. "Is Liz at home?"

Her father nodded. "Yes, she is, but you can't see her right now. She's busy in the kitchen. We've got to eat—nothing we can do about that—and getting food ready takes a lot of time."

Dan nodded, too. He remembered his mother working a lot

in her kitchen. He also remembered her grumbling about it. Chopping and cutting and plucking and gutting and tending the fires and cleaning up afterwards . . . Sometimes she'd dragooned him into helping, but women did most of the work in there.

"Ask you something?" Dan said.

"I make a point of never saying no to a musketeer who's carrying his gun," Liz's father answered. Dan wondered if he was telling the truth. Like the other trader, he was bound to have weapons of his own. But he wasn't showing any right now. And so . . .

"Why did you buy freaky magazines from that whiskery scoundrel?"

Liz's father looked startled for a moment. Then he smiled. "You must have run into Luke."

"If that's his name," Dan said. "But you didn't answer my question. Why did you? It could matter to the Valley." He wanted the trader to understand he wasn't just being snoopy on his own.

"I don't see how," Liz's father said. "I'm interested in those kinds of magazines myself, the same way Liz is. They remind me how much we lost when the Fire fell. And, after I look at them, I can sell them. I'll make good money when I do, too."

All you had to do was look around to see how much got lost when the Fire fell. The buildings, the rusting corpses of cars, the fancy firearms, the diseases people couldn't cure any more . . . "Why do you need to be reminded?" Dan asked.

"Like I said, I'm interested."

"Mrm." Dan made a noise deep in his throat. "Are you interested because you're trying to scope out plans for Old Time weapons?" People nowadays *could* imitate some of them.

But Liz's father just shook his head. "No."

"Can I see the magazines? I need to be sure of that," Dan said.

With a shrug, Liz's father said, "Sure. Why not? You'll probably arrest me if I try to tell you no. And the magazines really are what I said they are. Handle them carefully—that's all I ask. I paid more than a dollar apiece for them."

"So much?" That anybody would spend so much money for something to read blew Dan's mind. Yes, the trader said he would make money on the magazines sooner or later. How could he, though, when he threw away silver like that?

Into the courtyard Dan went. Savory odors wafted from the kitchen. Dan's nostrils twitched. If that wasn't going to be a mutton stew, his nose needed rewiring. He wondered why people said things like that. What did wires have to do with your nose? Wires had to do with electricity, and electricity was one more thing they'd had in the Old Time that they didn't any more. Somebody had once written that electricity would propel a streetcar better than a gas jet and give more light than a horse. The person who read that to Dan said it was supposed to be a joke, but neither one of them got it.

"Here are the magazines," Liz's father said.

The ginger-whiskered trader—Luke—had been right: they were funky. Some of them had rockets on their covers. Others talked about gas mileage for cars. Dan paged through them. He didn't see anything that had to do with weapons. Even if they were weird, they seemed harmless.

He gave them back to Liz's father. "I can't figure out why you think they're so cool."

"We were going to go to the moon." The older man pointed

up. There it was, a little more than half full, pale and white in the blue daylight sky. "To the moon, Dan. We'd already sent rockets up there. I've seen pictures that they took of craters and things, just before they crashed down onto it. And we were going to send people after them. People, all the way to the moon and back! And then we used the rockets to blow ourselves up instead. But we were so close." He held his index fingers maybe half an inch apart.

"What's that got to do with these?" Dan pointed to the magazines. The familiar musty smell of old, old paper came from them.

"They were sure we were going. They knew we could do it," Liz's father said. "What if we really had? What would we have done after that?" He tapped a magazine, one with a rocket on the front, with his finger. "These tell the stories of what might have been."

"And look what we have instead." All of a sudden, Dan's heavy matchlock didn't seem so wonderful. It was about as fancy a weapon as people nowadays could make. Everything else was on the same level. And they could have gone to the moon instead! Tears stung his eyes, tears of rage and embarrassment. "Isn't this a wonderful world we gave ourselves?"

"A little bit at a time, it does get better," Liz's father said. "The time right after the Fire fell, that was really bad."

"That's what they say," Dan agreed. "It'll be a lot better once King Zev gets done licking the Westside."

"Well, maybe," the trader said. "Do you think King Zev is the one who'll put the United States back together again?"

"Don't be silly!" Dan exclaimed. "Everybody knows Los Angeles is only a little part of the old United States. It would have to be Zev's son, maybe even his grandson."

"Right," Liz's father said, and Dan had left the house before he even thought to wonder whether the older man meant it.

Liz couldn't seem to poke her nose outside without seeing Luke. When she went up to UCLA, she would spot him sunning himself on the grass or playing solitaire. When she went into the market square to buy vegetables, he'd be gnawing on a baked potato or haggling over the price of a cheese sandwich.

He always looked innocent. Some people had a knack for that. He didn't quite have a halo glowing above his broad-brimmed hat, but he seemed as if one might pop out any minute. That made Liz suspicious. From what she'd seen, people who worked so hard to project that air of innocence were often chameleons. And what Luke might be hiding . . .

She had a pretty good idea there. Dad didn't want to spy for Cal and the rest of the Westside bigwigs who'd got thrown out of Westwood. If Luke could find out what Cal wanted to know, he'd get the payoff.

At first, that was the only thing Liz thought of. Then something else occurred to her, and she started to worry. "What if the Westsiders throw the Valley soldiers out again?" she asked her folks over supper. She'd earned her tacos. She'd made the tortillas from cornmeal, and she'd chopped up the beef that went into them. They tasted especially good to her because of that—and, no doubt, because all the ingredients were fresh as could be.

"Well, what if they do?" Mom said. "We did business with them before. We can do business with them again."

"But now they asked us to help them, and Dad told them no," Liz said. "How happy will they be about that?"

Her father paused to dab at his chin with a napkin. The tacos weren't neat, no matter how tasty they were. "The worst thing that happens is, we go back to the home timeline a little early," he said. "That wouldn't break my heart." He gave her a crooked smile. "And then Dan would be out of your hair, and it wouldn't even look bad. What's wrong with that?"

"Nothing . . . if they give you some warning first," Liz said. "Then we get away, sure. But what if they just grab you off the street or something? They can do whatever they want in that case."

One of the lessons Crosstime Traffic taught was, *Anything that can happen can happen to you*. People who worked in the alternates sometimes lost sight of that. They sometimes paid for losing sight of it, too. People everywhere lost sight of it too often. In the home timeline, the price might be your job or your lover. In the alternates, it could easily be your neck.

"I don't think that will happen," her father said. "They've got no reason to grab me, not like that."

"No? What about Luke?" Liz said. "Dan wondered about us before. And now he's asking questions about somebody who really does want us to spy for the Westside? That's not good."

"Luke's managed to live through a whole swarm of things we can't even imagine," Dad replied. "I don't think he'll lose any sleep about a Valley soldier who barely needs to shave."

The fuzz on Dan's chin and cheeks and upper lip was a pretty sorry excuse for a beard. "I wish the guy were dumb," Liz said. "He's just ignorant, though. Now I understand the difference."

Her father made clapping motions that produced silent applause. Liz's ears got hot. "Congratulations," Dad said, less sarcastically than he might have. "A lot of people never do figure that one out."

"That's 'cause most of them don't go out to the alternates, I guess," Liz said. "Everybody's ignorant in this alternate, but you can still tell who's smart and who isn't. Cal's pretty smart. Dan's pretty smart. Luke—"

"Would be a CEO or something in the home timeline," Dad broke in. "No flies on Luke, no, sir."

"How smart is King Zev?" Liz asked.

"Well, I haven't met him, so I don't know for sure," her father answered. "Finding that heavy machine gun in good working order won him the war. You don't need to be smart to have something like that happen—you just need to be lucky. He's got some pretty good officers—I do know that. But I have the feeling he's not the brightest bulb in the hardware store. How come?"

"I wondered," Liz said. Her father made an exasperated noise. She went on, "If the Westside and Speedro team up to try to take Westwood back, how well will Zev do against Cal and his buddies?"

"Ah. Gotcha." Dad nodded. "That's a good question. The only good answer I can find is, *We'll find out.*"

"Thanks a bunch. I could have done that well myself," Liz said.

"Sorry. I don't know what you want me to say." Dad spread his hands and shrugged. "I'm not a prophet, not from the Bible and not one of the new ones, either."

"I hope not!" Liz told him. "You're not dirty and shaggy enough, anyway." Dad laughed, not that she was joking. In the years since the Fire fell, plenty of people had said they knew why God let it happen. So far, none of their preachings held a very big audience. But who could guess what the holy books in this alternate would look like a thousand years from now? In the middle of the second century, how many people thought Christianity would turn out to be such a big deal?

"I wonder how much Luke has found out on his own," Dad said in musing tones. "Probably more than I could have told him. Cal will pay him plenty, I bet."

"But you've got Cal's money," Liz said.

"I've got some of it. I'd be amazed if Cal gave me all of it, or anything close to all of it," Dad said. "If he's going to get people in Speedro to do things for him, he'll have to pay them off. And he likes to live high on the hog, and that costs money, too—not as much as it would in the home timeline, but a lot, anyway."

Liz started to say something, then stopped. Dad had thought about a few things she hadn't. "What happens if what's left of the Westside and Speedro do beat the Valley?" she asked at last.

"I don't know that, either," he replied. "I'm not sure they can, because I don't know what all they've got. I didn't know the Valley had that heavy machine gun, and it made all the difference in the last round. Even if they do win, I don't think Cal can go over the hill and invade the Valley. He'd be nuts if he tried. The most he can hope for is getting Westwood back."

"Which means the shooting would all be right here," Liz said, and her father nodded, none too happily. She went on, "We never would have had any of this trouble if he hadn't built that dumb wall across the 405." The idea that there could be a wall across what was, in the home timeline, one of the two or three busiest freeways in the world told what a disaster this alternate had known.

Dad nodded. "And do you know what that shows?"

"No? What?" Liz said.

"That even smart people can do dumb things. He thought he could get away with it. He thought King Zev would put up with it. He thought he could beat the Valley if Zev didn't put up with it. And he was wrong every time."

"You should have talked him out of it," Liz said.

"Get real. For one thing, he didn't ask me. He was head of the City Council—he still is, for all the good it does him—and I'm just a trader. Besides, why do you think he would have listened even if I got a chance to talk to him about it? There's a particular kind of smart person who thinks everybody around him is a dope. Is that Cal, or isn't it?"

"Sure sounds like him," Liz admitted. "But that kind of smart person isn't as smart as he thinks he is."

"Not usually, no," Dad agreed. "You don't find that out till too late a lot of the time, though. A lot of really smart people go a long way on their own before they foul up. Afterwards, you wonder how much further they could have got if they realized other people are really people, not just ladder rungs for them to step on. You treat somebody like a rung, pretty soon he'll break under your foot."

"Then you go splat," Liz said.

"That's about the size of it." Dad sighed. "Way things are now, I wish we could bulletproof the walls here."

"You think the new fight's coming soon, then," Liz said in dismay.

"Don't you?" Dad said. "Cal wouldn't have sent Luke up here to find out what we know if he didn't aim to move. Luke wouldn't be sniffing around on his own if he didn't want to bring something back. He's sure Cal will pay off if he does. Cal wouldn't pay off if he weren't going to move. And so . . ."

"Yeah. And so," Liz said. Everything fit together, almost as neatly as in a geometry proof. But no geometry proof since the days of Archimedes had got anybody killed.

"Cheer up," Dad told her. "Like I said, you'll be rid of Dan. That's something, anyhow."

"Something, yeah," Liz answered. "I don't want him to get shot, though—I don't hate him or anything." She sighed. "You just want to yell at these people, you know? They had their great big stupid war, but they go on fighting these little wars that are even stupider. Don't they learn anything from history?"

"The first thing you learn from history is that nobody ever learns anything from history, or not for long," her father answered. "People used to say that in the home timeline, but now that we can look at a bunch of different histories we see it's true in all of them. People are like that. You wish we weren't, but we are."

"We already got stuck at the edges of one battle. I don't want to get stuck in the middle of another one," Liz said.

"Well, who does?" Dad said. "If it gets too bad, we disappear. I already told you that."

"Yeah, I know you did," Liz replied. If they were all here at the house when trouble came, they could do that. If they weren't, if one of them or two of them or all of them happened to be out in Westwood . . . But Dad was ignoring even the possibility. Liz called him on it.

He spread his hands. "I don't know what you want from me.

The fighting won't get here right away. We'll know it's coming ahead of time. And when we do know, we'll be able to come back to the house, so we won't get stuck. Right?"

"I sure hope so," Liz said.

"You have to have *some* confidence that things will work out. Otherwise, you can't do your job," Dad said.

"I guess," Liz answered. "I'd like that better if this weren't an alternate that's had an atomic war." She got the last word. Then she had to decide if she really wanted it.

Eight

"Musketeers . . . shoulder arms!" Sergeant Chuck yelled.

Proudly, Dan did. He wondered whether the other new musketeers had that tiny moment of hesitation, too. He still had to work to remember he was a musketeer, not a no-account archer any more. The few remaining archers in Captain Kevin's company were already carrying their bows ready to string and shoot.

"Riflemen . . . shoulder arms!" the sergeant shouted.

Their faces serious, the riflemen obeyed. With their fancy Old Time guns and cartridges, they could hit targets far beyond any a musketeer could hope to reach. But they took chances musketeers didn't, too. A musket wouldn't explode unless you loaded several charges of powder into it without lowering the match to the touch-hole. Old Time cartridges were just plain *old* nowadays. You never could tell about them till you pulled the trigger. Most of the time, they did what they were supposed to—you wouldn't dare use them if they didn't. Sometimes, though, they didn't do anything at all. And every once in a while, one would blow up in your face and wreck your rifle . . . and you. Riflemen needed steady nerves—and nerve, period.

Chuck nodded to Kevin. "All ready, sir."

"Very good, Sergeant." The company commander had the sling off, but his left arm still wasn't what it had been before he got shot. He raised his voice: "Forward . . . march!"

Along with the rest of the Valley soldiers, Dan tramped south down Westwood Boulevard toward the Santa Monica Freeway line. Some of the people on the sidewalk glanced at the marching men. Others just went about their business. Quite a few of them were bound not to like the Valley men. You couldn't tell which ones, though. They knew better than to show a company's worth of armed men that they were hostile.

Then the company had to stop, because a wagon full of beer barrels drawn by six big horses clattered across Westwood Boulevard from a side street. Sergeant Chuck yelled at the driver. So did some of the soldiers. The fellow on the wagon spread his hands, as if to say, *What can I do? It's my job.*

The pause let Dan glance over in the direction of Liz's house. He'd be going a couple of miles away—not impossibly far, but far enough. Too far, really. He would have felt even worse about it if he thought Liz cared. He sighed.

He didn't see her, even if he'd hoped to. He did see Luke the trader, who watched the Valley soldiers with keen attention. Was he counting them? For whom?

He caught Sergeant Chuck's eye. "See that scraggly fellow with the whiskers?" he said in a low voice.

"The guy with the pistols?" Chuck said. Dan nodded. "What about him?" the underofficer asked. "He looks like a tough customer, but so what?"

"He's a trader. He says he is, anyway," Dan said. "But he's mighty snoopy. I've seen him prowling around, kind of looking us over, know what I mean? And now he's doing it again."

"How about that?" Chuck said. "Well, when we get where we're going, I'll put a flea in Captain Kevin's ear. Maybe he'll want to pick this guy up, ask him a few questions. Sharp questions. Pointed questions. Hot questions." Chuck had a very nasty smile when he felt like using it. "What's the guy's name? You know?"

"He goes by Luke, I think," Dan answered.

"Okay. Well, we'll see what he goes by once we start finding out what's what." Chuck looked at the company and went from that special nasty smile to his usual sergeant's scowl. "Come on, you muttonheads! Straighten it up!" he bellowed. "You're not a herd of camels galumphing down the street. If you think you are, I'm here to teach you different."

They straightened up. Doing what Chuck said was easier than trying to get around him. Armies were made that way, and had been since the beginning of time. Dan didn't think about such things. As long as he stayed in step with the men around him, he didn't need to.

A couple of large Old Time buildings still stood on Westwood Boulevard, even if awnings and curtains and shutters replaced almost all the glass in their windows. Most of the buildings, though, were modern shops and houses. They were made from the rubble of what had stood there before. Stone and brick and wood and chunks of stucco with chicken wire in it made up the walls. The patchwork was odd if you weren't used to it. Dan was. A lot of stuff in the Valley was built the same way.

When they marched past a little place selling tacos and tamales and hamburgers, the soldiers' neat footwork faltered again. The smell of greasy, spicy roasting meat made spit flood into Dan's mouth. His stomach rumbled loudly, and his wasn't the only one.

"Keep moving! Keep moving!" Sergeant Chuck bawled. "It's all probably chopped-up kitty and lizard, anyway."

"I don't care," somebody behind Dan said. "I'm *hungry*."

"Who's the wise guy?" Chuck shouted furiously. "Was that you, Dan?"

"No, Sergeant." Dan could tell the truth with no trouble at all. That was a good thing, too. He might not have said anything out loud, but he didn't care what was in the savory-smelling goodies, either. If he meowed after he ate some of them . . . well, so what?

Chuck challenged several other soldiers marching near Dan. They all denied everything. Nobody blew the whistle on whoever had spoken up. Chuck fumed and swore, but that was all he could do. Dan, by contrast, noted just where the little cookshop stood. The freeway line didn't lie very far south of it. If he got some free time, he could come back and spend a dime or two.

The Santa Monica Freeway line was a good one for King Zev's soldiers to defend. The freeway had been built above the ordinary streets around it. That gave the Valley men the advantage of high ground in a lot of places. Here and there, though, the overpasses that let the freeway leap above the ordinary streets had collapsed. Maybe that happened when the Fire fell. Maybe earthquakes brought the overpasses down later. Or maybe they just fell because nobody had taken care of them for more than a century. Any which way, that cut down the number of possible invasion routes from the south.

Of course, there were far fewer routes from the north. King Zev's soldiers had broken through anyhow. Dan wished that hadn't occurred to him. He and his comrades took their place on the freeway itself west of Westwood Boulevard. No trouble could approach unless they saw it first.

But some trouble was already behind them. Chuck spoke to Captain Kevin about Luke. Dan couldn't hear what Kevin said. But a runner went pelting back into Westwood. A slow smile crossed Dan's face. From here on out, Luke wouldn't have a very happy time of it. *Too bad,* Dan thought.

A knock on the door in the middle of the night. How many books and movies and video games featured that kind of automatic suspense-maker? Liz had always thought it was such a cliché. But when somebody banged on the door to the house where she was living, her heart went *thud, thud, thud.* It was dark, so she had no idea what time it was. Ten o'clock? Midnight? Three in the morning? Groggy with sleep, she couldn't have said for sure.

A few watches and windup clocks with luminous dials survived from Old Time. None was in Liz's bedroom. She yawned and thought about sticking her head under the pillow. She decided she wouldn't imitate an ostrich—or what people said was true about ostriches. Besides, whoever was knocking out there didn't seem ready to go away.

She walked out into the hall, feeling her way in the darkness. She almost screamed when she bumped into somebody. Her father said something pungent. "What's going on?" she asked. In the face of unknown trouble, she felt like a little kid again.

"Don't know," Dad answered. "I think I'd better find out, though."

He was nothing but a darker shadow in a hallway full of gloom. Liz had never missed electricity so much as she did right then. "Do you have a gun?" she asked, a question she never would have thought of in the home timeline.

"You better believe it, sweetie," her father said. "Stay here, okay? That way I have one less thing to worry about it."

"What if you need help?" Liz squawked.

"I'm here, and I've got a gun, too," her mother answered out of nowhere. "Do you?"

"No," Liz said in a small voice.

"Then stay here, like Dad told you."

Muttering, Liz did. She listened to her father's soft footfalls as he approached the door. "Who's there?" he asked. The knocking stopped, which was a relief.

Standing there in the hall, Liz shivered. Even in summertime, Los Angeles nights could get chilly. Thinking this one was, gave her a reason not to think she was scared.

She couldn't hear the answer from whoever stood out there. She did hear Dad say, "Oh, for heaven's sake"—and then something stronger than that. A moment later, he unbarred the door and opened it. The man outside came in. Dad barred the door again in a hurry. Then he called, "Light a lamp!"

There was always a fire in the kitchen. Liz scurried across the courtyard. She lit a twig from the hot embers and used it to light a lamp. The smell of hot olive oil filled her nose.

The lamp didn't shed much light—even a toy flashlight would have put it to shame. Shadows jumped and swayed crazily as Liz carried the lamp toward the doorway. She didn't need much light to recognize the newcomer, though. "Luke!"

she said. "What are you doing here?" She'd more than half expected it would be Dan.

"Well, little lady, everybody's gotta be somewhere," the trader answered.

Her temper went off like a firecracker. "If you don't tell me what I asked you, you'll be out on the street again so fast it'll make your head swim," she snapped.

Luke blinked. She'd always played the girl who didn't speak up for herself. Most girls in this alternate were like that. But she was from the home timeline, and she had more self-respect. And her father nodded. "Yes, Luke. You'd better speak up. What *are* you doing here? Who's after you? Somebody is, right?"

The trader seemed to wilt. Reluctantly, he nodded. "It's those Valley clowns," he said. "They think I'm spying on them."

"Well, you are." Again, Liz spoke up where a local girl would have kept her mouth shut.

"That doesn't mean I want to get killed on account of it!" Luke exclaimed. He turned to her father. "You got some place you can, like, hide me, man?"

Nobody from this alternate knew about the subbasement or was likely to find it. All the same, Liz thought *No!* as loud as she could. She didn't want Luke going down there. That was where transposition chambers materialized. Nobody from this alternate had any business seeing such things.

"How far behind you are they?" Dad asked.

"Not far enough," Luke answered.

"They'll know to come here," Liz said. "People will remember he's visited us. Or maybe the Valley soldiers have bloodhounds."

"I took care of that—I put down ground pepper." The ghost of a smile crossed Luke's face. As if on cue, two dogs started baying frantically. "Well, that bought me a little time, anyways."

When he talked about pepper, he meant the red kind. It grew in the New World. Black pepper was a rare luxury here. Most of it came from Old Time supermarket shelves. The plants from which black peppercorns came grew only across the sea. Ocean traffic aboard windjammers was even more erratic than hauling goods overland.

Dad looked very unhappy, and pepper had nothing to do with it. "They *will* come here—Liz is dead right about that," he growled. "I ought to turn you loose and see how fast you can run."

"Wouldn't try that." Luke's right hand dropped toward a pistol.

"Wouldn't try *that*," Mom said from out of the darkness. Luke froze—her voice carried conviction. Very slowly and carefully, he moved his hand away. She didn't say anything else, not even, *That's better*. No point to letting him know exactly where she was.

"Well, come on," Dad said, and led Luke into the courtyard. *No!* Liz wanted to yell again. Biting her lip, she made herself keep quiet.

Dad didn't send Luke down to the subbasement. Instead, he got a ladder and nudged it up against the ceiling of a storeroom. "There's a hidey-hole up there," he said. "Push aside a couple of boards, get in, and put 'em back. And keep quiet from then on out, if you know what's good for you."

Luke touched the brim of his hat. "Much obliged to you, sir."

"Yes," Dad said. "You are. Now climb."

The trader from Speedro did, and disappeared into the hidey-hole. "I didn't even know that was there," Liz said in a low voice.

"Life is full of surprises sometimes," Dad answered, which might have meant anything or nothing.

Liz didn't get much of a chance to figure out *what* it meant, because more knocks came from the front door. "The Valley men!" she squeaked.

Dad took down the ladder. "Mm, I don't suppose it's the Tooth Fairy or the Great Pumpkin," he agreed. "We'd better answer it, don't you think?" He sounded almost indecently calm.

"Open up, in the name of King Zev!" the men outside shouted. Liz was pretty sure the Great Pumpkin didn't go around yelling things like that.

Dad did open the door. Liz went with him. Mom stayed out of sight—and kept the pistol where she could use it in a hurry. "Hello," Dad told the Valley men, who did have a couple of bloodhounds with them. "You probably want to know about Luke the trader, don't you?"

"Better believe we do," growled the sergeant who held the dogs' leashes. "You got him here? There's a twenty-dollar reward on his head."

Twenty dollars, in this alternate, was a lot of money. Dad sounded impressed when he said, "Good grief! What did he do?"

"Spied for the enemy, that's what," the sergeant answered, and he wasn't lying—Luke had done just that. "I'm gonna ask you one more time, buddy—you got him here?" He sounded tough and mean.

Dad looked sorry as he shook his head. He made a better actor than Liz would have given him credit for. "With that kind of reward, I wish I did. But I sent him off with a flea in his ear. I don't want any trouble with anybody."

"Can we track him?" another sergeant asked the dog handler. Then he asked Liz's father, "Which way did he go?" Liz thought she would have asked those questions in the opposite order.

"That way." Dad pointed south.

"I don't know." The sergeant with the bloodhounds looked almost as sorrowful as they did. "That person"—which wasn't exactly what he said—"has some kind of smelly stuff to mess up his trail. Rocky and Bullwinkle got all fubared before we came here."

Rocky and Bullwinkle? Liz thought. *They aren't dogs!* But they were here and now. And what was *fubared* supposed to mean? The English they spoke around here was mostly easy to follow, but every once in a while . . .

The bloodhounds did pick up a scent. It was probably the one Luke had left the last time he walked out of the house. The Valley soldiers seemed happy enough to let them follow it. One of the men nodded politely to Liz and her father as the group hurried off down the street.

Dad's shoulders slumped in relief when he reached for the bar to close up the door again. "I'm getting too old for this," he muttered.

"*I'm* getting too old for this, and I'm a lot younger than you are," Liz said.

That got her a weary grin. " 'Do field work,' they told me," Dad said. " 'You can't really understand anything without field work,' they said. I'll tell you what I understand—I understand how you can be scared out of your gourd all the time when you're doing field work, that's what."

"Yeah," Liz said. "And there are plenty of alternates worse than this one, too."

"Tell me about it!" her father exclaimed. "There are probably some of them where they give you your money back if you don't have a coronary the first day you're there." He snapped his fingers. "And I understand one more thing, too."

"What's that?" Liz asked.

"I'd better get Luke some water and a honey bucket," he answered. "With luck, a honey bucket with a lid."

"A honey bucket?" Liz said, and then, "Oh." Most of the time, euphemisms made her impatient. That one, though, she found she liked. She added, "You'd better let him know you're not giving him to the Valley soldiers, too."

"Sounds like a plan," Dad said. "I think he's liable to shoot first and ask questions later." He sang out as he hauled the ladder into place again: "It's just me! I've come with your fresh cauliflowers!"

Cauliflowers? Liz wondered. Dad could be weird sometimes. She didn't believe this was the right moment for it.

But maybe she was wrong. Luke opened the hidey-hole, and he didn't shoot first without bothering to ask questions later. "They gone?" he asked—quietly now, so his voice wouldn't carry. Questions first: the right way.

"For now, anyway," Dad answered. "How long do you want to stay there?" He asked questions, too.

"I was thinking till tomorrow night, if that's cool," the trader from Speedro said. "That way, they won't jump up and down so much, you know what I mean? If I went and split tonight, they'd still be all uptight, like."

"Groovy," Dad said, a small smile on his face. He *enjoyed* talking like a twentieth-century hippie. Liz was fried if she could see why. It made him sound like a jerk. She sure thought so, anyhow. "I brought you some goodies, then," Dad went on. He handed up the water and the . . . honey bucket. Then, from the top of the ladder, he told Liz, "Why don't you get our friend some bread and a chunk of that chicken we had tonight?"

Because I don't want to. Because I'm not more than fifty-one percent convinced he is our friend. Because I'd rather give him a clout in the teeth than a drumstick. All of that went through Liz's mind in a fraction of a second. None of it came out. The only thing that did was, "Sure, Dad."

As she hurried away, Luke laughed softly. "Don't think your daughter trusts me for beans."

"Don't be silly!" Dad played the good host. Well, of course he was a good host. If he weren't a good host, those bloodhounds would have been baying at Luke in here, pepper or no pepper.

How did he know? Liz wondered as she cut Luke a big chunk of bread and brought not a drumstick but a whole chicken leg back to the ladder. *How could he tell?* She was positive she'd been not just polite but even eager-sounding. But she hadn't fooled him—not even close. So what did she do wrong? She wanted to ask, but that would mean admitting she didn't trust him. She didn't want to do that—it would be too embarrassing.

"Thanks, dear," Dad said when she brought him the food. He handed it up to Luke.

"Thanks is right!" Luke echoed. "These are better rats than I'd see at most of the inns around town. If your room up here was just a little less cramped, you could make good money renting it out." He laughed again.

That's not rat! It's chicken! was Liz's first indignant thought. But she was listening to this alternate's English with ears from the home timeline. *Rats* came from military slang, not hippie talk. It had nothing to do with Mickey Mouse's bigger cousins: it was short for *rations*.

"This is the kind of room where, if you start advertising it, nobody wants to stay in it any more," Dad said. He was bound to be right about that. If everybody knew about a hiding place, what good was it?

"Well, friend, in that case I'm going to pull my hole in after myself again," Luke said. Dad took the ladder away. Luke put up the boards once more. As far as Liz could tell, the hidey-hole vanished completely.

Dad sighed. "Not the kind of game I like to play to settle my digestion." He set a hand on Liz's shoulder. "You did real well. Now . . . Do you think you're up to going back to sleep?"

"Beats me," she answered. "I sure aim to try, though." To her surprise, she did it. She didn't know what that proved—probably how tired she was to begin with.

When Dan saw a Valley patrol with bloodhounds working its way toward the Santa Monica Freeway, he wondered what was going on. "You guys looking for Luke the trader?" he called to them.

That won him more attention than he really wanted. The whole patrol converged on him. He was used to attention from

Sergeant Chuck. Now he had the undivided attention of two sergeants at once, and discovered it was at least four times as bad.

"How come you wanna know, kid?" demanded the one with the dogs.

"How'd you hear about Luke, anyway?" the other one growled. The bloodhounds didn't say anything, but in the torchlight their long, sad faces declared they were angry to have to pause in their search for even a minute.

"If it weren't for me, you guys wouldn't know about him." Dan spoke to the sergeants. He hoped they'd make the bloodhounds understand. "Have you been to the trader's house on Glendon?"

"Yeah, we were there," said the sergeant with the dogs. "You really do know too much, don't you? How'd you know about that house?"

"Well, it's the girl there." Now Dan knew he sounded a little sheepish. "Did you see her?"

"Oh. The girl." That was the dog handler. All of a sudden, things seemed to make sense to him. "I might've known." The other sergeant grunted. Even the bloodhounds seemed sniffy in a different way.

Dan wondered if his ears were on fire. They sure felt that way. "Don't you guys have girls?" he asked—not that he had Liz or anything. He just wished he did.

"We've got girls," the sergeant with the dogs said.

"But we don't have Westside girls," the other one added. "Not like that, we don't. For fun, yeah. Not for real."

To Dan's amazement, his ears got hotter yet. He hadn't thought they could. "How can you tell?" he asked. To make him feel like a complete idiot, his voice cracked in the middle of the question.

Both sergeants laughed themselves silly. Dan thought the dogs laughed, too, but maybe that was his imagination. The handler said, "You sound goofy when you talk about her, that's why."

Now Dan was the one who said, "Oh." Then he changed the subject as fast as he could: "What about Luke?"

"He was there, but he got away maybe three jumps ahead of us." The dog handler frowned. "I'm not sure how fresh this trail is, though. The dogs aren't all that stoked about it, and we know he's been down this way before."

"So why are you following it?" Dan asked. Yes, talking about Luke was a lot easier than talking about Liz.

"'Cause it's what we've got," said the sergeant who didn't take care of dogs.

"And 'cause that rotten villain messed up the trail before it got to the trader's house," added the one who did. "He put down something that almost made 'em jump out of their skins." That was saying something—the bloodhounds had a lot of skin to jump out of. The sergeant went on, "It was as bad as though somebody turned on an Old Time electric flashlight right in front of your face."

"Wow," Dan said. "Oh, wow." Electric lights were supposed to be bright, all right. He didn't know exactly how bright, because he'd never seen one work. He didn't know anybody who had, either.

"Yeah," the dog handler said. "So if we ever do catch this guy, we'll make him sorry. You bet we will."

"I bet he's sneaky," Dan said. "He looks sneaky. He sounds sneaky, too—I've talked with him." Was that really fair? Dan remembered Luke teasing him. If that didn't exactly make the trader sneaky, it came close enough, didn't it?

"He must be, or he wouldn't have got away from us," said the sergeant without the dogs.

"If we want to catch him, we'd better be sneaky, too," said the one in charge of the bloodhounds.

"If he's still here for us to catch," the other sergeant said. "If he got over the freeway line, he's a gone goose."

"How could he do that?" Dan asked. "We have it plugged tight."

Both sergeants looked at him as if he were still making messes in his drawers. "Kid, if he's that sneaky, chances are he can find a way," the one without the dogs replied. His voice was surprisingly gentle. He might have been explaining that the Easter Bunny wasn't real.

"Well, maybe," Dan admitted. The Valley soldiers were watching out for an attack from the south, not for one man trying to get past them and going that way.

"But if he *is* that sneaky . . ." the dog handler said.

"Yeah? What about it?" The other sergeant wasn't much impressed.

"Listen," said the three-striper with the bloodhounds. They put their heads together and talked in low voices. Dan did his best to listen without seeming to. The sergeants must have noticed, because they moved a couple of steps farther away. Dan muttered under his breath. He hadn't caught much anyway.

The older men both nodded. Then they headed back up Westwood Boulevard toward Westwood Village. They said not a word to Dan about whatever they'd decided. He thought that was rude. What did they figure? That he'd tell Luke what they were up to if he knew?

After a moment, he decided that had to be just what they figured. He couldn't remember the last time anything had made him angrier. He was a good Valley patriot. So what if he thought a Westside girl who knew Luke was cute? That had nothing to do with anything.

He could see himself explaining all this to the sergeants. He could see them both listening, and then laughing their heads off. And, because he could see all that so very well, he didn't even bother to try.

Nightfall in Westwood, the sun sinking towards and then into the Pacific. Far fewer tall buildings between Liz and the ocean than there would have been in the home timeline. The bomb that flattened Santa Monica into glass took out the ones that were there in 1967, and not many had gone up since.

As twilight deepened toward true night, Luke came down from his hiding place between the ceiling and the roof. He tipped his hat to the Mendozas again. "Like I said, much obliged to you folks. You saved my bacon there."

"When you go after somebody with dogs, most of the time you don't deserve to catch him," Dad said.

Luke started to say something, then checked himself. "You know what? I'm gonna have to think about that one for a while."

"Probably won't do you any lasting harm," Liz's father remarked.

Again, the trader started to answer. Again, he seemed to

think better of it. He sent Dad a cautious stare. "You're trouble, you know that?"

"Oh, no. He has no idea," Liz said before Dad could get a word in.

That made him and Luke both look at her. They both started to laugh at the same time. "Heaven help her boyfriends, man," Luke said.

"I don't know what you're talking about," Dad answered, deadpan. They laughed again, louder. Liz let out an indignant squawk. For some reason, her father and the hairy trader from Speedro thought that was funnier yet.

"Well, I'm gonna slide on out of here," Luke said when he was done with his uncouth guffaws. That was how Liz thought of them, anyway. Luke went on, "Thanks one more time for putting me up, my friend." He might have been talking about a night on the couch, not a day in a hiding place Liz hadn't even known about.

"Any time," Dad said, just as casually. "You want to be careful out there, you know what I mean?"

"I can dig it, man." As if to prove as much, Luke dropped his right hand to one of his pistols. "And I expect I can take care of myself."

"Okay, okay." Dad spread his hands to show he hadn't meant anything much. "I wasn't hassling you or anything. But in case those Valley guys haven't forgotten about you . . ."

The trader sneered. Liz didn't think she'd ever seen anybody more than twelve years old do that before, but she did now. "Negative perspiration," he said. She had to translate that into something that resembled the English she knew. *Don't sweat it,* he had to mean. Then why didn't he say so? He did go on, "If I can't give 'em the slip, I don't deserve to get out of here. They're from the *Valley*, after all." He laced the word with scorn.

"Yeah, well, just remember, that's what the Westsiders thought, too. Look what it got them," Dad said.

Luke didn't want to listen. "I'll send you a postcard, man," he said. That would have been snarky in the home timeline. Given what the mails were like in this alternate, it was a lot snarkier here.

Out the door he went. Dad barred it behind him, then let out a sigh. "Well, I'm not sorry to see him go," he said.

"And why is that?" Liz asked. "Just because he put us all in danger?"

"Might have a little something to do with it," her father replied.

Then things outside came unglued. Liz had heard the bloodhounds baying the night before. Now they sounded twice as excited—and twice as fierce, too. A voice with a Valley accent yelled, "Hold it right there, freak!"

After maybe half a second, another voice yelled from a different place: "Keep your hands away from your guns, or it's the last dumb thing you ever do!"

Dad said something under his breath that probably wasn't any hotter than what Liz was saying under hers. She didn't know why the Valley soldiers hadn't believed the Mendozas' story last night, but they hadn't. And that meant nothing but trouble.

Outside, Liz heard running feet. A gun banged—a matchlock musket, not an Old Time repeater. Someone shouted, "Hold it!" again. Then another matchlock fired. A cry of pain split the night. "Got him!" said the voice that had told Luke to hold it.

"Oh, wow!" Dad said, which fit what Liz was thinking almost

perfectly. For one thing, the Valley soldiers took a long chance. Their matchlocks weren't very accurate. They would have to reload after firing. If they'd both missed Luke, they would have been at his mercy. But one of them got him.

And *Oh, wow!* fit too well another way, too. Now the Valley soldiers knew Luke had come out of this house. They wouldn't be very happy about that. From their point of view, they had every right to be unhappy.

Liz didn't care about their point of view. She did care about the hassles that were bound to come.

And they did, in no time at all. Soldiers started pounding on the door. "Open up in the name of King Zev!" they shouted. "Open up in there!"

"What do we do, Dad?" Liz asked. "We can't let them in!"

"Tell me about it!" Her father was usually cool as an iceberg in January. Not now. She couldn't remember the last time she'd heard him so rattled. He raised his voice: "Sarah! Call for a chamber!"

"I'm doing it!" Mom answered. She didn't sound exactly calm, either.

"We hear you!" the soldiers yelled. "Open up!" When the Mendozas didn't, something thumped against the door—a man's shoulder, Liz thought.

"How strong is the bar?" she asked. It wasn't a question she'd ever thought she would have to worry about.

"We'll find out, won't we?" Now Dad sounded more like his usual self. But that wasn't the answer she wanted to hear, either. More quietly, he went on, "I think we'd better head for you-know-where."

That was smart. He didn't want the goons outside to hear

that they were heading for the subbasement. The goons didn't know the house *had* a subbasement. Maybe Luke would tell them about the attic hiding place. But he couldn't talk about the subbasement, because he also didn't know about it.

More thumps came from the door, and then one that brought a groan and a crackle as the hinges started to give way. The Valley soldiers bayed in triumph. "C'mon! Hit it again!" one of them said.

By then, Liz was hotfooting it down the stairs to the storerooms in the regular basement. The room with the computer link to the home timeline was there. When Mom came out, the door she closed behind her was all but invisible. Its hinges were a lot stronger than the ones to the front door. All the same, she carried the MacBook under her arm. "It's coming, which means it's here," she said.

The door to the subbasement was as well concealed as the one to the computer room. Dad latched it from below after Liz and her mother hurried down the stairs. Then he followed them, his shoes clattering on metal stairs. The transposition chamber waited for them. Its door slid open automatically.

"Trouble, eh?" the operator said as they got inside.

"Oh, maybe a little," Dad answered dryly—yes, he had himself back together again. After what felt like fifteen minutes and was really no time at all, they were back in the home timeline—which didn't mean their hassles were over.

Nine

Dan was pacing his patrol beat atop the Santa Monica Freeway when Sergeant Chuck and another private from the company came up to him. "Sidney will take the rest of your shift," Chuck told him. "Some guys down below need to talk to you pronto."

"What's happening?" Dan asked.

"If they needed to talk to me, they would've talked to me." Chuck jerked his thumb towards a ladder leading down on the north side of the freeway. "Go on. Get moving."

"Okay. Uh, yes, Sergeant." Dan corrected himself in a hurry. Chuck didn't even growl at him, which proved things were weird.

When he got to the bottom, he wasn't astonished to see the dog handler and the other sergeant he'd spoken with before. He was surprised to see a captain with them. He came to attention and saluted. "Musketeer Dan, reporting as ordered!"

"At ease," the captain said, and Dan let his spine relax. "Max and Mike here"—the captain pointed to the two sergeants—"and your Chuck say you probably know more about the traders on Glendon than anybody else from the Valley does. Is that the straight skinny?"

"I have no idea, sir," Dan answered. "I mean, I was over there a few times, but that's all."

"You liked the girl." The captain didn't make it a question. Dan nodded—it was true. He hoped it didn't land him in trouble. The captain said, "Well, that puts you one jump ahead of everybody else."

"Yes, sir," Dan said. When you were a common soldier, that was always the right answer to give an officer.

"Come on, then," the captain told him. "Maybe you'll be able to help us figure out where the devil they've gone."

"Gone?" Dan felt like somebody trying to play a game whose rules he didn't know. "I heard some gunshots last night. . . ."

"That was us, when we caught that so-and-so of a Luke," the captain said. "Max got him right where he won't sit down for quite a while." The sergeant who was usually in charge of the bloodhounds looked proud of himself. The captain went on, "Then we went and broke down the door to the Mendozas' house. They were in there—we could hear 'em talking to each other."

"They were—and then they weren't." Sergeant Max snapped his fingers. "Gone. Like that."

"Where'd they go?" Dan asked. "Did they have some secret way out?"

"Well, we turned Rocky and Bullwinkle loose in there to see if they could find the freshest trail." Max looked unhappy.

"What happened? Did they disappear into a wall or something?" Dan thought such things were impossible. He thought so, yeah . . . but you never could tell.

"Almost," the dog handler answered. "The hounds went down to the basement, and they just kind of parked there, right in the middle of the floor. And there's nothing there. So maybe the mutts are wrong. It can happen, I guess. But I sure don't know where else those people could've gone."

"They didn't get out the back door," Sergeant Mike put in. "We had somebody posted there, and they just didn't. Besides, that door's still barred from the inside."

"*Was* Luke in that house, sir? Did he have a hiding place there?" Dan asked the captain.

"We talked to him about that. He finally told us where it was at," the officer replied. Dan wondered how they'd persuaded Luke to talk. Some things, he decided, he might be better off not knowing. The captain still didn't look very happy. "We found the hideout. We could have looked for a month if we didn't know it was there, and we never would have. No sign the traders had used it, though."

"Oh." Dan chewed on that. "Where'd they go, then?"

"Good question." The captain looked hard at him. "C'mon back to the house with us. If anybody on our side has a chance of figuring it out, you're the one."

"Yes, sir. I'll try, sir." Dan felt he had to add, "I don't think I can promise you anything."

Up Westwood Boulevard he went with Sergeant Max and Sergeant Mike and the captain, whose name he still didn't know. Some of the other Valley soldiers on the street gave him stern looks, others stares full of sympathy. He felt embarrassed. A common soldier in the company of two sergeants and an officer almost had to be in dutch.

Well, maybe I am, Dan thought. *Maybe I just don't know it yet.*

They turned right on Wilshire and went over to Glendon, which was the next street east. Then up a couple of blocks, towards UCLA, and there stood the house, with soldiers outside the front door. They saluted as the captain approached.

If they couldn't find Liz and her folks, how am I supposed to? Dan wondered. *I don't know where they're hiding. Maybe they really did work magic and disappear*. He shrugged. He had to try.

He went inside with the officer and the underofficers. Everything was familiar, but everything was very quiet. The captain took him to a ladder leaned up against the inner courtyard wall. "Go on up," the older man said. "Have a look."

"Yes, sir," Dan said, and he did. Sure enough, it was a hiding place, about as comfortable as a cramped one could be. "This is where Luke was?" he asked.

"He says so," the captain answered. "Do you know about any others?"

"No, sir. I didn't know about this one," Dan said. "I guess the only way to find others would be to take a close look at all the walls and ceilings."

"We'll do that . . . eventually." The captain didn't sound thrilled about it. Dan had trouble blaming him. He went on, "Now come down from there and have a look at the basement."

"Yes, sir," Dan said again, and descended. He followed the captain and Mike and Max downstairs to the below-ground level. It held crates full of trade goods and sacks of beans and barley and parched corn—about what he would have expected.

Sergeant Max stepped on a flagstone. "This is where Rocky and Bullwinkle think they went," he said. "But it's just floor."

"I guess." Dan got down on his hands and knees. Only a couple of lamps burned in there. "Could I have one of those?" he said. Even though he forgot the *please*, Max handed him one.

The smell of the hot olive oil took him back to when he was a little tiny kid. He held the lamp as close to the floor as he could.

"What are you looking for?" Max asked.

"Beats me. Anything, really." Dan held his nose as close to the floor as he could, too. He squinted, staring as hard as he could. His sight hadn't started to lengthen, so he could peer closer than the captain or the sergeants could. He tried to stick his fingernail into a crack between flagstones. Then he thrust the blade of his belt knife into the crack. Excitement surged in him. "The dogs are right, I bet. This looks like a doorway, see?" He traced a rectangle with the knife. "And the cement here isn't just like the rest of it."

The captain stood on the rectangle and stomped hard. He cocked his head, considering the sound. "Might be something hollow under there. What do you boys think?" The question included the sergeants. It plainly didn't include Dan.

Mike stomped, too. He was a big, heavyset man with a lot of weight to put behind his boot. "Dog my cats if there isn't, sir. Now how do we go about prying it up?"

They tried the most basic way first: they wedged another knife in there and used it for a lever. The blade promptly snapped. It was Sergeant Max's knife. He had several unpleasant things to say.

They ended up needing army engineers. The engineers had trouble getting the door up, too. They dug up a flagstone beside the door, only to discover concrete beneath it. "Something funny's going on here," one of the engineers said. "I wonder if this is an Old Time fallout shelter."

Dan shuddered at the thought. Fallout was poison—he knew that much. Nobody in the Valley knew much more.

"If it is, it would make a perfect hiding place now, wouldn't it?" the captain said.

"Sure would," the engineer agreed. "I bet there's a lock on the other side of that trap door. Gonna take some work to break it. But with that other stone gone, we've got more room to pry."

They needed till late afternoon before they finally defeated the lock. "You found the door, kid," the captain told Dan. "You can go down there first if you want to."

Gee, thanks, Dan thought. But he couldn't look afraid, even if he was. "Yes, sir," he said. Holding a lamp, he went down into the blackness.

The soles of his boots clanged on metal stairs. He held the lamp high now, but it didn't throw much light. All it did was push the darkness back a little—he still couldn't see the walls of this chamber. He supposed it did have some.

He couldn't see the floor, either, not till just before his feet came down on it. It was hard, like asphalt or concrete—it felt too smooth for flagstones. He bent down with the lamp at the base of the stairs for a closer look. Yes, that had to be concrete.

"Well?" the captain called from up above. He wasn't coming down till he found out whether the fallout had eaten Dan.

"Well, what . . . sir?" Dan let a touch of impatience show. You couldn't come right out and say an officer had no guts. But he would have bet the sergeants got the message, even if the captain didn't. "It's a plain old room, that's all."

He straightened up, took a couple of steps forward, and proved himself wrong. It wasn't a plain old room, whatever else it was. When he walked out toward the middle, the lights in the ceiling went on.

He stopped and stared up at them, his mouth falling open like a fool's. Who could blame him? Those had to be electric lights—they were too bright for anything else. But he was as sure as made no difference that nobody had seen electric lights since the Fire fell and ended the Old Time.

"What did you just do, soldier?" the captain asked in a very small voice.

"I didn't do anything, sir," Dan said, even if he wasn't exactly sure that was true. "They came on all by themselves." He looked around. Here were these miraculous lights, but they sure didn't light up much. He might have been inside a concrete box with a glowing lid. The floor had yellow lines painted on it. Outside of the lines were words, also in yellow paint, and plainly done with stencils. KEEP CLEAR—CROSSTIME TRAFFIC REG. 34157A2.

Dan scratched his head. What was that supposed to mean? Did it mean anything? Not to him, it didn't.

Slowly, cautious, the captain and the two sergeants descended. "What is this place?" Sergeant Max asked in a low voice.

"Beats me," Dan said. "I don't think anybody's hiding here, though."

Sergeant Mike walked over to a wall and thumped on it with his fist. He got back a good, solid thunk. He moved over a couple of feet and did it again. Thunk. And again, and again, till he'd gone all the way around the chamber. "I don't *think* there are any secret rooms," he said.

"Didn't sound like it," Max agreed. "I wonder what Rocky and Bullwinkle would tell us."

"Why don't you go get them, Sergeant?" The captain kept staring up at the lights in the ceiling. They weren't bulbs, or what Dan thought of as bulbs. They were more like tubes of light seen through the kind of glass that survived here and there in bathroom windows. "How do those work?" the officer whispered. "How *can* they work?"

"There's electricity somewhere in this house." Dan looked at the floor again, as if expecting to see it sneak along there. Maybe it did. He wouldn't have recognized it had he seen it. Had he seen anything strange then, he would have called it electricity.

But he didn't. The floor was only a floor, with that big painted rectangle and some kind of funky warning on it.

The captain looked at that, too. "What's 'Crosstime Traffic'?" he asked, as if Dan were supposed to know.

"Can't tell you, sir." Dan denied everything.

"D'you think it's something the Westsiders know about? Electricity!" The captain's gaze went back to those impossible ceiling panels.

Dan could answer that question: "No way, sir. Nohow. We haven't seen anything like this anywhere else." The two sergeants solemnly nodded. Dan went on, "Besides, if the Westsiders had it, they'd use it above ground, wouldn't they? They wouldn't hide it in a basement under a basement."

"*I* sure wouldn't," Sergeant Max agreed.

"Well, neither would I," the captain said. "So that means these traders aren't ordinary Westsiders. What *are* they, in that case?" He looked at Dan, as if still expecting the common soldier could come right out and tell him.

But Dan said, "Sir, I only wish I knew," and that was nothing but the truth. Who was Liz, really? *What* was she, really? He wondered if he'd ever find out. And then he stared up at those magical glowing electric tubes again. Looking at them, blinking at the impossible light they shed, he realized Liz was only part of the question, and probably a small part at that.

Part of Liz was glad to be back in the home timeline again. Cars. Cell phones. Hot showers. Microwaves. Supermarkets. TV. Radio. The Net. Fasartas. Flush toilets. You didn't know how much you missed your comforts till you went without them for a while.

The home timeline held other pleasures, too. A UCLA campus that wasn't a crumbling ruin overgrown with weeds. A Santa Monica that wasn't grass trying to push up through the glass that nuclear strikes had fused. A Los Angeles that wasn't divided up into a bunch of squabbling little kingdoms.

No, the home timeline wasn't perfect. Not even close. She knew that all too well. But her time in that post-atomic alternate had taught her more than she'd ever imagined about the difference between better and worse.

But . . .

"We ought to go back," she told her father a couple of days after they'd escaped from the Valley soldiers.

"I know," he said. "We were really getting close to finding out what started the war there. That's what the grant was for. If we give incomplete results . . ." He sighed. "Well, if we do, we won't see any more research money for crosstime travel, that's for sure." He sighed again. "Stuck in the home timeline."

If you had to be stuck anywhere, there were lots of worse places. Liz understood that, in ways she never had before. Even so, she said, "I don't want to be stuck anywhere."

Dad smiled. "You aren't, sweetie. Even if I turn out to be, you aren't. They won't come down on you because of this. I got the grant, so I get the blame. And I deserve it. If I didn't hide Luke—"

"They would have shot him!" Liz broke in.

"They shot him anyway," Dad reminded her. "But for you it's no harm, no foul. You've still got to go to college and get your career going. Nobody'll hold anything that happened when you were eighteen against you. It's not like you robbed a store or something."

"*I* blame me, even if nobody else does," she said. "If Dan hadn't kept coming around, he wouldn't have got suspicious of us. I'd bet my last benjamin that that's what made them come looking for Luke the second night."

"You don't know for sure. You can't know for sure," her father said. "Besides, what you're really blaming yourself for is being a pretty girl. There's nothing wrong with that. Believe me, there isn't."

There is when it causes trouble. And it does, Liz thought. But that didn't want to come out. Instead, she said, "I should have told him to get lost when he started visiting all the time."

"You would have been out of character if you did," Dad said.

"I didn't think he'd turn out to be such a pest," she said, as if her father hadn't spoken. "After all—"

"He's just a barbarian from an alternate where everybody's a barbarian," Dad finished for her. She wouldn't have put it quite the same way, which didn't mean she thought he was wrong. He went on, "And yeah, he *is* a barbarian. He's ignorant. He has fleas and lice and bad breath. And he doesn't smell good. But none of that makes him dumb. He can see when things are peculiar."

"He sure can!" Liz interrupted in turn. "I kept making little mistakes, and he kept pouncing on them."

"Making little mistakes and getting pounced on because of them is the biggest problem we have going out to the alternates," her father said. "Almost everybody does it. It's like going to a foreign country. You can speak perfect French, but you'll still have a devil of a time making a real Parisian believe you grew up on the Left Bank."

Speaking perfect French, or almost any other language, was easy. Like everybody else, Liz had a computer implant behind her left ear. It interfaced with the speech center in her brain, so software could feed her the words and the grammar and the logic behind a language. She wished learning history and math and literature were that simple. Maybe one day they would be. Software engineers improved implants all the time.

But that was a distraction now. She said, "*Can* we get back to that alternate without giving ourselves away? A lot of people know who we are."

"Tell me about it!" her father said unhappily. "I wish we had another outlet for a transposition chamber closer than Speedro." He muttered to himself. "Maybe I should count my blessings. A lot of alternates, there's only one for the whole world."

"We can't be traders again, not if we go back up into Westwood. What would we be instead?" Liz liked acting. She was pretty good at it. She had to remind herself her life would depend on her performance here.

"Maybe just people looking for work," Dad said. "There are always people scrounging in that alternate, because there isn't enough to go around."

Liz wasn't so sure she liked that. People looking for work

would go hungry a lot of the time. People pretending to look for work would go hungry, too. And . . . "How do I get back to the UCLA library for more research? The people there know me, too."

"Well, they're Westsiders. They wouldn't give you away to the Valley soldiers." But her father checked himself and did some more muttering. "Only they might. It just takes one to sell you out, and we've never yet found an alternate where some people won't do things like that."

"People who didn't wouldn't be human," Liz said.

"No, I guess not," Dad agreed. "We haven't gone to any alternates where the people aren't human beings. There are bound to be some, but the transposition chambers haven't traveled that far yet. Probably just as well."

"What do you mean?"

"If we make little mistakes in the alternates where people are just like us, how would we pretend to fit in where they're really, really different?"

"Oh." Liz chewed on that. "I don't know. But I bet we could be back up to the Westside in disguise. I always wanted to see how I'd look in a blond wig."

"You'd look silly, that's how."

He wasn't wrong, not when Liz was slim and dark like most people in the home timeline's Los Angeles. The Westside and the Valley in the bomb-ravaged alternate had many more fair-skinned people. Lots of waves of immigration hadn't happened there. But even if Dad was right—maybe especially because he was right—Liz gave him a dirty look. "You're mean!" she said.

"Why? Because I told you the truth?"

"Sometimes telling the truth is the meanest thing you can do."

That brought Dad up short. He thought it over, then nodded. "Well, you've got something there. But I don't think I'm guilty this time around. Honest, I don't. I'd look silly in a blond wig, too."

Liz eyed his close-cropped black hair. He was starting to get some gray at the temples. When did that happen? *Some time when I wasn't looking,* Liz thought. What did her parents think they were doing by getting older behind her back? That was pretty sneaky. She nodded to herself. They should cut it out.

"Blond wigs or no blond wigs, do you think we can get back up to the Westside without giving ourselves away?" she asked.

"Sure," Dad said. "What could go wrong?"

"They could recognize us and shoot us for spies?" Liz suggested. "They could torture us before they shoot us for spies?"

"How many bad adventure videos have you downloaded lately?" he asked. "That kind of thing doesn't happen if you're careful."

"If we were careful enough, they never would have got suspicious of us in the first place," Liz said.

"Well, do you want to stay behind when your mother and I go back?" Dad asked. "You can do that. It won't look bad on your record or anything. You can just start college a quarter earlier than you would have."

"No!" Liz didn't even need to think about that. "I don't want you sticking your necks out if I'm not there. And I do want to go back and find out what *was* going on in that alternate in 1967." She paused, looking inside herself. "And I want to find out how things turn out there now, too."

Her father gave her a sly smile. "And you want to find out how Dan's doing, too, right?"

She sniffed. *I won't let him get my goat,* she told herself. *I just won't.* "Dan can do whatever he does, as long as he does it a long way from me," she said. "If he sees me after we go back, that's trouble."

"Mm, so it is," Dad agreed. He nodded, as if making up his mind. "Okay. We'll see what we can set up."

"Cool!" Liz grinned. "Speedro, here we come!"

The strap on Dan's binoculars was new. The binoculars themselves dated back to the Old Time. TASCO, they said, whatever a TASCO was, and *Made in Japan.* He knew where Japan was: he'd been to school, after all. It was on the far side of the Pacific, thousands and thousands of miles away. Once in a blue moon, a sailing ship from Japan would come in to Speedro. But those were fishing boats, blown off course in storms. He tried to imagine a steamboat—there still were some steamboats, for coastal trade—or a big sailing ship crossing the ocean full of binoculars.

And what would America have sent back to Japan in that steamboat, or in another one? Guns, maybe? Or automobiles? He knew he was just guessing.

He raised the binoculars to his eyes and peered south from the Santa Monica Freeway. Everything there leaped closer. Binoculars weren't magic, any more than Old Time guns were. Still, even though he'd been to school, he didn't understand how they worked. He did understand *that* they worked, which was all that really counted.

He scanned back and forth, looking for any signs that the Westsiders were getting frisky. He spotted one fellow who was plainly a soldier. The man was standing on the roof of a tall building maybe half a mile south of the freeway. He was looking north . . . through binoculars.

Do his say TASCO, *too?* Dan wondered, and then, *Is he looking straight at me?* He raised his left arm and waved. After a moment, the guy on the rooftop waved back. Why not? They might be enemies, but they both had the same job. And nobody was shooting at anybody right this minute.

A gong stood only a few feet from Dan. If he did see anything that looked like trouble, he was supposed to clang on it for all he was worth. That would send Valley soldiers running to help him . . . if nobody'd shot him before they got here.

In the meantime, he waved to the other soldier again and fought against a yawn. This wasn't a very interesting duty. Necessary, maybe, but dull. But he could still think about all the mysteries at Liz's house. He understood those even less than he understood how binoculars worked which only made him more eager to try to figure them out.

Electric lights! Nobody in the world had electric lights, as far as Dan knew. But Liz's house did. And they came on when you went down onto that floor and moved around. When you walked back up the stairs, they went out. How did they know? Was somebody watching, to make them go on and off? Dan didn't see how that was possible. He couldn't imagine any other way it would work, either.

Does that make me dumb? he wondered. If it did, everybody else in the Valley was as dumb as he was. Sergeant Max and Sergeant Mike were floored, and weren't too shy to admit it. The captain—Dan had finally found out his name was Horace—was baffled, too.

Captain Horace had gone looking for scholars at UCLA.

He'd brought back one fellow who claimed he understood electricity. The scholar wore a dirty white coat and a frayed necktie from Old Time. He looked like a bright man. He talked like a bright man.

And when he saw those ceiling lights come on? Dan had been down there with him, and watched him stare the way everybody else did. "Impossible," he said.

"You're looking at it. It must be possible," Captain Horace said. That sure made sense to Dan.

Not to the guy from UCLA. "Impossible," he said again. "No battery could hold its charge from the time when the Fire fell till now."

"Maybe these are new batteries," Dan had suggested. Captain Horace beamed at him.

By the way the scholar looked at him, he was an idiot who'd never wise up enough to become a moron. "I know what batteries can do. I know what kind of batteries we can make nowadays," the man said, fiddling with the knot on his tie. "I'm familiar with the research not just here, but in Frisco and Vegas and as far away as Salt Lake City. Nobody can do anything like this. Nobody."

"How long does it take for research news to get from Salt Lake City to here?" Captain Horace asked.

"Less time than you'd think," the scholar said. "The telegraph between Salt Lake and Vegas works most of the time. Of course, you only get an outline on the telegraph. The real journal articles arrive after a couple of years. But people couldn't keep anything like this a secret. And why would they want to?"

Captain Horace had no answer for that. Neither did Dan. The officer did have a question of his own: "If this stuff is impossible, what's it doing here? Kindly tell me that."

The scholar couldn't. He just stared up at the glowing ceiling some more. "As far as I can see, it's a miracle," he said.

A lot of people believed God was angry at the world, and stopped working miracles after the Fire fell. Didn't that explain why things were so messed up nowadays? But some people said it was a miracle *anybody* lived through the Russian-American war. Dan didn't know what to believe.

He did know thinking about that stuff was a lot more interesting than sweeping the southern horizon with his binoculars. He wondered what was going on at Liz's house right this minute. He didn't want to be on duty here in the sun. He would rather have gone back to the basement under the basement and stared at the electric lights.

Fluorescents. They were called fluorescents. So the scholar said, anyhow. It was an awfully fancy name. He tried to explain how they were different from ordinary light bulbs, but Dan didn't get it. He wondered if the scholar made up the word to sound smart. Captain Horace didn't seem to think so, though.

Right now, they were fluorescing or doing whatever fluorescents did. *And I'm not there to see them,* Dan thought angrily. *I have to stay out here to try to make sure Cal's soldiers don't sneak up and murder us.* It hardly seemed fair.

You couldn't tell you were going anywhere when you rode in a transposition chamber. And, in a very real sense, you weren't going anywhere. You got out in exactly the same place as the one you'd left. The same place, yes, but not the same alternate.

Details, details, Liz thought. Traveling between alternates was as boring as flying coach. More boring, really. You didn't have a video screen inside a transposition chamber, and you couldn't look out the window. Transposition chambers had no windows. And if they did, all you'd see out of them was Nothing, with a capital N. She sighed. She just had to sit in her seat and sog, like breakfast cereal soaking up milk.

Going between the home timeline and the nuked alternate didn't seem to take any longer than coming back had. In reality, neither took any time at all. But the body perceived something that felt like time while the chamber shuttled between worlds. Duration, the chronophysicists called it.

A few lights on the control panel at the front of the chamber went from amber or red to green. "We're here," the operator announced.

Liz and her mother and father stepped out of the transposition chamber. The bare, concrete-walled chamber in which they stood was a lot like the one from which they'd departed. But it wasn't the same chamber. And, even if they were in the same place, they were also in a new place. They'd left San Pedro, the harbor district of Los Angeles, in California, in the United States. Now they'd come to the independent Kingdom of Speedro.

Behind them, the transposition chamber disappeared. Chambers never hung around long once they'd delivered their passengers. They always had something else to do, some other alternate to go to.

"Hello, there," someone called from up above, where the trap door opened. "We knew you were coming, so we baked a cake!"

The Stoyadinoviches, who ran Crosstime Traffic's Speedro

trading center, turned out to be very nice people. A lot of the sailors and fishermen in Speedro were descended from Serbs, so the Stoyadinoviches fit right in. And, just as George said, his wife—her name was Irma—really had baked a cake. It was sweetened with honey and raisins, because sugar was rare and expensive here. That didn't mean it wasn't good.

George Stoyadinovich had an amazing mustache. Asterix and Obelix and even Vitalstatistix would have envied it. The ends hung down onto his chest. He also had a good grasp of what was going on in Speedro. "Yeah, they're all hot to help the Westside," he said. "If Cal gets Westwood back, Speedro will take some of the South Bay as payment for giving him a hand."

"And if Cal doesn't get Westwood back, Speedro will grab some of the South Bay anyhow," Irma Stoyadinovich added. "In that case, the Westside won't be strong enough to do anything about it."

"Can we get over the border between Speedro and the Westside?" Dad asked.

"Sure." Mr. Stoyadinovich nodded, which made his soup-strainer waft up and down. "Long as you're carrying something the Westside army can use—bullets, boots, whatever—they'll give you a big hug and a kiss."

"What's going on up at the Santa Monica Freeway line?" Liz asked.

Both Stoyadinoviches frowned. "Well, that's a long way off," Mrs. Stoyadinovich said. It wasn't more than forty-five minutes by car, unless the traffic was bad. But that was in the home timeline. Here, it was a couple of days away, at least.

"Yeah, we aren't so sure about the news we get from up there," George Stoyadinovich agreed. "Most of the time, it's gone through six or eight people by the time it gets to us. Who knows how weird it gets while it's doing that? It's like playing telephone at a party, you know?"

Liz nodded. By the time a phrase got whispered from a dozen mouths into a dozen ears and came back to the person who started it, it sounded nothing like what that person said at first.

"There isn't much shooting right now—we're pretty sure of that," Mr. Stoyadinovich went on. "You guys are going to try to sneak back up into Westwood, right?"

"Gotta do it," Dad answered. "We got the grant to see why things went kablooie here, and the YRL's the best place to look."

"The URL," Mom reminded him. "It's the URL here."

Dad made a face. He hated making mistakes—Liz took after him there. Mom was more easygoing about it. But if he said that around locals, they'd wonder where the devil he came from. And it was such an easy slip to make. Liz shook her head. No wonder Dan got so curious—or suspicious—about her. Did she betray herself every time she opened her mouth? She could hope not, anyway.

That mustache made Mr. Stoyadinovich's frown a fearsome thing. "Well, you know what you're doing, I guess. But if they chased you out of there once, I sure wouldn't want to go back so soon."

"If the grant runs out . . ." Dad didn't go on, or need to.

Mr. and Mrs. Stoyadinovich both nodded. "Yeah, I know that song," he said. "But watch yourselves just the same."

"You've got a wagon and a team for us, don't you?" Mom said.

"Sure do," the Stoyadinoviches said in chorus. George went

on, "You'll dig it. Body's made from an Old Time station wagon, so it'll hold a lot, and you'll look rich. And the horses are as gentle as you please."

To Liz, that mattered more than the rest. Till she came here, horses were animals that ran races or lived on farms. She'd never dreamt how important they could be in alternates where machines didn't work. Oh, she'd *known*, but she hadn't seen with her own eyes. That made all the difference in the world.

Now how will I get back into the URL? she wondered. Somebody from her family would have to figure out a way. Well, they still had some time to think about it. They wouldn't get up to the Westside right away. In an alternate like this, nothing happened in a hurry.

Ten

Dan pulled the trigger on his matchlock. The serpentine swept down. The glowing end of the match set off the priming powder around the touch-hole. The charge inside the barrel of the gun exploded. The matchlock bucked against Dan's shoulder.

Sergeant Chuck went down the range to examine the target.

"How'd I do?" Dan called after him.

"Well, you hit it." Chuck didn't sound as happy as he should have. Like a lot of sergeants, he was allergic to sounding happy, no matter what. And he had another bone to pick with Dan: "I don't see *how* you hit it. You aren't getting enough practice, and you know you aren't."

"I can't help it, Sergeant," Dan said. "They want me to help them find out stuff about the traders' house." He didn't mention Liz's name. That would only have set Chuck off again.

Chuck turned out to need zero help from him. "So they found electric lights there. Big deal!" he said. "All I've got to tell you is, they may have found electric lights, but they're ruining somebody who was a pretty good soldier."

That might have been the first time he'd ever said he thought Dan made a pretty good soldier. It was just like him to say it so it suggested Dan had been but wasn't any more. "If I'm all ruined and everything, Sergeant, how did I hit the target?" Dan asked.

"Luck," Chuck answered at once. "Nothing but dumb luck."

"I bet I do it again." Dan knew he was taking a chance. The matchlock wasn't a very accurate weapon. Even a good shot could go astray. If his did, Chuck would make him pay for it. Oh, would he ever!

But the sergeant shook his head. "Nah, don't bother. Even if you hit, it doesn't really prove anything. Besides, you're getting soft because you're not exercising enough. You can't tell me you are, either."

Since Dan couldn't, he tried to change the subject: "I'm just doing what the officers tell me to do, Sergeant."

"Yeah, like officers know anything," Chuck said scornfully. "Are they gonna figure out electric lights? Get serious! Are you gonna help 'em figure those lights out? What do you know about electricity?"

"Nothing, Sergeant." Dan gave the only honest answer he could.

"Well, then!" Triumph filled Chuck's voice.

"But neither does anybody else," Dan said.

"And *you're* gonna be the one who finds out? Ha! Don't make me laugh."

Even though Dan didn't think that was real likely, either, he didn't like the sergeant teasing him about it. And he had a good way to get Chuck off his back: "I do need to go back. They want me there."

"The more fools them," Chuck said. But he couldn't tell Dan not to go, not when Dan had orders. He did tell Dan to clean his musket first. Dan did. He took keeping the musket clean very seriously.

Then he hurried off to the traders' house on Glendon. Even if Liz hadn't lived there, he would have been glad to go. Every time the electric lights came on (and how? by magic?), he felt as if he were back in the Old Time. If he only had some gasoline, he might have gone looking for an automobile, to see if he could make it start.

Captain Horace had put sentries at the front door. He didn't want anybody who wasn't supposed to be there getting in and gawking at the lights. The sentries knew who Dan was. He had no trouble getting past them.

Sergeant Max and his bloodhounds were in the courtyard. By now, the bloodhounds knew who Dan was, too. They came over and sniffed his boots. He patted their heads and scratched them behind the ears. They looked as happy as you could if your face was made for saying your grandmother had just died.

"Do you expect them to find anything here after all this time?" Dan asked Max.

The sergeant shook his head. "Nah, not really. But I can give 'em a rest from running around, so that's cool, you know? They're good dogs. They won't get into any trouble."

"Okay," Dan said. If you argued with a sergeant, you lost unless you were an officer. Sometimes you lost even if you were an officer. A lot of young lieutenants let their sergeants run their platoons. More often than not, that was smart, too, because sergeants usually had a better notion of what was going on.

Dan went downstairs. He wanted to look at the electric lights again. Even if he didn't understand them, he liked being around them. They told him something about how marvelous Old Time really was. To have lights like those whenever you wanted them . . . How cool was that?

Captain Horace was down there, too, with a gray-haired man whose hair stuck out in tufts that went every which way. Dan recognized him straight off. Dr. Saul was the closest thing to a scientist the Valley had. Up till now, Dan had thought he was the smartest man in the world.

Maybe he was . . . these days. But now Dan couldn't help wondering how he stacked up against a real Old Time scientist. Was he still smart, or nothing but a bumbling fool? Then again, no matter how clever the Old Time scientists were, they went and blew up the world. How smart did that make them, really?

Right now, Dr. Saul was pitching a fit. "Those lights have got to have a power source somewhere!" he shouted at Captain Horace.

"Where?" the officer asked—reasonably, Dan thought. "What does it look like?"

"*I* don't know!" Yes, Dr. Saul sounded plenty peeved. "If I knew things like that, I'd be able to do them myself. Where do the wires from the fluorescent tubes go?"

"Beats me." Captain Horace sounded cheerful admitting how ignorant he was. "Far as I know, nobody's looked. There are wires up there, you say?"

Dan thought Dr. Saul would blow a gasket. He wasn't quite sure what a gasket was, but the scientist sure looked ready to blow something. He tore at his hair. Dan had never seen anybody do that before, though people talked about tearing their hair all the time. No wonder Dr. Saul's looked as if he'd never heard of a comb. Maybe he was lucky to have any hair at all.

"Nobody's looked?" he roared, loud enough to raise echoes in the basement under the basement. "Are you people blind, or just really, really stupid? *Why* haven't you looked?" He suddenly rounded on Dan. "Why haven't *you* looked?" he demanded, as if it were all Dan's fault.

"Sir, I don't know anything about electricity. I don't know anything about wires," Dan answered. "I'm still learning how to take care of a matchlock."

"Well, do you suppose you can learn to get me a ladder?" Dr. Saul said. "*Somebody's* got to do the work around here." By the way he said it, he meant he had to do everything himself. But he didn't have to find a ladder and then lug it down two flights of stairs. That was work for the likes of Dan.

Once the ladder was in place, Dr. Saul climbed it as nimbly as a monkey. That was one more thing people said without thinking about. How nimble *were* monkeys? Dan had never seen one. He didn't know anybody who had, either.

The scientist got a cover off so he could look right at the fluorescent tube under it. He cautiously reached out and touched the tube. "Isn't it hot?" Dan asked.

"No. I didn't think it would be." But Dr. Saul sounded relieved enough to show he hadn't been sure. He gave the tube a twist, and it came away from something set into the ceiling. It also stopped glowing, which made the underground room noticeably gloomier.

"Did you kill it?" Captain Horace asked.

"No, no, no." Dr. Saul shook his head. His hair went on moving after his head stopped. "I want a look at the socket." Cautiously, he tugged at the socket. "It's set into the concrete, confound it. The wire must go through there."

"Are you sure there's a wire?" the officer said.

"Of course I am. Of course there is," Dr. Saul said. "This isn't magic, you know. But we'd have to chip away that concrete to get at the wire and trace it back to the power source." He muttered to himself. "We'd probably break something."

If "we" suddenly started chipping concrete, who would do the real work? It wouldn't be Dr. Saul. He thought about things—he didn't actually do them. It wouldn't be Captain Horace or any sergeant. No, it would be somebody a lot like Dan, somebody who wasn't good for anything else. They'd look at it like that, anyhow.

Dan slid up the stairs and out the trap door while Dr. Saul was still talking. Nobody noticed him go. Who paid attention to common soldiers? When you needed one, you went and grabbed him. Otherwise, forget it.

By the time they might have thought about needing Dan, he was already back on the Santa Monica Freeway line with the rest of his company. He could hope they would grab somebody closer to chip concrete.

They likely did. They didn't come grab him, anyhow. That suited him fine.

Liz had seen several wagons like the one the Stoyadinoviches gave the Mendozas. It was made from an old Chevrolet, a brand still alive in the home timeline. The engine and the fenders and the roof were gone. Losing the engine saved a lot of weight. Losing the fenders saved weight, too, and let the wainwright install big wooden wheels with iron rims to replace metal wheels and rubber tires that had rotted away. And in place of the roof were iron hoops and a cloth cover that reached up much higher and let the auto body hold more.

When Liz looked at the team hitched to that contraption, she cracked up. "What's so funny?" George Stoyadinovich asked. "They're good horses—you won't find better ones this side of Santa Anita."

"I'm sure they are," she said. "But . . . It's a car, right? And what's a car? A horseless carriage, right? And so this is a horseless carriage—with horses! How crazy is that?"

Mr. Stoyadinovich thought about that for a few seconds. Then he started to laugh, too. "I never looked at it that way before." He turned to Dad. "Keep an eye on her. She's dangerous."

"Really? I never would have noticed," Dad said, deadpan. Mr. Stoyadinovich laughed harder than ever. Liz stuck her nose in the air and sniffed. That only made Mrs. Stoyadinovich and Mom bust up. Liz glared at her mother, who ignored her. Sometimes you couldn't win.

"You've got a pretty good cargo there, too," Mr. Stoyadinovich said. "People go out and party when they find Old Time Levi's in good shape. And they should, because it doesn't happen very often any more. And the ones you're taking north, they're just like new." He winked.

Liz knew what the wink meant. The jeans in the wagon weren't just like new, from some unearthed clothing store. They *were* new, from the home timeline. The locals wouldn't know the difference. These were special trade Levi's, made in a style that wouldn't have been out of place in the 1960s.

The Chevy wagon's doors and front seat were still intact. The windshield could have survived, but the driver needed to be able to use the reins when he sat behind the steering wheel.

"Is that a cool set of wheels or what?" George Stoyadinovich said, winking again.

By the standards of this alternate, the wagon was without a doubt a cool set of wheels. By the standards of the home timeline . . . "I think it's what," Liz said.

For a moment, George didn't get it. Then he did, and laughed twice as hard to show he did. "You *are* a troublemaker," he said. He aimed his right forefinger at Liz and brought his thumb down. "Bang!"

She mimed being shot, and staggered all over the place. "Too much ham in your sandwich," Dad told her.

"Let's go." Mom was the relentlessly practical one in the family. "The sooner we get started, the sooner we make it up to the Westside again."

Dad sat behind the wheel. Springs creaked when Liz got in beside him. The old upholstery had long since rotted away. The new upholstery was leather, which made Liz a little queasy. People in the home timeline didn't think leather was quite so bad as fur, but they used imitations almost all the time. There were no imitations here. All the Old Time Naugahyde was long gone, and Naugas seemed to be extinct in this alternate. So the locals used the real stuff, and didn't lose any sleep about it. This couldn't have been any more real—it smelled powerfully of cow.

"Giddyap!" Dad flicked the reins. He had a whip, too, in case the horses didn't feel like moving. But they leaned into the traces and started to pull. Slowly at first, then at a more respectable speed, the wagon headed toward the Harbor Freeway. It had its southern end in Speedro.

In the home timeline, people called the Harbor Freeway

the 110 as often as not. It was part of the U.S. Interstate Highway system. Here, it hadn't joined that system when the Fire fell. A sign left over from the Old Time told the world it was State Highway 11.

They had to pay a twenty-five-cent toll to get on what was still known as a freeway even if it wasn't free. Dad passed the silver coin to the toll collector without a murmur. Old as it was, beat-up as it was, the Harbor or 110 or 11 or whatever you called it was far and away the best route north.

Not far from where the Harbor Freeway joined the 405—also called the San Diego Freeway—a hot-air balloon floated five hundred meters in the air, tethered to the ground by a rope. Speedro kept it up there to watch for trouble from a long way off. Seeing it made tears sting Liz's eyes. In the home timeline, a Goodyear blimp took off and landed right about there. She wondered if the balloon's gas-tight skin had once been part of a blimp.

The San Diego Freeway swung northwest. The Harbor Freeway went straight north. In the home timeline, it went straight north to downtown Los Angeles. In this alternate, it went straight north to . . . nothing. Several big bombs had taken out downtown here. The stump of City Hall still stood. It looked like a candle that had burned most of the way down and then slumped over.

In the home timeline, Los Angeles County had more people than forty-two or forty-three states. Liz couldn't remember which. Even with cars burning clean hydrogen, that Los Angeles still had smog. And so did this one, even with far less than a tenth as many people. The way the mountains and the breezes worked, air pollution always got trapped here. When the Spaniards first saw

Santa Monica Bay, they called it the Bay of Smokes. So tears of sorrow weren't the only things bothering Liz's eyes.

The horses plodded up the 405. When you lived in a world without cars, without phones, without TV and the Net, nothing happened in a hurry. Dad tried to use the steering wheel to keep the Chevy wagon's wheels from going into potholes. Sometimes he could, and sometimes he couldn't. When they did hit a bump, Liz's teeth came together with a click. The springs were as old as the rest of the chassis.

Other wagons used the freeway. So did people on horseback, people on foot, people on bone-shaking bicycles, and one guy on a skateboard of sorts. He'd found Old Time roller skates and nailed them to the ends of a board. When he pushed himself along, he could go faster than he would have walking.

Dad eyed his style. "He's not ready for the X Games—that's for sure."

"They have the sense to wear helmets when they do those stunts," Mom said. "Knee pads and elbow pads, too. If he falls down, it's just him and the asphalt. I bet the asphalt wins."

"People aren't nearly as safe here as they are in the home timeline," Liz said. "They worry about it a lot less, though. It's funny."

"It's crazy," her mother said.

"But it's true," Liz insisted.

"People here figure something's going to get them. And it usually does," Dad said. "In the home timeline, they think they ought to stay safe, so they try more. And you know what? Sooner or later, something gets them anyway."

"That's true. But it usually takes longer than it would here," Mom said, and Dad couldn't very well disagree.

They pulled off the freeway at the Rosecrans ramp, which was still in decent shape. A large sign directed them to GORDON'S GOOD EATS. Liz knew that offramp in the home timeline, because her family used it to visit cousins. A Denny's sat at that corner there. She stared at Gordon's. "Oh my God!" she said. "It's the same building!"

"It sure is," Mom agreed.

"Prices will be better here," Dad said, which was bound to be true. He added, "I wouldn't be surprised if the food is, too."

You couldn't get a hamburger with avocado and vine-ripened tomatoes at a Denny's. On the other hand, you couldn't get an ice-cream sundae or even a Coke at Gordon's Good Eats, though the orange juice was better than Denny's. When it came to restrooms, Denny's won hands down. As she usually did in this alternate, Liz came out of this one wrinkling her nose.

There was a guarded campground next to Gordon's. Camping behind barbed wire cost another quarter. To stay in character, Dad grumbled when he paid it. Afterwards, he winked at Liz. There hadn't been quarters in the home timeline for years and years. There, a quarter wasn't enough to worry about. Neither was a dollar, even if they still had dollar coins.

Dad asked people coming south what things were like on the Westside. "There's gonna be a rumble, man," one traveler said. "Hasn't happened yet, but there's gonna be." Another man nodded.

"Can we get through?" Dad didn't say anything about stopping. You never could tell who was a spy, or for whom.

The traveler coming down from the north shrugged. "You can try, like. I wouldn't give you no money-back guarantee."

Some of the phrases of Old Time advertising had stuck in the language here.

The back of the seat reclined in the Chevy. It went back farther than an airplane seat would. You could sleep on it . . . after a fashion. Liz and her parents lay side by side. One of them wiggling was liable to wake somebody else. Liz had passed plenty of nights she enjoyed more.

By what had to be a miracle, Gordon's Good Eats had coffee the next morning. Liz didn't usually like it, but she thought of it as medicine now. Her folks poured down cup after cup. It wasn't cheap, not by this alternate's standards, but Dad didn't say boo.

They got back on the 405—they didn't have to pay a toll this time—and started north again. With luck, they would get up to Westwood as the sun was setting. Liz thought that was good for all kinds of reasons. If it was dark, the Valley soldiers would have a harder time recognizing them.

Then Dad passed Mom the reins. He ducked into the back of the wagon. When he returned, his beard was gone. He didn't look like the same person any more. After he took back the reins, Mom did up her hair instead of letting it fall down over her shoulders. She put on a pair of glasses to replace her contacts. She looked different, too, even if not so much as Dad did.

"Your turn, Liz," she said when she got through.

Liz put her hair up, too. Mom showed her how she looked in a mirror from an Old Time compact. She did seem different, but different enough? Maybe for somebody who'd met her only a couple of times.

"If Dan sees me, he'll know who I am," she said gloomily.

"Well, what are the odds?" Dad said. "There's only one of him, after all, and we won't be going right back to where we were."

"Besides, they're probably still trying to figure out how we disappeared," Mom said. "They can't think we'd come back again."

"I sure hope not," Liz said.

Curiosity drew Dan back to the house that had been Liz's. He knew what they said about cats. He knew he ran the risk of hard, unpleasant work. He went anyway. He was a soldier, but he wasn't an *old* soldier.

Sure enough, somebody—a luckless common soldier not named Dan—had chipped away a lot of concrete from the roof of the basement under the basement. Some other soldier—or maybe the same one—had swept up most of it. Most, but not all. Little chunks still gritted under the soles of Dan's boots.

Dr. Saul was up on a ladder again. He was poking around up there with a stick. He'd said something about electricity not biting wood. Dan didn't follow all of that, but Dr. Saul knew his own business best.

Or maybe nobody knew anything. "This can't be the power pack that keep these lights going," Dr. Saul insisted. "It *can't* be, I tell you! It's too small—way, way too small."

"Well, if it's not, what is?" Captain Horace asked.

"*I* don't know!" Dr. Saul yelled, and then he said something Dan wouldn't have expected to hear from a distinguished scientist.

Captain Horace was about to say something just as lovely

when somebody yelled from up above: "They're clanging the alarm!"

What Horace said then made Dr. Saul's remark seem like sweet talk by comparison. What *Dan* said made both the officer and the scientist gape at him. He never knew it, though. He was clattering up the stairs, and paid no attention to whatever went on behind him.

He dashed up the stairs from the basement to ground level, too. By then he noticed Captain Horace wasn't real far behind him. But the captain couldn't catch him. Dan ran out of the house, down Glendon to Wilshire, down Wilshire to Westwood Boulevard, and down Westwood Boulevard to the freeway line.

The shooting had already started by the time he got there. Westsiders to the south were banging away at Valley soldiers up on the freeway. "Take your place!" Sergeant Chuck yelled when he saw Dan.

Dan did. He started loading his matchlock. He could see plumes of smoke that showed where enemy musketeers were firing. He worried more about what he couldn't see. Riflemen with Old Time weapons could shoot at him from ranges at which he couldn't hope to reply. They used smokeless powder, too. Unless he saw a muzzle flash, he wouldn't even know where they were shooting from. And if they hit him . . . No, he didn't want to think about that.

Then he heard a bigger explosion and saw a bigger flash from a distant window. "Good!" Chuck yelled. "Dog my cats if that wasn't an Old Time rifle blowing up!" Ammunition two long lifetimes old could get touchy—could and did. Yes, riflemen needed several different kinds of courage.

A more familiar boom made Horace duck. A cannonball

flew over his head and landed with a crash somewhere north of the freeway. Westside artillerymen—or would they be from Speedro?—started reloading their piece.

"Where are *our* rifles?" Chuck yelled. An Old Time rifle could shoot as far as one of those cannon. A matchlock couldn't come close. Dan didn't waste ammunition trying. The Valley's fearsome .50-caliber machine gun could make hash of the enemy gun crew in nothing flat. Where was it? Nowhere close enough to use, anyway.

Valley riflemen did start shooting then. Every round they fired meant scrounging for more. What would happen when it all finally ran out or grew too unstable to use? The matchlock musketeer would reign supreme, that was what.

In spite of the riflemen, the cannon boomed again. This time, the roundshot thudded into one of the freeway supports. It felt like an earthquake to Dan. The supports had to be strong. They'd stood up through real earthquakes. But Dan was pretty sure they weren't meant to stand up to cannon fire. What would happen if one fell down?

Then a stretch of freeway falls down, too, dummy. Then you *fall down.*

He wanted to do what any soldier in a spot like that would want to do. He wanted to run away. But he couldn't. His superiors would hang him for being a coward—unless they decided to do something even more interesting and painful. That wasn't his biggest worry, though. Letting his buddies down was.

So he stayed where he was posted. Under cover of the rifle and cannon fire, enemy soldiers ran toward the freeway line. He fired at one of them. The fellow went down. Maybe Dan's bullet hit him. Maybe someone else's did. Dan never knew for sure, and didn't much care. All he knew was that he had to reload as fast as he could. And he did.

The Chevy wagon had come a long way up the 405 when the gunfire to the north started up. "Oh, dear!" Liz's mother said.

"Oh, no!" Liz said.

What Liz's father said meant about the same thing as *Oh, dear!* and *Oh, no!* Still, it was a good thing the wagon that had been a car carried no more gasoline. What Dad said would have made the stuff explode.

Then he said something a little calmer but no less disgusted: "Timing is everything, isn't it?"

"How are we supposed to get through that?" Mom asked.

"Carefully?" Dad suggested. Mom and Liz both gave him the same kind of look, the look you gave somebody being difficult on purpose. He sounded hurt as he went on, "Well, I don't see how else we can make it through that unless we feel like getting filled full of holes. Which isn't what I had in mind."

"Let me put it another way," Liz said. When Dad was being difficult, sometimes the best thing to do was be difficult right back. "How do we go *around* that? Or how do we get to Westwood without getting shot?" Those were two other ways, as a matter of fact. And the second one let Dad keep on being difficult if he felt like it.

Mom's warning cough worked as well as a lion's warning growl would have. "Did I say anything?" Dad asked plaintively.

"Not yet," Mom said. "I suggest you don't, unless it helps."

"Okay. The only way to get to Westwood by going around the fighting is probably by going through one of the dead zones."

Liz wasn't sure that helped, even if she was pretty sure her father was right. Dead zones were the places where bombs had landed. They were the reason the Harbor Freeway didn't make it up to downtown Los Angeles in this alternate. They were the reason the Santa Monica Freeway didn't make it all the way into Santa Monica. They weren't radioactive any more, not after 130 years. But they were still so battered that hardly anybody lived in them.

"Can we get the wagon through?" Mom asked.

"Won't we stand out like bugs on a plate?" Liz said at the same time.

"I don't know," Dad told Mom. To Liz, he said, "No, we won't stand out that bad. Things are flat in the dead zones, but not *flat* flat, if you know what I mean. That's not what worries me about the whole thing."

"And what worries you about the whole thing is . . . ?" Mom prompted.

"Whether the Westside and Speedro will try to sneak soldiers through the dead zone and get into Westwood that way," Dad said. "Does the Valley have troops looking west? If they don't, the other side will turn their flank just like that." He snapped his fingers.

A split second later, so did Liz. "I bet that's what Luke was trying to find out!"

"I bet you're right," her father said. "One thing we can be pretty sure of, though—if he did find out, he didn't pass it on to the people farther south. Of course, we don't know if he was the only spy they had. If they were smart, he wouldn't have been."

"I don't like the idea of maybe needing to leave the wagon

behind," Mom said. "How can we be traders if we don't have trade goods? And *does* the Valley have soldiers posted at the edge of the Santa Monica dead zone?"

"Good question," Dad said. "If there are no other questions, class is dismissed."

"You say that when you mean you don't know," Liz said.

"I never worried about it. Did you?" Dad said. Liz had to shake her head. He added, "Besides, they could have sent them out after we, uh, disappeared from this alternate. What it all boils down to is—"

"Which stupid chance do we want to take?" Mom finished for him.

He nodded. "Couldn't have put it better myself."

The Santa Monica Freeway line held through the first day of fighting. Valley riflemen and musketeers kept Westside and Speedro soldiers from breaking through for a couple of hours. Then the heavy machine gun arrived. It fired off a burst—*pock! pock! pock! pock!* Those big, heavy booms couldn't be mistaken for anything else. Neither could the way the big, heavy bullets chewed through wood and bricks—and flesh—out to a mile and beyond. As soon as the machine gun opened up, the enemy lost his enthusiasm for advancing.

"Ha!" Sergeant Chuck yelled. "Thought we forgot about it, did you? Well, let's see how you like it!"

The Westsiders didn't like it a bit. One of their cannon thundered. The ball flew over the machine-gun crew's heads. You couldn't hide a cannon, not with all the smoke it spat. The machine gunners started banging away at it as soon as it fired.

If Dan had served the cannon, he would have run for cover as soon as it fired. But what did you do then? You couldn't shoot once and vanish, not if you wanted to win. And so the cannoneers had to come out again and try to reload their piece. One of the men in the machine-gun crew had binoculars much like the Tascos Dan used on sentry duty. As soon as he saw the artillerymen stirring, he let out a yell. The machine gun fired several more bursts.

Another cannon fired, and another. One cannonball cut a Valley soldier in half about six feet from the machine gun. Dan tried not to look at that, but it had a sick fascination to it. The poor man's top half didn't die fast enough to suit Dan—or, probably, the fellow himself.

But the near miss was also just one of those things to the machine-gun crew. They went on shooting as if nothing had happened. Before Dan went into battle himself, he wouldn't have understood that. He did now. If the machine gunners had the shakes, they didn't have time to indulge them. Doing your job, doing what you could for your friends, came first.

That was also true for the Westsiders and the soldiers from Speedro who seemed to be their allies. They pushed forward again and again, even though the terrible machine gun and the Valley riflemen and musketeers—and, once or twice, even the archers—punished them when they tried. Medics with red crosses on their smocks dragged the wounded to cover. You weren't supposed to shoot at medics—it wasn't sporting. Accidents did happen. For the most part, they were real accidents, not cheating.

Dan glanced at the sun, which was sliding down toward the Pacific. That was how he thought about it. He didn't worry about the earth turning. He worried about . . . "What'll we do when it gets dark?"

"Depends on what those sweet and charming people do," Sergeant Chuck said, or words more or less to that effect.

"Okay, cool. Far out, even, man," Dan said. "What'll *they* do? What do we do if they try a night attack?"

"Gotta have fires," Chuck answered. "We get some big fires going, they'll show us anybody who tries sneaking up." He went on, thinking out loud: "Gotta get fuel together, then. We should have done that already, but I don't think we have, or not enough." He eyed Dan in a . . . sweet and charming way.

"Hey!" Dan squawked. He didn't like shooting at people. He *really* didn't like people shooting at him. But he didn't want to chop wood and carry it, either. "C'mon, man—cut me some slack. I was the one who made you think of this!"

"Well . . . yeah," the sergeant admitted. He wasn't even slightly used to backing down. After a moment, he reached over and thumped Dan on the arm. "Anybody who'd sooner stay and fight than get out of it's okay in my book."

"Mm." All of a sudden, Dan wondered whether squawking had been such a good idea. But once you chose something, you didn't get to take it over. If you got to try again, to do things differently, wouldn't you have another world after a while? Maybe better, maybe worse, but for sure not the same.

Sergeant Chuck went to talk to Captain Kevin. Maybe Kevin had to talk with higher-ups, too. Any which way, some of Kevin's company and some of the reinforcements came down off the freeway line. Before long, Dan heard them hacking away with axes. He heard them cussing, too. They liked their new duty no more than he would have.

Like it or not, they got the job done. The .50-caliber machine gun laid down covering fire so they could move the wood out in front of the freeway line—out to the south. A couple of soldiers got wounded doing that, but only a couple. At sunset, the Valley men lit the bonfires.

The wind had been coming out of the west, off the ocean. It swung around after the sun went down, and started blowing from the mountains to the sea. If flying embers spread the fires toward bomb-ravaged Santa Monica . . . well, so what? Dan watched them burn that way with, if anything, a certain sense of relief. Anybody trying to sneak through the dead zone would be sorry.

Eleven

Once upon a time, in both this alternate and the home timeline, the section of Los Angeles called Venice had really had canals. They were long gone there, and they were long gone here, too. The Mendozas' wagon rolled north through Venice toward the wasteland that was Santa Monica.

Liz tried not to think about the gunfire to the north—to the northeast, now. Not thinking about it wasn't easy, because it got louder and closer every minute. She wasn't calm, or anything close to calm. To keep from driving her parents crazy, she had to pretend she was.

After a while, she wondered if they were pretending, too, so they wouldn't drive her squirrely. If they were, they made better actors than she did.

The farther north she and her folks went, the stranger the looks people gave them. "You fixing to go into the dead zone?" a cobbler called, looking up from the boot he was resoling.

"What if we are?" Dad said.

"Well, plenty of folks go in there," the local answered. "Not so many come out again. You look like nice people. Wouldn't want to see anything bad happen to you."

A ferret-faced fellow coming out of the tavern next door

leered at the Chevy wagon. "Wouldn't want to see anything bad happen to you while we ain't around to grab the leftovers," he said.

"Oh, shut up, Stu," the cobbler said, and then, to the Mendozas, "Don't pay him no mind. He's got as much in the way of brains as my cat, only I don't have a cat."

"Er—right," Dad said. "Any which way, I expect we can take care of ourselves." He displayed a modern copy, made in the home timeline, of an Old Time Tommy gun.

"Well!" said the cobbler, who didn't seem to know quite what it was. "Pretty fancy piece you got there, buddy." He turned. "Ain't it, Stu? . . . Stu? Where the devil did he go?"

He'd turned green and ducked back into the tavern. Liz watched him do it. He knew exactly what Dad was showing off, and how many bullets it could spray. He clearly wasn't a predator—he had no taste for a fight. He was a scavenger. If somebody else did the Mendozas in, he'd scrounge what he could from the things the real robbers didn't want.

"Are you sure that was a good idea?" Mom asked as the wagon rolled on. "One of those guns is worth a mint here. We may have people coming after us on account of it."

"Anybody who tries will be sorry," Dad said. "We don't just have one Tommy gun—we've got three."

Liz was anything but thrilled about shooting people. But she wasn't thrilled about people shooting her, either. She supposed she could pull the trigger if she had to. If she did end up killing somebody, she'd probably heave her guts out right afterwards.

When she said so, Dad replied, "As long as it *is* afterwards. In the meantime, do what you've got to do. You can be sorry about it later."

"You don't talk like a history professor," Mom said.

"I hope not," he told her. "I know enough history to know thinking like a history prof from the home timeline while we're here is liable to get us killed. I don't want that to happen. It's too permanent."

Houses and shops with people in them got thinner and thinner on the ground. Piles of rubble and obviously empty buildings grew more and more common. But just because a building was obviously empty, that didn't mean it really and truly was empty. Maybe—probably—bandits lurked in some of the sorry structures that looked about ready to collapse under their own weight.

Dad handed Mom and Liz their submachine guns. That put a lot of firepower on display. Were the bandits on vacation? Or did they figure they didn't want to tackle a wagon defended by three Tommy guns? Liz had no way to know. She did know she was glad things stayed quiet.

And then they got into the dead zone. Where the bomb hit, there mostly wasn't enough of anything left to make rebuilding worthwhile. Everything looked charred and melted, even after 130 years. The scrubby weeds pushing up through cracks in the glassy crust didn't do much to hide that. Nothing could. It was like looking at a dead body in a threadbare suit.

Liz thought about Santa Monica in the home timeline. She thought about the beach and the malls. She thought about all the people, especially on weekends. And she thought about the RAND Corporation. The Russians had likely used a bomb here to make sure they knocked it out.

Well, they did. Along with the United States, they knocked almost everything out. Liz started to cry.

"What's the matter?" Mom asked.

"It's all ruined." Liz sniffed. "No matter what we do, we can't fix it. It'd be like unscrambling an egg."

"I wish I could say you were wrong, sweetheart," Dad told her. "But you're not. All we can do is help a little and try to find out what went wrong."

"It's not enough!"

He nodded. "I know. It's what we can do, though. And it's more than most of the bombed-out alternates ever see. Easier and cheaper just to leave them alone. We don't have the people or the resources to do anything else."

"We don't want to bother." Liz made it into an accusation. "We don't care."

Dad only nodded again. "Mostly we don't," he agreed. "We're spread too thin the way things are. And Crosstime Traffic needs to show a profit, not a loss. And so . . ."

"So we make like a bunch of vultures and watch things die," Liz said.

"We do pass on antibiotics when we can." Did Dad sound defensive? If he didn't, why not? "And we showed them how to make the anthrax vaccine. More of their cows and sheep live, so more of them live, too."

"Oh, boy."

Liz's sarcasm was largely wasted, because the gunfire from the Santa Monica Freeway line changed note. Dad paid more attention to that than he did to his own daughter. His head came up like a wolf's when it took a scent. "The Valley soldiers are using that heavy machine gun again," he said.

"Heaven help anybody coming at them, then," Mom said.

"Yeah." Dad nodded one more time. "Only thing I worry

about now is whether Cal's boys will try an end-around through the dead zone. If they do, we've got problems."

But they didn't, not while the light held. Liz wondered why not. Scavengers and scroungers did come in here sometimes. Most people in this alternate stayed away from places where H-bombs had fallen, though. They had to know the fallout wasn't poisonous any more, or the scavengers wouldn't go in. Still, lingering fear or superstition kept almost everybody away.

The sun went down. The stars started coming out. Dad stopped the horses and gave them their feed bags. They chomped happily on oats and hay. The Mendozas, not so happily, ate bread and smoked pork and sauerkraut and raisins. They drank rough red wine that would have got any vintner in the home timeline fired. It was safer than the local water, which was guaranteed to give you the runs.

"Isn't this fun?" Dad said as they got ready to sleep in the cramped wagon. "Isn't this cozy?"

"Fun?" Liz said. "As a matter of fact, no."

"Too blasted cozy, if anybody wants to know what I think," Mom added.

"Everybody's a critic," Dad said. Liz gave him a dirty look. He could fall asleep in thirty seconds and keep sleeping through anything this side of the crack of doom. Trouble was, he thought everybody else could do the same thing. Most normal human beings couldn't, and he didn't get it.

"Warmer tomorrow," Mom said. "Breeze isn't off the ocean any more."

"That's true." Dad sniffed. "You can smell the smoke from all the fires."

The horses could smell it, too, and they didn't like it. They snorted and shifted their feet, as if to say they would rather be somewhere else. Liz would rather have been somewhere else, too. Then she noticed a red-gold glow on the eastern horizon. She watched it for a little while, and decided she wasn't imagining things.

Pointing, she said, "That fire's getting closer."

"Don't be silly. It's—" Dad broke off. He started watching the fire, too. After a few seconds, he said something incendiary himself. Then he said something even worse: "You're right."

He jumped out of the wagon. "What are you doing?" Liz asked.

"Harnessing the horses," he answered. "No fire departments around here worth the paper they're printed on. We've got to get away, because nobody will put that out before it gets here. And horses are faster than people."

That all made good sense, however much Liz wished it didn't. She also wished he could hitch up the horses faster. The job looked easy, but it wasn't, not if you wanted to do it right.

While he worked, of course, the flames didn't stop. Mom said, "You want to hurry that along there?" She sounded much calmer than she could possibly have felt.

"I *am* hurrying," Dad snapped.

"Well, hurry faster," Mom told him.

The breeze blew harder. It sent a puff of smoke that made Liz cough. *Stop that*, she thought, but it didn't. After what seemed forever, Dad jumped back into the wagon. He flicked the reins. The horses went off at a trot without so much as a giddyap. They'd probably wondered what was taking so long, too.

From everything Liz had heard, fire made horses stupid.

From everything she'd seen, horses were no big threat to get fives on their AP tests anyway. But, this once, panic worked for the Mendozas, not against them. The horses wanted to get away from the fires, and so did the people they were pulling.

It was going to be closer than it had any business being. In the home timeline, Dad would have been on his cell phone yelling his head off. A water-dropping plane or helicopter would have splatted the leading edge of the flames. That would have slowed them down enough to let endangered people get away. And, of course, in the home timeline, they wouldn't have been stuck in a horse-drawn wagon to begin with.

No cell phones here. No water-dropping airplanes or copters, either. And the wagon was the fastest way to escape they had. The only other choice was getting out and running. If the horses freaked and stood still, they would have to try that. Liz didn't think it seemed like a whole lot of fun.

Things ran past them in the night. Coyotes and raccoons and feral cats hated the fire, and feared it, too. So did rats and mice and hamsters and squirrels and . . . everything, really.

When she looked back on that night, none of it stuck in her mind as a whole lot of fun. The fire got closer and closer and hotter and hotter. The smoke got thicker and nastier, till she felt as if she were smoking about ten packs of cigarettes every time she breathed in. Mom gave her a hanky soaked in water to put over her nose and mouth. It helped some—till it dried out. That didn't take nearly long enough. She soaked it herself the next time. Mom splashed the fabric of the wagon to keep embers from catching.

Mom also rigged makeshift breathing masks for herself and Dad. "Shall I make some for the horses, too?" she asked.

"I don't think they'd put up with it," Dad answered. "Besides, do you want to stop and find out?"

Mom automatically looked back over her right shoulder. So did Liz, and wished she hadn't. The flames were much too close, much too big, and much, much too hot. Dad's question kind of answered itself. In case it didn't, Mom took care of things: "Now that you mention it, no."

"About what I figured." Dad snapped the whip above the horses' backs. They were already doing all they could, but he wanted to make sure they kept on paying attention.

"What happens if the smoke gets them?" Liz asked through the bit of cloth that wasn't keeping as much smoke out of *her* lungs as she wished it would.

"We jump down and we hold on to each other and we hustle," Dad said. "Next question?"

Liz decided she didn't have a next question. The answer to the one she'd just asked gave her plenty to chew on all by itself.

Mom looked over her shoulder again. Liz admired her nerve. *She* didn't want to know exactly how close those leaping, crackling flames were. If things were going to turn out badly, couldn't it be a surprise? If you *knew* you were about to get roasted . . . Well, what could you do? Scream, maybe, and then stick an apple in your mouth.

Except she didn't have an apple. She didn't think the flames would stop when she was just done to a turn, either—not that it would matter to her one way or the other at that stage of things.

Then Mom said, "We're gaining."

"What?" Liz wasn't sure she'd heard right. Nobody ever talked about how loud a really big fire was up close. The people who knew things like that were mostly either firefighters or dead.

"We're gaining," Mom said again. Liz could hear her better this time. Maybe Mom talked louder. Maybe they were a little farther from the flames. If they were . . .

"We're gaining!" Liz said joyfully.

She looked over her shoulder then. The flames were still too close, but they weren't *way* too close any more. That looked like progress, all right.

"Just hope sparks and embers don't set the wagon roof on fire," Dad said. Liz gave him a reproachful stare, not because that wasn't possible but because it was. They couldn't stop it if it did happen, so she didn't want to hear about it.

Heart pounding as loud as the flames were roaring, she looked over her shoulder once more. The fire was definitely farther away now. She approved of that. She would have approved even more if it were a mile beyond the moon.

A few minutes later, Dad let the horses slow down. "I'm pretty sure we're good," he said. "It's burning straight west, pretty much, and we've got north of it."

"What do we do now?" Mom asked.

"How about we sleep for a week?" Dad said.

"Works for me," Liz said. "And you know what else? I bet we've got so much soot on our faces, nobody can recognize us."

"That works, too," Mom said. "I was going to say we should wash in the morning, but maybe not. In the meantime . . ."

In the meantime, Liz had no trouble at all falling asleep in the wagon.

Back in the Valley, Dan hadn't thought about sleeping on asphalt wrapped in no more than a blanket. That didn't mean he couldn't do it. If you got tired enough, you could sleep anywhere. He proved that: Sergeant Chuck had to shake him awake when the sun came up the next morning.

Yawning, Dan started to sit up straight. Then he didn't. You never could tell whether Westside snipers were waiting for somebody to do something that dumb. Chuck was on his hands and knees. He'd been ready to push Dan down if Dan forgot where he was. Since Dan didn't, Chuck relaxed.

Relaxed or not, he didn't look so good. He needed a shave, and smoke from last night's watchfires streaked his cheeks and forehead. "Boy, Sarge, you ought to clean up," Dan said.

"Look who's talking. You'd stop a clock at fifty yards," Chuck retorted. He was probably right. Dan had been firing a matchlock musket all day. Every time the gun went off, it belched out a great cloud of fireworks-smelling gunpowder smoke. How much of that was he wearing on his face?

"What do we do today?" Dan asked.

"Wait and see what our loving neighbors to the south try," Chuck said—or something like that, anyhow. "If they want more trouble, we can give it to them. If they sit tight, we're not going to go after them or anything. What would the King of the Valley do with land south of the Santa Monica Freeway?"

Rule it? Dan thought. As soon as he did, he wondered, *But how?* It would take a long time to get messages and orders back and forth between Zev's palace up in Northridge and these lands way down here. Back in the Old Time, people said, you could talk to anybody right away, no matter how far apart the two of you were. Radio, TV, telephones . . . Dan believed in them, but they weren't around any more. The telegraph survived—where people didn't steal wires for their copper, anyway—but who really wanted to pay attention to orders in Morse code? Dan knew he wouldn't.

"Have they started shooting yet?" he asked.

"No, but it's still early," Sergeant Chuck answered. "I don't know that they won't, and neither does anybody else."

Dan's stomach growled. It had ideas of its own, and wasn't shy about letting the rest of him know about them. "Will anyone bring us breakfast?" he asked.

"I heard they were supposed to be making sandwiches, but I sure haven't seen any." Chuck looked around. "Wait—speak of the devil."

Kitchen helpers with big cloth sacks crawled up and down the freeway dealing out sandwiches and Old Time soda bottles full of watered wine. Dan's sandwich was smoked pork and pickled tomato on a hard roll: something that wouldn't go bad in a hurry. He made it disappear in a hurry, so how long it would keep didn't matter. Chuck's breakfast was the same, and vanished even faster.

"It's not bacon and eggs and hash browns, but it'll do," the sergeant said.

"Yeah, Sarge, but think what army cooks'd do to bacon and eggs and hash browns," Dan said. Chances were the cooks would do fine by them. He didn't let that bother him. Complaining about army cooks probably went all the way back to the Old Time.

"They're pretty lousy, all right," Chuck agreed. Sergeants complained about cooks, too. Sergeants complained about everything. It was part of their job.

Here and there, Valley soldiers started standing along the freeway line. When nobody fired at the first few, more men did the same. Dan and Chuck stood up at the same time: not soon enough to take a big chance, and not late enough to seem yellow. Getting shot wasn't part of anybody's job . . . except when it was.

"Dan! Musketeer Dan!" somebody farther down the freeway called.

"I'm here!" Dan sang out. "What's happening, man?"

"They want you back at the traders' house, so step on it," the messenger answered.

"May I go, Sergeant?" Dan asked.

"How can I say no?" Chuck replied. "If the Westsiders attack, we'll just have to try and fight the war without you. I don't know that we've got much of a chance then, but we'll do our best."

Propelled by such pungent sarcasm, Dan was glad to get away. He let the messenger lead him down to the level of the ordinary streets and take him back to the house where Liz had lived. (Of course, her parents had lived there, too, but he didn't think about them very much.)

With electric lights down there in the bottom basement, could they have had TV and a telephone, too? A moment's thought made Dan decide that was silly. What would they watch? Whom would they call?

He couldn't ask the messenger. You weren't supposed to gossip about what was in that house. He would be violating an order if he did, and he'd be making the other soldier violate one, too. He kept quiet.

When he got to the house, he asked Captain Horace, "What's up, sir?"

"You know the way you found the door down into the room with the electric lights?" the Valley officer said.

"Yes, sir."

"Well, we found another door like that," Horace said.

"Under the basement, sir?" Dan asked. "What's in it?" He could imagine all kinds of things, each more marvelous than the last. A TV set that worked? An auto that worked? Why think small? What about an airplane that worked? If only you could fly!

But Captain Horace shook his head. "No, not under there. It's set into the wall in the regular basement, the room above the one with the lights."

"Oh." Dan knew he sounded disappointed. A room there wouldn't be so big. You couldn't put a car into it, let alone an airplane. But maybe you could put other cool stuff in there. "How do we get in?"

"I hope you can help us figure that out," Horace said. "So far, we haven't had much luck."

As if to show what he meant, somebody started banging on the wall with what had to be a sledgehammer. *Boom! Boom! Boom!* The racket made Dan's head ache. "Got to be a better way than that," he said.

"It'd be nice if there were," the captain agreed. "What can you come up with? If you can get us in there without tearing the place apart, I'll make you a sergeant on the spot."

Dan imagined three stripes on his sleeve. He imagined the look on Sergeant Chuck's face when the underofficer saw him with three stripes on his sleeve. That look would be worth ten dollars—no, twenty. And twenty dollars was a lot of money. "I'll do what I can," he said.

"See what you come up with, that's all. We don't expect miracles." Horace's mouth twisted in a crooked grin. "I sure wouldn't mind one, though." He went to the top of the stairs and shouted down to the basement: "Knock it off! . . . *Knock it off!*" Mercifully, the banging stopped. Horace breathed a sigh of relief. "That's better. Now the top of my head doesn't want to fall off."

"Yes, sir," Dan said again. He'd had the same idea. He thought like a captain—or the captain thought like him! What would Sergeant Chuck say about that if he were ever rash enough to mention it out loud? Something interesting and memorable—he was sure of that.

He went downstairs. A burly Valley common soldier was leaning on the handle of his sledgehammer. The musclebound man didn't look sorry to take a break. Nodding to Dan, he said, "You're the guy with smart ideas, huh?"

"I don't know. We'll see," Dan said. "Where's this door at, anyway?"

"In the wall there. If you look real close, you can *just* see the crack," the other soldier answered, pointing. "I sure hope you psych something out, man. This wall's gotta be reinforced concrete, or else whatever's tougher than that. I could keep banging away at it from now till everything turns blue, and I don't know if I'd ever bust in."

"Okay." Dan peered at the wall the way he'd peered at the floor when he found the trap door. He wasn't sure he would have spotted this hairline crack if the muscular man hadn't pointed it out. He wondered how anybody'd found it in the dim light down here.

When he said as much, the guy with the sledgehammer said, "Dr. Saul went over the whole wall with a magnifying glass. That's how."

"Oh," Dan said. "How . . . scientific of him." You had to be thorough to do something like that. You also had to be a little bit crazy, or more than a little bit. Except if it paid off, the way it had here, you weren't really crazy, were you? Or maybe you were, and lucky, too.

"What are you gonna do?" The other soldier didn't sound as if he thought Dan could do anything. A moment later, he explained why: "Dr. Saul tried everything under the sun. He sure couldn't get in."

"Groovy." Dan had just been thinking how lucky Dr. Saul was. Well, so much for that. He eyed the almost invisible door. He eyed the sledgehammer, and the broad-shouldered, sweaty soldier who'd been swinging it. He eyed the tiny handful of concrete chips on the floor. No, brute force didn't seem to be the way to go.

What then? If you couldn't break down a door, how did you go about tricking one? He remembered a story he'd read, one that seemed to have been all the rage right around the time the Fire fell. It wasn't a true story—or people nowadays didn't think so, anyhow. But the wizard and his followers had got stuck outside a door into a mountainside that didn't want to open.

Dan pointed at this one. "Friend!" he said. Nothing happened. He laughed at himself. He might have known. Then another idea struck him. What was that word?

Before he could remember it, the guy with the sledgehammer started laughing at him. "I know what you're doing," he said. "My folks read me that story, too. But it's only, like, a story, man."

Never argue with somebody with a sledgehammer, especially when his shoulders are twice as wide as yours. That was an old rule Dan had just made up. Instead of arguing, he said, "Yeah, it's only a story. What have I got to lose, though? I mean, do you *want* to pound reinforced concrete for however long it takes?"

The other soldier looked at the pitifully small bits of concrete he'd managed to break loose. He looked at Dan. His wave of invitation was almost a bow. "Go for it, man."

"I will, as soon as I . . ." Dan snapped his fingers. The Elvish word *did* come back to him! He pointed at the doorway, even though he had no idea whether that made any difference. "*Mellon!*" he said.

Silently and without any fuss, the door swung open.

Valley soldiers did guard the west-facing approaches to Westwood. Liz supposed that made sense. With all the fighting the day before, the Westsiders might have tried to sneak a column through the dead zone. But she'd hope she and her folks would be able to get into Westwood and start selling their jeans before the occupiers noticed they were around.

No such luck. The soldier who seemed to pop up out of nowhere didn't have a matchlock. He carried an Old Time rifle. His U.S. Army helmet was two lifetimes old. "Halt!" he called, and his voice said they'd better do it. "Who are you people, and what are you doing here?"

"Whoa!" Dad called to the horses. He pulled back on the reins. The animals stopped. Then he said, "We were coming up here with a load of denim pants—genuine Old Time Levi's, fresh like they were made yesterday—when all the shooting started. We couldn't go through, so we went around. And here we are."

"Levi's fresh like yesterday, huh?" The rifleman laughed.

"I've heard traders sling it before, but you've got more nerve than anybody. How about telling me one I'll believe?"

"Pull out a pair, Liz," Dad said, cool as a superconductor. "Let Doubting Thomas here see for himself."

"Sure." Liz scrambled over the seat and into the back of the wagon. She grabbed a pair of jeans and showed them to the soldier. "See? With a zipper and everything." The only trousers in this alternate that didn't close with buttons used zippers recycled from Old Time clothes. But not many zippers still worked, and not many tailors bothered with them. Buttons did the job. Zippers were mostly for show, the way cuff buttons on suit jackets were in the home timeline.

Before asking for a closer look, the Valley soldier called, "Hey, Harvey!"

"Yo!" A voice came from nowhere. "What's happening, man?"

"Cover me. I need to check something out."

"You got it." Harvey still didn't show himself.

"Now let me see those jeans," the soldier who'd challenged the wagon told Liz. She didn't make any sudden moves when she handed them to him. Maybe his father was a tailor, or maybe he was when he didn't carry a gun. He felt the fabric. He held the pants up against the sun to see if they had any thin spots. He worked the zipper several times and peered at the way it was sewn to the rest of the fly. The more he examined them, the more surprised he looked.

"See?" Liz said.

"Yeah." The Valley rifleman seemed to nod in spite of himself. "Unless this is just one supercool pair to show people . . . You've got a whole bunch of these in the back there?"

Liz nodded. "You better believe it. Look for yourself if you want to. We're no ripoff artists." She made herself sound angry, the way a trader who'd been unfairly challenged naturally would.

"I'll do that," the soldier said. His expression said a lot of the people who protested hardest were the biggest thieves. That only made Liz mad for real. Nobody liked getting called a liar, even if just by a raised eyebrow.

And she wasn't lying. She walked around to the back of the wagon and pointed to the big old stack of Levi's. "Go ahead. Pick any pair you want."

The rifleman trusted her far enough to sling his weapon for a moment, anyhow. He leaned forward and pulled a pair out of the middle of the stack. He gave them the same once-over he had with the ones Liz offered him. When he finished, he said, "Well, I take my hat off to you." And he really did lift the old-fashioned steel pot off his head. "These are the real McCoy. I don't know where you found 'em, but I bet we'll want to buy 'em. Pass on, Miss. Pass on."

They didn't go to the market square just south of the UCLA campus. That was too close to their old house. There was another market square, a ritzier one, north of Sunset Boulevard in Brentwood. The only reason that square was ritzier was that the neighborhood had been ritzier before the Fire fell—and still was.

As Dad guided the horses towards it, he said, "If we were proper traders, we'd go to the other market. It's bigger, and there are more Valley soldiers around."

"All the more reason for staying away," Mom said.

"That's what I was thinking," Dad agreed. "The people who do buy from us may think we're kind of dumb for setting up there, but they won't think we're anything more than kind of dumb."

"You hope," Mom said.

Dad nodded. "You bet I do."

"It's not too bad," Liz said. "The library's up near the north end of campus. We won't be any farther from it than we were before . . . as long as the librarians don't tip off the Valley soldiers as soon as I go in there."

"I know it can happen. I hope it won't," Dad said. "They're all people who've been there since the City Council ran things. Maybe there's a quisling or two, but we can hope not, anyhow. With a little luck, we'll get the job done yet."

"That would be good," Liz said.

"That would be *wonderful*," Mom said. "Not seeing this alternate again wouldn't break my heart."

"Get used to it, hon. If we land another grant, we'll be back one of these days," Dad said. By the look on her face, Mom had no trouble curbing her enthusiasm. Ignoring her expression, or at least pretending to, Dad went on, "That's what happens when you have an academic specialty: you keep coming back to it. I'll be coming back here when the beard I'm not wearing right now is all white—if I can keep getting grant money."

"And if you don't have WANTED posters with your face on them in every little kingdom from Frisco all the way down to Teejay," Mom added.

"Well, yes, there is that." By the look on his face, Dad kind of liked the idea. He glanced over at Liz. "Of course, by then we won't have Liz to help get us in trouble."

"Hey, what are you blaming me for? You were the one who decided to hide Luke," Liz said.

"Yeah, but if Dan didn't think you were cute, none of the

other Valley soldiers would have paid any special attention to us," Dad said.

"I can't help that!" Liz knew her voice went higher and shriller than she would have liked.

"I didn't say you could," Dad answered, which was . . . sort of true. "But you won't come to this alternate to stir up the boys here by the time my beard's all white. You'll be through with school by then, and you'll find some other alternate to be especially interested in—or maybe something in the home timeline: who knows?—and then you'll—"

"If you say I'll stir up the boys there—well, *don't* say it, that's all," Liz broke in.

"You can't prove I was going to," Dad said.

"You're lucky she can't, too," Mom told him. "If she could, you'd be in even more trouble than you've already got yourself into."

"And they said it couldn't be done!" Dad sounded proud of himself for being such a pest. He probably was. *He's not the stuffy kind of professor, anyway,* Liz thought. *That would be worse . . . I think.*

Dad sure wasn't stuffy after they got set up in the Brentwood market square. He put some Levi's out on a card table with folding legs that could have come from the Old Time. (Like the jeans, it really came from the home timeline.) Then he started yelling and carrying on about how wonderful they were. He even pulled out a bugle. Heaven only knew where he'd got that. Maybe from the Stoyadinoviches? Wherever, he blew a long, tuneless blast on it. He couldn't have been hokier if he tried. And he *was* trying . . . all kinds of ways.

And it worked. The people who lived in Brentwood put

down silver for the Levi's. Pair after pair disappeared. Before too long, a Valley sergeant strode over to inspect the goods. He wasn't a warrior. He was at least fifty, with a pot belly and shrewd eyes. He was a quartermaster sergeant: somebody who got fighting men what they needed to fight with. No army in the world kept going without people like that, and they won exactly zero glory.

This one didn't seem to care. He examined the jeans even more carefully than the Valley rifleman had. He carried a magnifying glass to help his aging eyes look at them up close. Once he was satisfied, he said, "How many pairs have you got left?" Dad told him. He nodded and asked, "What's your price?" Again, Dad told him. Liz waited for the sergeant to pitch a fit. He just said, "Okay. I'll take fifty pairs, assorted sizes."

It was as simple as that.

Twelve

When Dan stepped into the room he'd found with a word from *The Lord of the Rings*, lights in the ceiling came on. They were just like the ones in the room under the basement, so they had to be electric lights. Somehow, he wasn't much surprised. And then, a moment later, not being surprised . . . surprised him.

The room was full of strange, mostly plastic furniture. A rectangular metal box sat against the far wall. The front had hinges and a handle, which made it likely to be a door.

"Oh, wow, man." The guy with the sledgehammer pointed to it. "Like, what is that thing?"

"It's one of those refrigerators, isn't it?" Dan said. You found them in houses every now and then. They could be dangerous. Little kids sometimes got them open and went inside. For some dumb reason, refrigerator doors didn't work from the inside out. Too often, kids playing games suffocated before anybody found them.

"Yeah, I guess you're right. They kept stuff cold in the Old Time, right?" the other soldier said.

"I think so. I wonder if this one still works." Dan looked up at the bright ceiling. "The lights do."

"Oh, wow," the muscular soldier said again.

"Go get Captain Horace," Dan said. "He needs to see this."

"Okay." The other guy let the sledgehammer fall over with a clatter. Dan was half surprised he didn't carry it with him.

Horace came down the stairs on the double. He walked through the newly opened door. He looked at the furniture, at the refrigerator, and then at Dan. "Congratulations, Sergeant," he said.

Now Dan was the one who said, "Oh, wow!" Then he said, "Thank you, sir!" And then he walked over to the refrigerator. "Could this thing work?"

"Beats me," Captain Horace said, which struck Dan as a pretty honest answer. The officer continued, "Why don't you open it and find out?"

Why don't you . . . sir? Dan thought. What if it didn't work? What if it blew up instead? The captain would say, *Well, so what?* He was a captain, while Dan was only a just-promoted sergeant. Everybody in the whole Kingdom of the Valley would agree with him. Well, everybody but Dan. And nobody would care what he thought.

He reached out, grabbed the door handle, and pulled. Obviously, that was what you were supposed to do. The door wasn't real easy to open, but it sure wasn't hard, either.

As soon as it swung open about three inches, a light came on inside the refrigerator. *Where does it go when the door closes?* Dan wondered. But he had other things to worry about by then.

He felt chilly air on his legs. "It does keep stuff cold!" he exclaimed.

Captain Horace came up beside him. Why not? Now the

captain knew it was safe. "It sure does," he said. He reached out to touch a shelf. Then he jerked his hand back. "It's as cold as a winter night in there."

Dan was eyeing the cans on the shelf. He'd seen tin cans before. In L.A.'s warm, dry climate, they didn't rust away very fast. These, to look at them, might have been made yesterday. They were red, with fancy, swirly letters that ran along the whole length from top to bottom. The letters were so fancy, they were hard to read. When Dan finally puzzled them out, he said, "Oh, wow!" one more time.

"Coca-Cola?" Captain Horace read the name as if he had trouble believing it. Well, so did Dan. There were lots and lots of wasp-waisted green glass bottles around, all of them carrying that same swirling script. "You don't think . . . ? Is there real Coca-Cola inside those things?"

Nobody'd tasted Coca-Cola since the Old Time, or not long after it. Dan picked up a can. It had to be the coldest thing he'd ever touched: so cold, he almost dropped it. "How are you supposed to open this thing?" he wondered. But the can had a metal tab on top. He worked it with his thumb to see how it operated. If you pushed up from under it, the other end went down and . . .

Ssss! The sudden hiss nearly made Dan drop the can again. Some brown bubbly stuff came out of the opening he'd made. He started to taste it, then paused and sniffed instead. What if it was rotten or something? But it smelled spicy—intriguing. He took a cautious sip.

It had bubbles. They tickled his tongue, and then tickled his nose from the inside out. It tasted like . . . he didn't know what it tasted like. It was pretty good, though. He took another sip—a bigger one this time.

"Well?" Captain Horace asked. Dan handed him the can. He sipped, too. "It's like sweet champagne!" he said.

"Is it wine, then?" Dan asked. He knew champagne was wine with bubbles in it, but he'd never had any. It was expensive stuff.

"No way," the officer said. "You'd taste the booze in it if it were." Dan nodded. He was like anybody else. He drank beer or wine—often watered down—instead of water whenever he could. Water would do at a pinch, but you always took a chance with it.

"What is it, then?" Dan said. "It isn't water, it isn't wine, it isn't cider or grape juice. It isn't *anything*." He wanted things to fit into their own neat little slots. Well, who didn't?

Captain Horace took a bigger swig. "It's Coca-Cola, that's what it is." He handed the can back to Dan. Dan drank some more, too. Horace wasn't wrong. Something like this deserved a name for itself, all right. It wasn't like anything else. It was something out of the Old Time. How did it end up here in the modern world?

The captain let out a loud burp. A moment later, so did Dan. He looked at the can of Coca-Cola. "It's the bubbles, that's what it is," he said.

"Well, sure," Captain Horace said indulgently. Then his gaze sharpened. "How did these traders get their hands on Coca-Cola, though? It's an Old Time thing. It doesn't really belong here."

"Neither does a refrigerator that works. Neither do electric lights," Dan said.

"I know." The officer took the can back again and drained it. Dan almost got mad, but the impossible refrigerator held more impossible cans. Captain Horace belched again. "It's all righteously freaky, man."

"Really," Dan agreed. His mind leaped. "What if the traders aren't from now? What if they're really from the Old Time? That would explain why they acted funny sometimes, too. They were trying to, like, fake it, you know? They didn't exactly grok how we do things nowadays."

"I don't know. That doesn't sound very scientific to me," Captain Horace said. "It doesn't sound very likely, either."

"Sir, none of this stuff is very likely, either." Dan's wave took in the lights, the refrigerator, and the can the officer was still holding. "But it's here. What's that thing the Great Detective says?"

" 'When you have eliminated the impossible, whatever remains, *however improbable*, must be the truth.' " Captain Horace knew what he was talking about, all right. He went on, "But *everything* here seems impossible! How do we go about eliminating any of it?"

"It may be impossible, but it's *here*." Dan reached in and took out another can of Coca-Cola. This one was easier to open than the last one had been—now he knew how. He drank from it. It tasted like the real thing, all right.

Going back onto the UCLA campus brought Liz the usual, almost pleasant, pain. They still respected learning there, even if they embalmed it instead of helping it to grow. That was good. A lot of the buildings were familiar, which wasn't true down in Westwood. But it was like looking at an old friend filthy and starving and dressed in rags. It *did* hurt.

"Haven't seen you for a while," one of the librarians said when she walked in.

"Life's been . . . complicated," she answered. The librarian nodded. Liz had the feeling that was true no matter which alternate you visited.

Just *how* complicated was life, though? Did this bespectacled fellow report to the Valley soldiers occupying Westwood? If he did, would he slip away to let them know she was back? One thing for sure: he couldn't phone them in this alternate.

She went upstairs and started going through the bound issues of *Newsweek*. She had a pretty good notion of what had happened in 1967 in the home timeline. Most of what had happened in this alternate seemed about the same.

Maybe the Soviet Union really had started the war here. Maybe the Communist leaders reacted differently to something—Vietnam? the Six-Day War?—from the way they did in the home timeline. If that was so, American news magazines wouldn't have such a good idea of what was happening on the other side of the Iron Curtain.

Or would they? *Something* would have leaked out, wouldn't it? Here was a story about Vyacheslav Molotov going back to Moscow from his post at the International Atomic Energy Agency for consultations. Molotov's name rang a bell with Liz from the AP Euro course. He was the longtime Russian foreign minister in the middle of the twentieth century. She didn't remember that he'd been on the IAEA in 1967.

Excitement tingled through her. Maybe, in the home timeline, he hadn't. What did that mean? Did it mean anything?

She couldn't be sure. She didn't know enough. But she made sure she scanned the story. She was mighty glad these

Newsweeks hadn't crumbled to dust between the time when the Fire fell and now. How many people had looked at them in those 130 years? Not many—she was sure of that. One reason they were still around was that not many people ever looked at them.

Liz wanted to find the missing puzzle pieces and put the whole thing together herself. She knew that wasn't real likely. Mom and Dad knew more about the 1960s in the home timeline than she did. And they knew as much as anybody—including the natives of this alternate—about the 1960s here. It wasn't enough yet to let them know what went wrong.

She didn't think they knew about Molotov, though.

Well, they would once she told them. And she had the data inside the little handheld scanner. From what she remembered, Molotov was a hardliner, a tough guy. If he had a more important slot in this 1967 than in the home timeline, that said something about the way the Russians' minds had worked here.

Did it say enough? There was no transposition chamber that ended in this alternate's Moscow or Leningrad—or was it Petrograd here, or St. Petersburg? She couldn't remember. It had got nuked, too. Most major cities here had. Any which way, there wouldn't be a chamber that could reach either place here unless somebody waved lots and lots of benjamins under Crosstime Traffic's nose. CT wasn't in business for its health.

No way the Mendozas could come up with that kind of money on their own. But if they landed another grant . . .

Maybe finding out about Molotov would help them do that. Liz could hope so. She didn't think she wanted to make a career out of studying this alternate, but her folks already had. If she could give them a hand while she was working with them—well, why not?

She closed the bound volume of *Newsweeks*. A scrap of old, brittle paper fluttered down and fell to the floor. She didn't think it had any printing on it, but sooner or later—probably sooner—all these magazines would get too fragile to read, and then they'd crumble to dust and be gone forever.

Except for what I've scanned, she thought. That was a funny feeling. She had history in her scanner. She didn't just have it, either. She felt like its custodian. What she and her folks took back to the home timeline had a better chance of lasting than anything that stayed here.

Maybe this alternate would rebuild two or three hundred years from now. It would want to know what had made the Fire fall. Maybe people from the home timeline could give back this information then. *We're custodians, all right*, she thought.

Sed quis custodiet ipsos custodes?—a bit of Latin came back to her. Who *would* watch the watchmen? There was no guarantee that the home timeline would be in great shape by the time this alternate was ready to find out about its past. Not long before her folks were born, the home timeline was right on the edge of going down the tubes. Too many people, not enough resources. Finding out how to go crosstime saved everybody's bacon.

Which didn't mean everybody in the home timeline was happy all the time. Old political and religious rivalries remained very much alive. And national governments were still figuring out how to deal with Crosstime Traffic, which was as big and as rich as any of them.

Well, complications came with being alive. The simplest

alternates were the ones where the atomic wars had killed everybody and everything. A graveyard the size of a planet. . . . Liz shivered. This alternate hadn't missed by much.

She got the next volume of *Newsweek* down from the shelf. Paging through the ads in the first issue, she thought about how confident everybody seemed. No one had any idea the USA and USSR were on the edge of blasting each other to kingdom come. No one seemed to suspect that, even if the superpowers left each other alone, the alternate would have run out of energy and food and drinkable water inside of a lifetime.

Would they have found out how to go between alternates here? She doubted it. She doubted it like anything, in fact—that had happened only once. (Or if it had happened more than once, nobody from Crosstime Traffic had ever found any evidence of it.) Other high-tech alternates exploited the rest of the Solar System as best they could. Too bad it was a less inviting place than science-fiction writers from the mid-twentieth century thought it would turn out to be.

Still other high-tech alternates ruthlessly limited population and energy use. If they couldn't get more, they'd make do with less. That worked, after a fashion, but Liz was glad she didn't live in one of those alternates. They were tyrannies, and tight ones. They had to be, to keep people from having too many babies and consuming too much. She'd grown up free, and was glad of it.

She scanned all the stories she could find about Russia and Vietnam and the Middle East. None of them grabbed her by the arm and yelled, *Hey! Look at me! I'm different!* She had the data, though. Maybe her folks could run with it if she couldn't.

When the sun got low in the west, she put away the bound

volume and left the library. No electric lights here. None anywhere in this alternate except in the secret rooms of the house the Mendozas had used and at the Stoyadinoviches' place down in Speedro. The locals would never find any of those.

Dan didn't know why he came back to the UCLA campus. He was tempted to go into the big, fancy library. If he could find out anywhere whether time travel was possible, that would be the place.

But he didn't think he could. If somebody back then knew how to do that, it would have been a heavy-duty secret, a bigger secret than the Fire. And something else occurred to him as he tramped along the cracked, weed-infested concrete. Why would anybody from the Old Time want to see *this*? They had things so much better back then. Everybody knew that. Next to what they'd had and thrown away, what was left was just a mess. People were lucky anything at all was left—if this counted for luck.

That was one side of the dime. The other side was, where did all that stuff in the traders' house come from if it didn't come from the Old Time? Nobody nowadays could make any of those things and keep them working. Fluorescent lights? A refrigerator? Coca-Cola? A door that opened when you said the right word? No, none of that was part of the world Dan knew.

He laughed at himself. He didn't know which world he was really in, not any more. If *Mellon* hadn't made the door open, the next thing he would have tried was *Open, sesame!* He was pretty sure *Ali Baba and the Forty Thieves* was nothing but a made-up story. But when you ran into marvels like the ones under the traders' house, how could you be certain about anything?

You couldn't. It was that simple.

There was Bunche Hall. The University Research Library sat a little north and a little west of the taller building. Dan still wondered how the devil Liz and her folks had managed to disappear from her house. So did a lot of other people from the Valley. If they didn't have a time-travel machine, what *did* they have?

He laughed again. He told himself he wouldn't have been real surprised to see Liz come out of the URL, just the way she had before all this weird stuff started.

Two heartbeats later, Liz came out of the URL, just the way she had before all this weird stuff started. Dan turned out to be wrong. He was so surprised, he tripped over his own feet and barely saved himself from falling on his face.

The wild stumble and flail kept him from yelling out her name. As he caught himself, he realized that might not be such a good idea. She and her folks were fugitives, after all. They wouldn't want anybody to know they were back in Westwood. If Liz found out he knew, wouldn't she disappear right before his eyes?

Could she do that? He shrugged. He didn't know she couldn't, and he didn't want to take the chance.

So instead of yelling, he followed her. She headed north—away from the house where she'd been staying—as if she had not a care in the world. He skulked along behind her, using everything he'd learned as a soldier not to be noticed. It was getting dark, which helped him.

What to do, what to do? If he just trailed her, she'd have a chance to get away when he went off to tell somebody about it and get help. If he grabbed her, she might disappear. When all your choices were bad, which one did you pick? The one that didn't look worst, whichever that happened to be.

He decided she had less chance of disappearing if he grabbed her than she did of getting away if he left her alone for a while. Maybe he was right, maybe he was wrong. But at least he was doing something. She'd almost got to Sunset Boulevard when he broke cover and ran toward her, calling, "Halt in the name of King Zev!"

She whirled. There was just enough light to let him see that she looked as astonished as he had a few minutes earlier. Then he was on her. If she wouldn't halt, he had to make her do it.

Next thing he knew, she'd grabbed his outstretched arm. He went up over her shoulder, flew through the air with the greatest of ease—and with a startled grunt—and landed, *thump!*, on his back.

Liz made a mistake then. She had pretty good combat reflexes, but not perfect ones. Instead of getting out of there as fast as she could, she stood and admired what she'd done. And Dan had combat reflexes of his own. Crashing to the ground made them kick in. He snaked an arm around her ankle and brought her down. She let out a startled grunt of her own, and then a squawk when her bottom bounced off the dirt.

He was bigger and stronger than she was. She had more skill. She didn't mind fighting dirty, either. She tried to do something that would have ended the fight in a hurry, but he took her knee on the point of his hip instead. It hurt, but it didn't ruin him.

"Is that how they fought in the Old Time?" he panted.

"Are you nuts? What are you talking about?" she said, and then, cautiously, "Truce?"

He thought about it. As cautiously, he nodded. "Truce."

They both got to their feet. She didn't try to kick him again where it would do the most good. He couldn't try to shoot her—his matchlock wasn't loaded. Just clouting her with the musket took a moment to cross his mind. By the time it did, she'd moved back too far to let him do it. Could he run her down if he had to? Maybe. Probably, even. Did he want to? That was a different question.

"What am I talking about? . . . I'll tell you what." Dan was still panting. Liz didn't seem to be. Did that mean he *couldn't* run her down? If they just talked, he wouldn't have to find out. "Coca-Cola. Electric lights. *Mellon*. That's what."

She looked almost comically amazed. "You've read *The Lord of the Rings*!"

"I didn't know I wasn't supposed to," Dan answered.

"But the movies are from the start of the twenty-first century," she said, more to herself than to him. "Are the books *that* much earlier?"

"*What* movies?" Dan asked. He had only a vague idea of what a movie was—sort of like TV, only bigger; sort of like a play, except it wasn't really there in front of you. It was like a photo that moved. He knew what photos were. He'd seen them. People still knew how to take them, even if not in color any more. How they were supposed to move . . . that, he didn't understand. He didn't know anything about movies of *The Lord of the Rings*. He was sure nobody else did, either, especially not movies from around the year 2000. Nobody could make movies then—it was after the Fire fell.

And Liz clapped both hands over her mouth, the way somebody would after blurting out a secret she didn't mean to tell. "Oh—!" she said, and then something that would have made Sergeant Chuck's ears turn green.

Dan was almost too surprised to be shocked—that was *not* the kind of thing he expected to hear from a girl he liked. But neither was talk about movies. "You really *are* a time traveler from the days before the Fire fell!" he exclaimed. "Nobody wanted to believe me. Everyone said I was nuts."

"You *are* nuts," Liz said. "You can't travel forwards and backwards in time—it's impossible." She had a scratch on her cheek, and a bigger one on the heel of her hand.

Dan noticed he had sore ribs along with an ache on his hipbone where her knee had got him. She'd hurt him other places, too, but those were the bad ones. "Yeah, sure," he said. "So how did you get here—sideways?"

Liz didn't look amazed this time—she looked horrified. "If I tell you the answer to that, I'll have to kill you," she said, and she sounded dead serious.

"It wouldn't do you any good." Dan hoped he was right.

He didn't like the calculating look in Liz's eyes. "No? You said nobody believed you. If you had an accident . . ."

If she really intended to kill him, she'd just try to do it. She wouldn't warn him she was thinking about it—would she? No way, Dan decided. Liz was a lot of things, but not even slightly stupid.

And the way she'd looked when he guessed sideways . . . He'd hit on something there, even if he didn't know just what. "How could you be from sideways in time?" he asked. "What's sideways from here?"

"I'm not supposed to tell you," Liz answered seriously. "It won't do you any good if you find out, and it won't hurt me any, but I'm not supposed to."

"Why not?" Dan said. "Knowing stuff is supposed to help, isn't it?" That was what they taught in school, anyhow.

"How much can knowing something help when you can't do anything about it even if you know?" Liz said. Dan only shrugged—he couldn't imagine anything like that. She must have seen as much, because she sighed before going on; "Okay. Remember, you asked for it."

"I promise," he said.

"Yeah, right," she told him. But she didn't stop talking: "I'll tell you what's sideways from here. *Everything* is, pretty much. There are alternates where the Nazis won—you know who the Nazis were, right? There are alternates where the Russians won and there was no atomic war. And there's the one I'm from. In my world, there was no atomic war, and the West won. And we just kept going forward from the way things were in 1967. What looks all superscientific and cool to you seems silly and old-fashioned to me. There. That's the truth. What are you going to do about it?"

"You've got—your people have—all the stuff they had back in the Old Time and then some?" Dan said slowly. If he hadn't seen the secret rooms in her house, he never would have believed it. But he had, and he did.

Liz nodded. "That's right. You aren't so dumb after all."

He'd just thought the same thing about her. "Gee, thanks a lot," he said. But he had a hard time feeling insulted. "Why aren't you helping us more, then?" he demanded. "Look at us! We're a mess! You could make us more like you."

Maybe for the first time since he'd known her, Liz looked embarrassed. "I'm sorry," she said. "I really am—I'm sorrier than I know how to tell you. But there's no money in fixing up an alternate. It's that simple. There just isn't. Besides, do you have any idea how big a whole world is? You can't go and fix something that size once it's messed up. Too much to do. Too much even to try."

"No money in it." Dan paid the most attention to the first part of what she said. "What are you doing here, then?"

She looked even more embarrassed. "Well, my dad got a grant."

"A grant?" It sounded like the English word Dan understood, but he didn't know what it meant here.

Liz nodded. "That's right. He teaches at UCLA—the UCLA in the alternate I come from. We call it the home timeline, but never mind that. Somebody's paying him money to come to this alternate and find out why you guys blew yourselves up."

"The Russians did it!" Dan said automatically. "The Reds! The Commies!" He didn't know quite what a Commie was, but it had something to do with being a Russian. He was pretty sure of that.

"As a matter of fact, I think you're right—here," Liz said. "But there are some other alternates where we're pretty sure America launched first. And there are a few where the Chinese started the big war, and some where the Nazis did, and even one where the Kaiser's Germany did—and won the war, and still is top dog today. All kinds of different possibilities."

Dan thought one of the possibilities, right then, was that his head would explode. It wasn't that he thought Liz was lying to him. He didn't. Nobody could make up a story like that and have so many details straight. But . . . he'd heard people talk about getting their minds blown. Now he knew exactly what that meant.

He stabbed out an angry forefinger at her. "What if I tell my officers about you people, about all this?"

She only shrugged. "What if you do? Who'll believe you? And even if somebody does, what can he do about it?"

"I'll show you!" He sprang.

Next thing he knew, he was on the ground again, with the wind knocked out of him. He fought to breathe. Anything more than that? Forget it. Liz said, "I probably ought to kill you for real, but I won't. You're just doing what you're supposed to do."

He tried to knock her off her feet once more, but she was wary this time. He wanted to tell her off, or to yell for help, or to do anything else that might be useful. What with struggling to breathe, he couldn't.

"Besides, I know you were sweet on me," Liz added. At this stage, it was insult on top of injury. He thought so, anyway, till she kicked him in the head. He spiraled down into blackness.

Dad and Mom were taking down the display when Liz came back to the Brentwood market square. "We've got to get out of here," she said. "Sorry, but we do."

"What went wrong?" Dad assumed something must have—and boy, was he ever right.

Liz told him what had gone wrong. She finished, "If he were only a little bit better—I mean, a *little*—the Valley soldiers would be asking me questions instead of you." She hadn't counted all her bruises and scrapes yet. She did count herself lucky that they were only bruises and scrapes.

"How soon will he wake up? How much will he remember when he does?" Mom asked.

"I don't know. I kicked him pretty good." Liz's foot hurt, too—Dan had a hard head. "But I don't think we ought to waste any time, you know?"

"Maybe he won't remember anything about the other alternates. We can hope not, anyway." Dad sighed as he walked over to the horses and led them back to the wagon. "Did you have to tell him about that? We aren't supposed to spill the crosstime secret, you know."

"Yeah, yeah, yeah," Liz said impatiently. "But even if they've got it here, what can they do about it? They won't have the technology for hundreds of years, if they ever do. And even if they do by then, this'll be a legend if they haven't forgotten all about it."

The horses snorted. They didn't want to go back to work at night. Some other merchants were eyeing the Mendozas. The locals had to be wondering why they were getting ready to bail out. That wasn't so good. If the Valley soldiers asked them, they might say which way the wagon went.

"I did find some stuff about Molotov at the International Atomic Energy Agency in 1967," Liz said. "We aren't leaving with no answers, or I hope we aren't."

"Molotov? At the IAEA? In '67?" Dad fired questions in bursts. Liz nodded after each one. He whistled. "That does sound important."

"It shows this alternate had already split off from the home timeline by then," Mom agreed. "So the breakpoint's somewhere earlier."

"Well, we won't worry about where it is right now," Dad

said. "When Dan comes to, the Valley soldiers will all want to find out what *our* breakpoint is."

Liz wouldn't have put it like that, which didn't mean her father was wrong. "How long will he be out?" Mom asked.

How were you supposed to answer a question like that? "About *this* long." Liz mimed how hard she'd kicked him.

"No way to tell for sure, not with something like that," Dad said. "Maybe a few seconds, maybe a few minutes, maybe longer. Maybe—with a little luck—he won't remember what you were talking about before you punted him."

"I wish you didn't have to do that," Mom said. "In this culture, guys feel ashamed when girls beat them. I know he liked you, but now all he'll think of is getting even."

"In *this* culture?" Liz and Dad spoke in the same breath. "It's the same way in ours," Liz added, though she admitted, "It is worse here." As far as she was concerned, everything was worse here. Sexism sure was. Of course, without an industrial society and modern medicine, women really were the weaker sex. There were plenty of alternates more sexist than this one, which still kept memories of more nearly equal times. But there were also plenty that did better.

"We can worry about that later, too," Mom said, and then, to Dad, "Don't you have those horses hitched *yet*? You said it yourself—no telling when Dan will come to. We don't want to be here when he does."

"We're ready." Dad got behind the wheel of the Chevy wagon to prove it. Liz and Mom jumped in behind him.

As they rolled away from the Brentwood market square, Mom said, "It's kind of a shame. For somebody from this alternate, he wasn't bad."

"I guess," Liz said, which was politer than *Are you out of your mind?* but meant the same thing. Dad lit a lantern and set it in a holder on the dashboard. You were supposed to show a light if you drove at night. He hadn't in Santa Monica, but nobody enforced traffic rules there. Here, a wagon without a light was likely to get stopped because it didn't have one. He wanted to look as normal as he could.

"You didn't tell Dan what kind of wheels we had or anything?" Mom asked.

"No way." Liz started to laugh. "I told him all the big secrets, but none of the little ones."

"Well, the big ones will freak him out even if he does remember them," Dad said. He turned right on to Sunset Boulevard. Sunset ran all the way to the ocean here, the same as it did in the home timeline. The resemblance ended there.

"I was thinking the same thing," Liz said. "Let him tell whoever he wants. Nobody'll believe him. And even if somebody does, what can they do about it?"

"Be more alert for people from the home timeline," Dad answered, which was something Liz hadn't thought of. "We need to warn the Stoyadinoviches about that."

A squad of Valley foot soldiers came east on Sunset toward them. Liz tensed. One of the soldiers called, "You folks are out late." The men kept marching. Liz tried not to be too noisy with her sigh of relief. She must have done well enough—none of the Valley men stopped and looked back at her.

When they got to the 405 and Sepulveda Boulevard, Dad turned right again and went down onto Sepulveda. "What are you doing?" Mom asked with exaggerated patience. "Speedro's the other way."

"I know," Dad said. "If they're looking for us anywhere, they'll be looking at the Santa Monica Freeway line and at the edge of things between Westwood and Santa Monica. If we go north instead—"

"We go up into the Valley," Mom broke in. "Is that where we want to be?"

Good question, Liz thought.

But Dad said, "Sure. Why not? It's the last place the soldiers down here will look for us. And we can go east from there, go around the dead zone in downtown L.A., and get back to Speedro. That's better than trying to sneak south through Santa Monica, don't you think? What else would they be looking for?"

That was also a good question—a better one than Liz wished it were. Dad liked to take a backwards slant on things. Sometimes that worked really well. Sometimes it didn't work at all. But Santa Monica, especially after the latest fire, wasn't any place Liz wanted to be.

"How much can they learn from what they find in our house?" Mom asked.

"Not enough." Dad sounded confident as he guided the wagon up the onramp to the 405. "They'll see that electric lights shine, that refrigerators keep things cold, and that Coke tastes good. And what can they do with any of that?"

A horse-drawn wagon plodding along a freeway built for speeding cars seemed almost unbearably sad to Liz. It also went a long way toward proving Dad's point.

Thirteen

When Dan woke up, he felt as bad as if somebody had kicked him in the head. "Oh, yeah," he said, and then, "Oh, wow!" Somebody *had* kicked him in the head—he remembered that much. And now he wished his head would fall off so he didn't have to put up with the pounding, throbbing ache in there.

Somebody . . . Who? That didn't come back right away. But he hadn't decided to lie down here on the ground in the gloom by himself. No. He'd been talking with someone, and they'd had an argument, and then a fight.

"I lost," he said sadly. "I must have lost." That didn't make him feel like much of a soldier. He looked around, though turning his head hurt, too. Come to that, almost everything hurt. Twilight hadn't altogether faded. The sun had been setting when whatever happened, happened. So he hadn't been out too long.

Whoever'd licked him hadn't taken his matchlock. That was good. He imagined trying to tell Sergeant Chuck how he'd lost it. That would have hurt worse than the thumping he'd taken. Hard to believe, but it would have. What would Chuck have done to him for losing his gun to a Westside rebel? Nothing pretty.

Or was it a Westside rebel? "Liz!" he exclaimed, and with

the name things started flooding back. He hadn't just lost—he'd lost to a girl!

And what were they talking about before she tried using his poor aching skull for a football? He had trouble coming up with that. It made him mad—it was important. He was sure it was. It was even more important than his humiliating defeat. *Where* did she learn to fight like that?

"Must have been in the home timeline," Dan muttered. For a second, the words didn't mean anything to him—they were only words. Then he remembered what lay behind them. A whole world where the Fire didn't fall! A whole world where they still had electricity and refrigerators and Coca-Cola! A whole world . . . that didn't give two cents for this one. A whole world . . . that just wanted to find out what had gone wrong in this one, that didn't care anything about fixing it up.

Rage filled him. Was that fair? Not even close! If they could catch Liz and her folks, maybe they could . . . *Do what?* Dan wondered. Something, anyhow. They had to be able to do something. He heaved himself to his feet and started dogtrotting back to the house where the traders—the traders from that other world—had lived.

He was in good hard shape, the way a soldier needed to be. He should have made it back to that house without even breathing hard—it wasn't much more than a mile. He took about three strides and then stopped, fighting not to be sick. He'd never got kicked in the head before, not by a girl, not by a horse, not by anybody or anything. He didn't know how very badly that kind of injury could mess someone up—adventure stories didn't talk about such things. He might not have known, but he found out in a hurry. Trying to do anything fast left him dizzy and wondering if his skull would split in two. As a matter of fact, he hoped it would.

But he had to get back, even if he couldn't do it fast. If he couldn't run, he would walk. *If I can't walk, I'll crawl,* he thought. It didn't quite come to that. He *could* walk, as long as he didn't try to hustle.

Little by little, he realized he was glad the sun had gone down. The torches and lamps he saw as he got into Westwood seemed to pierce his eyes and stab his brain like needles. Cooking odors and the general town stink were much stronger than usual, too. He gulped several times. He was hungry, but maybe it was just as well he had an empty stomach.

The traders' house still had guards posted in front of it, and torches in the sconces by the front door. Dan narrowed his eyes against what felt like an intolerable glare. The torchlight let the sentries get a good look at him. "Look what the cat dragged in," one of them jeered.

"Drinking on duty?" the other one asked.

"I've got three stripes now. You can't talk to me like that," Dan said. The men stiffened to attention—rank *did* have its privileges. That his speech wasn't slurred also helped. He went on, "Is Captain Horace still in there?"

"Yes, Sergeant," the sentries chorused—they didn't sound snotty any more. One of them ventured, "Uh, what happened to you, Sergeant?"

"What's it look like? I got beat up." Dan didn't say Liz had done it. He supposed he would have to tell Horace, but he didn't want these yahoos being the first to know.

He went inside. He went downstairs. He had to squint even harder against electric lights than he had against the torches—

they were that much brighter. Captain Horace stared at him. As the sentry had, he asked, "What happened to you?"

"Sir, I saw Liz—you know, the traders' daughter—coming out of the UCLA library. I came up to her, and I . . . I lost the fight, that's all."

Horace's eyebrows leaped for the sky. "How in blazes did a girl whip you?"

"Sir, she fights better than our dirty-fighting coaches. That's the truth."

"Where could she have learned to fight like that?" the officer demanded.

"In the home timeline, sir," Dan answered. "It'd have to be."

"What the devil is the home timeline?"

Dan explained—as well as he could, anyhow. Looking back, he didn't know how good a job he did. All he knew was the little Liz had told him. And he was trying to remember it after she'd knocked him cold.

When he got done, Captain Horace said, "That's the craziest thing I ever heard in my life."

"Yes, sir," Dan said. You didn't want to argue with officers. Even when you were right, you were wrong if you did something like that. But the electric lights overhead hurt his sensitive eyes. Pointing to them, he went on, "Where in *this* world do we have lights like that? Where do we have all the other stuff here? Where do we have Coca-Cola?"

"That's a . . . good question, Sergeant," Horace said slowly. "And I wish I had a good answer for you. This Liz was heading north, you say?"

"Yes, sir."

"Then she and her folks are likely at the Brentwood market

square, eh? We'll send some men up there right away." The captain scowled. "But chances are they'll already be gone. I wouldn't hang around, anyway, not after I got into a fight with one of King Zev's soldiers." In his own way, he was tactful. He didn't remind Dan that Liz had not only got in a fight but won it. "So we'll also pass the word to the border stations. They must have come up from the south, right?"

"I'd think so, yes, sir," Dan replied.

"Then we'll catch 'em when they try to escape, that's all. No one can assault a Valley soldier and expect to get away with it." Captain Horace sounded plenty confident.

"That all sounds good, sir. The only thing is . . . The only thing is, they're sneaky." Dan had the feeling his superior was missing something. Trouble was, he had no idea what. It had something to do with Liz and her folks and how sneaky they were. But what? His poor battered brain wouldn't tell him.

"I don't care how sneaky they are. They can only go one way," Horace said. "And when they do, we've got 'em."

The Chevy wagon reached the top of Sepulveda Pass. This was the place where the Westside had built its stupid, greedy wall, the one that touched off the war with the Valley. Looking north, Liz could see all the lights of King Zev's domain flickering in the darkness.

What she saw was how few and faint those lights were. When you came to the top of the pass in the home timeline and started down toward the Valley, all the neon and fluorescent lights blazed out at you. These fires seemed pathetic by comparison.

"Doesn't seem to be anybody after us," Mom said.

"Nope." Dad sounded smug. "We would've heard people on our trail. With no motors or anything, you can hear a long way in this alternate." As if to prove his point, an owl hooted in the hills off to one side of the pass. Liz never would have heard that driving along in a car with a million other cars all around. Now they had the old freeway almost to themselves.

"They must think we *are* heading down to Speedro," Liz said.

"Sometimes the fastest way to get somewhere is the long way around," Dad said. That sounded as if it ought to make sense, in a Zen kind of way. Almost everything Dad said sounded as if it ought to make sense. Sorting out what really did from what didn't could be a full-time job, though.

"We can sell jeans to King Zev himself," Mom said. "Who wouldn't want a pair of brand new Old Time jeans? They'd be fit for a king."

"If we have a pair that fits him," Liz said. "Isn't he supposed to be sort of short and round?"

"He's a bowling ball with a mustache," Dad said, which gave her a case of the giggles. "But he is fairly smart, I think—which won't help him fit into denim."

Mom started to snore. Liz was jealous. She was also way too wound up even to try to sleep. Escaping from occupied Westwood was bad enough. But that she'd been in a fight with somebody she knew, that she'd hurt him . . . She didn't like the idea, not even a little bit.

If she'd lost, Dan and his buddies would be questioning her right now. They wouldn't be gentle about it. She understood all that perfectly well. She'd done what she had to do if she wanted to stay safe. Remembering that truth made her feel better—but not enough better.

The owl hooted again, or maybe it was another one. A coyote howled at the moon, for all the world as if it were a dog. She wouldn't have heard that zooming along in a car, either—or stuck in traffic not zooming at all. No morning and afternoon rush hours in this alternate.

Mom stirred. "I think we're all right," she said sleepily. "If they were going to come after us, they really would have done it by now."

"It's my fault. I feel bad about it," Liz said. "If Dan hadn't liked me too much, nobody would have paid any attention to our house. Then none of this would have happened. It would have been like another alternate."

"Maybe it is. Maybe it's one where we know the breakpoint," Dad said. "Maybe there's a whole Mendoza family going on about its business in an alternate almost like this one—except Dan didn't like you or didn't meet you, and we never ran into any trouble."

"I don't *think* so," Liz said. They hadn't found any alternates with breakpoints after the discovery of crosstime travel. Otherwise, there wouldn't be *a* home timeline. There would be a bunch of home timelines, each a little different from all the others. And if that didn't make your head want to explode . . .

"Probably not. It's not a big enough deal," Mom said. "But that kind of thing could happen one of these days."

"It'll be a mess if it does, too," Dad said. "We've never found another alternate that goes crosstime, right? If we can't find others, we'll just have to make our own." He might call it a mess, but he sounded cheerful about it.

"Brr!" Liz shivered, though the night was mild. The idea

gave her the horrors. They didn't talk about that kind of thing in school. She knew why not, too. It would give people even more to worry about than they already had. As if life wasn't complicated enough!

After a while, Dad said, "I think we can pull off onto the shoulder and stop. They haven't realized we might have headed north."

"A good thing, too, or we'd be in even more trouble," Mom said. But she turned around on the seat and grabbed a couple of blankets. Sleeping in the wagon was cramped, but it wouldn't be chilly.

The horses seemed glad to stop. Some scraggly grass grew by the side of the road. They nibbled at that. Dad spread some oats on the ground, too, and put out a water bucket for each animal. "They aren't like cars," he remarked. "You've got to take care of them all the time, not just lube and oil them every seventy-five thousand kilometers."

"They might as well be people," Liz said. "And I sure could use a lube and oil change right now." She shifted under the blankets, trying to get comfortable.

Next thing she knew, it was dawn. She yawned and stretched. She'd meant it about the lube job—she really was stiff and sore. By the way her folks grumbled, so were they. Yeah, they were older than she was. But they hadn't had a Valley soldier try to throw them into the middle of next week and almost succeed.

Down the north side of the Sepulveda Pass went the wagon. Dad had to ride the brake, which made the wheels squeal. Otherwise, on the downhill slope, the wagon would have bumped the horses' backsides. He breathed a sigh of relief when the terrain leveled out.

He got off the 405 at Victory. "Here we are, in the wonderful, romantic Valley," he said.

It didn't look wonderful or romantic to Liz. It looked a lot like Westwood: a relative handful of people living in what had been part of a great city. Without imported water and food, the Los Angeles basin couldn't support anything close to the population it had in the home timeline.

Ruined, tumbledown houses and shops spread as far as the eye could see. The dead zone in the Valley lay off to the northwest, where the aerospace factories had stood. The Russians knew that, of course, and gave them a bomb.

A man selling avocados on a street corner called, "What have you got?"

"Blue jeans—genuine Old Time Levi's," Dad answered. "Top quality, too. I don't have many left."

"How many avocados you want for a couple of pairs?"

"Whoa," Dad told the horses. Not stopping would have been out of character. He and the man with the avocados haggled for a while. Levi's were hard to come by, while avocados grew all over the place in Southern California. On the other hand, as the local pointed out, you couldn't eat blue jeans. When the man threw in a beat-up basket to hold the avocados, Dad made the deal. "We can eat some on the way and give the rest to the Stoyadinoviches," he said.

"Do we have more to worry about than avocados?" Mom pointed up the street. Marching their way came a platoon of Valley soldiers: archers, musketeers, and a few tough-looking riflemen.

"Well, I hope not." Dad steered the wagon over to the curb, the way you'd steer a car in the home timeline if an ambulance or a fire engine or police car came at you. The platoon tramped past with no more than a couple of sidewise glances toward the traders.

"Whew!" Liz said as the wagon started rolling again.

"I didn't *think* the soldiers in Westwood would have got word about us up here so fast," Dad said. "Still, I wouldn't have liked to find out I was wrong."

That made Liz look back over her shoulder. She saw the Valley troops, other people on foot, people on horseback, and a few carts and carriages and wagons. Everything looked normal—normal for this alternate, anyhow. She told herself she was jumpy about nothing. Then she told herself to *believe* she was jumpy about nothing. Herself laughed at her.

"I wish you could step on the gas and make the horses go faster," Mom said. That made Liz feel better—she wasn't the one one with the jitters, then.

"Matter of fact, so do I," Dad said. "But I can't." He flicked the reins. Maybe the horses went a tiny bit faster. And maybe they didn't.

Step on the gas. That was a funny phrase. Cars in the home timeline burned clean hydrogen, so it made sense there. But people in this alternate also said it when they meant *hurry up*. Cars in 1967, when the Fire fell, hadn't burned hydrogen—they'd burned nasty, stinky, polluting petroleum. Petroleum wasn't a gas—it was a liquid. She knew that. She needed a moment to remember that the part of the petroleum Old Time cars burned was called gasoline. People must have clipped that to *gas*, even thought the stuff wasn't.

Victory went east, straight as a string for a long way. Dad stopped to rest the horses and bought lunch at a roadside taco stand. He could have done that in the home timeline, too, though people there would have had conniptions if he'd driven a team of horses on the street. The tacos were pretty good. They were handmade, not cranked out in a factory and nuked when the order came in. That helped.

Nuked. In the home timeline, you nuked something when you threw it in the microwave. Oh, it meant using nuclear weapons, too, but most people didn't dwell on that. The home timeline had escaped atomic war, and with a little luck would go right on escaping it.

They didn't have microwaves here. Nuking something meant just one thing in this alternate—destroying it altogether. Studying the way languages changed from one alternate to another was a field that was just taking off.

On they went, on and on and on. Right where Victory finally curved a little south, two customs posts straddled the road. The Mendozas needed only a couple of minutes to clear the Valley post. The men at the other one wore green uniforms, not King Zev's khaki. "Welcome to beautiful downtown Burbank," one of them said.

It didn't look beautiful to Liz. It didn't look like downtown, either. It looked like the border between a couple of tinpot kingdoms that had forgotten they should have been suburbs.

For some reason, Dad seemed to think the Burbank customs man's greeting was funny. Liz could tell, but she hoped the local couldn't. Dad certainly sounded serious enough when he said, "Thank you, sir."

"Anything to declare?" the customs man asked.

"Well, we're traders," Dad answered. "We've got what's left of a nice load of Levi's in the back of the wagon. We sold a good many in the Valley, and I expect we can move some more of them here."

The customs man took a look at them. "Those are pretty fine, all right. Anybody can see they come from the Old Time. We charge duty on things we make ourselves, so our people will buy from Burbank craftsmen instead of foreigners. Clothes like that, though, with the zippers and everything . . . We can't make anything quite like 'em ourselves, even if we are getting closer. I don't know where you found these, pal, but I'm jealous. They look like they're brand new."

"They do, don't they?" Dad still kept his face straight.

"Yeah." The customs man sighed. "I wish I had the cash to buy clothes like that. They probably aren't dutiable, but. . . . Maybe I'd better check the regulations."

"Why don't you find a pair that fits you, sir?" Dad said smoothly. "Why don't your other inspectors do the same?" A real trader from this alternate probably would have been furious at the polite shakedown. He wouldn't have dared to show it, though. Dad really had no reason to get upset, and plenty of reason to keep these people sweet.

"That's mighty nice of you, pal," the Burbank customs man said. He turned to his colleagues. "Melvin! Frodo! C'mere!"

Frodo, Liz thought. Yes, they knew about *The Lord of the Rings* in this alternate. No wonder the password in the basement hadn't been good enough.

As soon as the Burbank customs men found jeans that fit them, the senior man swung aside the gateway. "Pass on!" he said.

Dad called, "Giddyap!" to the horses. They pulled the wagon through. The customs inspector closed the gate. Liz and Mom and Dad all grinned at one another. They were out of the Valley! They weren't home free yet, but they were on their way.

Captain Horace was not a happy man. "Where the devil are they?" he growled. "They aren't at that Brentwood market square—people saw them go. They aren't anywhere in Westwood that we've been able to find. And I swear they haven't sneaked past us heading south. So where are they?"

"Sir?" Dan said.

"What?" No, Horace wasn't happy, not even a little bit.

"What if they didn't go south, sir?" Dan said—it was about the worst thing he could think of. "What if they went north instead?"

"North?" By the way the officer said it, it might have been a dirty word. "Why the—dickens would they want to go and do a stupid thing like that?"

"If it throws us off the track, like, is it really stupid?" Dan asked.

Captain Horace bit down on that like a man crunching into a cherry pit. His expression was as dour as if he really had bitten down on something painful. "It could be," he said at last, each word plainly tasting worse than the one before. "Yes, it could be. And if it is, we've wasted an awful lot of time waiting for something to happen when it won't. Why didn't you think of this sooner, confound it?"

"Sir?" was all Dan said. The unfairness of the crack took

his breath away. *Me? I just made sergeant. You're so smart, Captain Horace, why didn't you think of it for yourself?*

But then Horace let out a sheepish laugh. "Well, you weren't the only one here—I admit it. Why didn't I come up with it on my own? I wonder if the telegraph between here and army HQ in the Valley is working."

"Maybe we'd better find out, sir," Dan said. The telegraph worked by electricity, and modern people still managed to use it . . . some of the time, anyhow. Dan didn't understand how they could do that but not make things like electric lights and refrigerators. He asked Captain Horace.

"As I understand it, those need a lot more power than the telegraph does," Horace said. "But just because I understand it that way doesn't prove it's so. I know a lot about electricity—for an army officer. If you want to get the straight skinny, though, you need to talk to somebody like Dr. Saul."

"I'd like to do that, sir, one of these days," Dan said. "For now, we probably ought to see if we can catch the traders."

"Right." Going to the telegrapher took more time. Somewhere—was it really somewhere up north, somewhere in the Valley?—the traders' wagon was getting farther and farther away.

Will I ever see Liz again? Dan wondered. His head still ached dreadfully from the kick she'd given him. *Do I want to see her again, after she did that?* He did. In spite of everything, he did. The things she could tell him about the way her world worked—and the way this one did!

He still thought she was cute, too.

How could you think somebody was cute after she almost fractured your skull? He didn't know, but he did anyway. He was also sorrowfully aware that she didn't think he was cute.

She probably looked at him the same way he looked at the wild men who'd lost all traces of civilization. Dan didn't think that was fair. Well, the wild men probably didn't think his opinion of them was fair, either.

He didn't care what the wild men thought. Liz was much too likely not to care what he thought.

Captain Horace had him describe Liz and her parents for the telegrapher. He knew them better than anyone else from the Valley. *But do I know them at all?* he wondered. The captain described their wagon. Neither he nor Dan had seen that—they relied on what they'd heard from the traders in the Brentwood market square. Would it be enough? Dan couldn't know. He had to hope.

The telegrapher's clever finger sent Morse code north. Not long after he did, his clicker started making noise in reply. It wasn't magic, though Dan didn't fully understand why it wasn't. "They have the message, sir," the telegrapher told the captain. "They'll do what they can."

"Right on," Horace said. "Far out."

How far out was it? Dan had his doubts. The brass up in the Valley hadn't seen the marvels down here with their own eyes. How hard would they try to catch Liz and her folks? Would they put real effort into it, or just go through the motions? And how much did any of that matter? If the traders had headed north, wouldn't they be long gone by now?

Dan hoped not. They knew so much. They could *do* so much. How much could they help this world if only they wanted to? But they didn't—Liz had made that much too clear. There was no money in it for them. If they hadn't been studying this alternate, they wouldn't have come here at all.

Alternates . . . The idea made Dan's head spin even worse than Liz's foot had. All those possibilities, and each one coming true. A world where the Fire didn't fall. That one by itself was plenty to take Dan's breath away. But it was far from the only thing that might have happened. He could see that, too.

He had a friend who'd become a secretary because a teacher praised his handwriting. If the teacher hadn't, Norm probably would have been a leatherworker like his father. And there were the guys who just happened to wind up at the wrong spot in a battle. If they'd stood a couple of feet to the left or right, they would have been fine. As things were, they stopped a bullet with their chest or their head.

So easy to see how changes, big changes, could turn a person's life upside down and inside out. And if a person's life could change that way, why couldn't a country's or a whole world's? No reason at all, not that Dan could see. When he thought about it in those terms, he had no trouble understanding why he believed Liz.

Besides, how could anybody make up a story like hers? And even if somebody did, how could she back it up with things that had been gone since the Old Time? Dan didn't think it was possible.

"Maybe we'll catch them yet," Captain Horace said. "I bet we do."

"Yes, sir. Maybe we will," Dan answered. *What else can I say?* he wondered, and didn't see anything else. But he didn't believe it. The traders had too long a start. And they could disappear—they really could. What else was traveling between alternates but disappearing from one and appearing in another one? How were you going to catch somebody who could do that?

Very late that afternoon, a wire came in about somebody who'd got two pairs of denims from some people who might have been Liz and her folks. They were heading east, toward beautiful downtown Burbank. If they got there, King Zev's soldiers would never lay a hand on them again.

Zev might threaten war to get them. . . . Dan laughed at himself. Not a chance. With the Valley still fighting the Westside and Speedro, Zev couldn't make beautiful downtown Burbank mad at him, too. Fighting one war was bad enough. Fighting two wars at once had to be four times as bad, or maybe eight.

"Do you think they'll stay in beautiful downtown Burbank?" Horace asked him. "Or are they more likely to go somewhere else from there? If they do go somewhere else, where do you think it would be?"

This is the stuff you're supposed to worry about—you're the officer. Dan was learning to think like a sergeant in a hurry. But he did know Liz and her family better than the captain did. "Well, from what we found out, they came up from the south," he answered "My guess is, they'd go back that way, too. Maybe they've got another watchamacallit—a transposition chamber—down there somewhere."

"How far down there?" Captain Horace persisted. "The part of the Westside we didn't take? Speedro? Sandago? Teejay?"

"Sir," Dan said mournfully, "I have no idea." So many things about Liz and her folks he didn't know. So many things he wanted to know. So many things he knew he'd never find out. So many things he'd wonder about for the rest of his life.

One surfaced right now. *If she came from this world or I came from hers, would she have liked me better?* He could hope so, anyhow. And that led to another thought. If she was still working in the UCLA library, she and her folks hadn't found all of their answer, whatever it was. Maybe she'd be back one day to look for it. *If we make this world more like the one she comes from, would people from there and people from here get along better?*

Again, Dan could hope so. And he could do more than hope: he could work to make it so. He realized he suddenly had something to do with however much time he had left. He'd never known a feeling like that before. He . . . decided he liked it.

"Be it ever so humble, there's no place like . . . the Stoyadinoviches' trading post." Dad looked pleased with himself. "That's an old saying I just made up."

"I never would have guessed." Liz grinned as she zinged him.

"Now, children." Mom sounded amused, or maybe just resigned. Liz thought about asking which, then decided she'd rather not know.

"I wish we could have stayed longer this time around, but we did pretty well, anyway," Dad said. "That stuff we found out about Molotov—nobody knew that about this alternate before."

"Who's this 'we'?" Mom wondered. "You and your tapeworm? Liz did all the finding. You're just the guy who'll write the articles about it."

"Guilty," Dad agreed. "That's guilty, guilty, guilty—always quote from the classics if you can't make up your own old sayings. But I will give her credit. I may borrow, but I don't steal—much. And it's definitely an important lead. If the Soviet government here was more hard-nosed than in the home timeline . . . Well, it's not a smoking gun, but—"

"A smoking mushroom cloud, don't you mean?" Liz put in. "Or don't I get to make up old sayings, too?"

"That one fits this alternate too well," Mom said.

Gulls wheeled overhead. You could see the ocean—and, when the wind blew in, as it did more often than not—smell it, too. Its clean salt tang helped cut the usual city reek of Speedro. Sailboats and a few wood- or coal-burning steamboats glided across the water.

Those were only details, though. For the most part, Speedro was like any other part of L.A.—any other part of this whole alternate—after the Fire fell. The buildings were put together from some new bricks and a lot of pieces of what had been here in 1967. There were lots of open spaces, because far fewer people lived here now. Groves of citruses and olives and almonds and avocados grew where houses and shops and factories had stood once upon a time. Pigs and chickens and ducks and turkeys made a racket. So did stray dogs and scrawny children. Speedro's flag—a white sailing ship on a blue background—flew over it all.

The Stoyadinoviches greeted the Mendozas like long-lost siblings. In this alternate, they were. The two families shared 130 years of experience no one else here had. "What's the password for your safe room down below?" Liz asked.

"'Rosebud,'" George Stoyadinovich answered. "Why? You want to get a soda or something? Long as you stay down there to drink it, help yourself."

"No, thanks. I was just thinking it's from before the break-point, so maybe you ought to change it." Liz told him what had gone wrong up in Westwood. "We never imagined they could figure out something like that, but they did. The movies of *The*

Lord of the Rings are from the start of this century, but the books are older."

"I don't *think* 'Rosebud' is a problem," Dad said. "It's from before the breakpoint, yeah, but it's from a movie. I don't believe there *is* a book to *Citizen Kane*. And nobody here has watched any movies since before the big war."

Liz hadn't thought about that. Slowly, she nodded. The risk with the Stoyadinoviches' password was bound to be smaller than with the one her family had picked. She didn't think there was no risk at all, though.

"We'll change it," Mr. Stoyadinovich said. "I know what we'll use—'Shaquille.' He was from long after the breakpoint."

"He played . . . baseball, didn't he?" Liz knew she was guessing.

Mr. Stoyadinovich and Dad grinned in a way that told her she'd guessed wrong. "Basketball," they said together. She shrugged. As long as he came from after '67, it didn't matter.

"Did you get any research done up there?" Irma Stoyadinovich asked. "You weren't gone very long."

"We did quite a bit, matter of fact," Dad said. Mom coughed. "Well, Liz did the digging," he acknowledged. "Looks like the Soviets were more hardline here than they were in the home timeline, so chances are they did push the button first. Can't nail it down a hundred percent, but it seems a lot more likely."

Mr. Stoyadinovich nodded. "Makes sense. So coming back turned out to be worthwhile?"

"Sure did." Dad nodded, too.

Mom set a hand on Liz's shoulder. "Tell them what else your darling daughter did, dear."

"She KO'd the Valley soldier who recognized her and tried

to grab her." Pride rang in Dad's voice. "That bought us the time we needed to get away."

"Good for you, sweetheart!" George Stoyadinovich boomed.

"I guess," Liz said. "I mean, I know it was, but it's sad, too. The only reason Dan did recognize me is because he liked me."

"Which didn't keep you from kicking him in the head when he needed it," Dad said.

"I know. But even so . . ." The fight embarrassed Liz more than it made her proud. It was something she'd needed to do—Dad had that right—but not something she'd wanted to do. "I mean, he was nice enough. If he came from the home timeline, he wouldn't have been too bad."

"That's more than you ever said before," Mom told her.

"Well, I'll never see him again, so I can say what I think," Liz answered. "And even if I did see him again now, he'd want to shoot me, I bet, and not just 'cause he's a Valley soldier. Guys don't keep on liking girls who knock them cold."

"Well," Mr. Stoyadinovich said solemnly, twirling his mustache, "you're right."

Liz didn't tell him how much of the crosstime secret she'd spilled to Dan. She didn't aim to say anything about that to anyone but her folks. Not that the locals could do anything with it, but all the same. . . . If Crosstime Traffic found out they knew more than they should, the company could assume it was because of what they'd found in the underground rooms.

If Dan hadn't liked her, he wouldn't have listened anyhow. He would have gone on trying to deck her, and he might have done it. She'd needed the breathing space, maybe more than he did. And if he'd decked her, the Valley soldiers might have got her folks, too.

She knew she was talking herself into something, but she didn't much care. A Greek philosopher had called man the rational animal, and that was true. But man was also the rationalizing animal. You did what you had to do or what you wanted to do, and you worried about why later, when you had the chance.

"I got away. We got away," Liz said. "It wasn't pretty, and it wasn't neat—what is in this alternate? But we did it."

"That's what counts," Dad said. Everybody nodded. The Mendozas would go back to the home timeline soon, and Dan . . . Poor Dan. Liz did feel sorry for him. She wondered what he thought he ought to do now. She was absolutely, positively, sure she'd never find out.